BONE FACTORY

Also by Steven Sidor

Skin River

BONE FACTORY

Steven Sidor

To Pete

one of my 1st best readers.

— Steve

9/1/05

St. Martin's Minotaur New York

 For information, address St. Martin's Press, 175 Fifth Avenue, New York, N.Y. 10010.

www.minotaurbooks.com

ISBN 0-312-32951-2
EAN 978-0-312-32951-8

First Edition: September 2005

10 9 8 7 6 5 4 3 2 1

In memory of Joe Strummer (1952–2002)

Every cheap hood strikes a bargain with the world . . .
—"Death or Glory" (STRUMMER, JONES)

Acknowledgments

The following people helped me to put the black stuff on the white stuff and live to fight another day.

Steve Hamilton, extraordinary writer
and hell of a nice guy.

Brian Padjen, former boss, poet, critic, and friend.
Not necessarily in that order.

Dawn and Gary Heinz, good companions and
providers of quiet space.

The Howard brothers, Jamie and Pat, in Galway.
And Jack in Jersey too.

Ann Collette, my agent and friend,
who even met me at the airport.

Ben Sevier, my fine editor.

The owners, managers, and staff of the
independent mystery bookstores.

Lisa, Emma, and Quinn. The reasons I get out of bed
in the morning. Eventually.

Final thanks to the Everlast heavy bag in my basement.
For never calling the cops.

BONE FACTORY

1

DEAD GIRL SCOUT

Coulter Street

The man said he was a sailor. He wore a Navy peacoat, unbuttoned, and a white, V-necked T-shirt underneath. Blue slacks, shiny black shoes, but no sailor's hat. Gia guessed he could be a sailor like he said. The snow fell heavier. It blew down the front of the Hotel Hippolyte in icy bursts.

"Let's go around the corner."

"Sure."

They walked around the corner of the building for some protection from the weather and curious eyes. He showed her he had money. He bounced the bill roll in his outstretched palm. He wore bike gloves. The man who said he was a sailor paused under a bright light overhanging the back door to a bar. Gia noticed acne scars on his face. His eyes were green and didn't look real, but people wore colored contact lenses and Gia guessed he was one of those.

"You ain't a cop, sailor man?"

"Me? No, I'm no cop. Are you?"

"Nah-uh. I'm Gia."

"Hi, Gia. You have a place we can go? A room?"

Gia decided she didn't like his smile. Straight white teeth and Gia could tell he had a face that changed with how he felt. Or how he wanted you to feel. An animated face. Gia had one too. But the sailor gave off a bad vibe and Gia said no to the idea of her room. This sailor was going to be quick and outside in the alley. She wasn't spending too much time with him. She wasn't taking him into the hotel either.

"We do it right here. Down where that doorway goes into the brick wall. See? We do it there or nowhere."

"It's so cold."

"Not with Gia it isn't. C'mon. What you want tonight? I bet I know."

The man stuffed his hands into his pockets. Gia watched the money disappear.

"Hey, it'll be good, sailor. Gia satisfies."

"We have to be in a room. Not out here in the snowstorm."

"You ain't cold, sailor. Coat's all open. And look." She brushed her fingers on his cheek. "You warm. Gia's getting warm too. The doorway's nice and dark. Nobody looks in there."

They held hands as Gia led him to the narrow gap where a brown steel door was chained shut and empty wine bottles stood in paper sacks. The man looked up and down the alley.

Snowflakes were sticking in the man's blond buzz cut. Gia could see his pink scalp and veins like pipe cleaners twisted at his temples. He was chewing gum. Gia smelled mint when he laughed. A pretend laugh like a salesman uses.

"Gia, Gia. Today's your lucky day."

The man turned and walked back to the street. Through the falling snow Gia saw him go north half a block, and she continued to watch until the storm erased him, finally, from her view.

Girl Scout Beach

"Who found the body?"

"A jogger. Lady's over there."

Detective Eliza Ochoa followed the patrolman's gloved finger to a slim-hipped redhead wearing fluorescent lime sweats. She was talking to another uniformed cop. They were about twenty yards uphill, out of the wind, huddled inside the opening of a tunnel. The tunnel connected the city park to the trails along Figg's Pond and the river. Eliza turned and started walking. The patrolman frowned when the detective angled away from the witness.

Eliza wanted to take a look at the playground first.

Tornado slide. Two swing sets. Red, white, and blue jungle bars shaped like a rocket. Between the rocket and the river, a pair of gold-jacketed men moved together, then apart, pulling a tape measure.

The Booth City crime techs had finished taking their first set of photos in the dim morning twilight. They had to hang an extra spotlight on the rocket's nose. Its brilliance fanned into the soft gray murk. Eliza stepped over a half-dozen pale blue extension cords snaking along to the curbside and the Crime Scene van. The techs were busy recording distances around the body, how far it came to rest from the street, the water, and the trail.

Dr. Lu, the Medical Examiner, did her work from the morgue and rarely made an appearance at a crime scene. The detectives would need a good reason to bring her to the river.

A body's length from the foot of the rocket, on a gentle slope curving down to the water, knelt Tom Gandy, the assistant ME. His black bag gaped next to him like a mouth he had to feed. He looked happy. Eliza knew it was Gandy's game face, always smiling over the dead, and it meant nothing about the circumstances. He motioned for her to come closer. The spotlight neutralized colors, pushed them into camps of black and white. Gandy had wax hands. A strip of mud guarding the river behind him shined like congealed grease. Eliza's eyes locked on the dark mound he huddled over.

"Morning, Detective Ochoa."

She took the pair of gloves he offered. Gandy pulled aside the rubber cloth he'd placed over the victim.

Eliza's partner, Detective Ike Horner, walked out of the gloom, ducking under one of the swing sets and swallowing the last of his gas-station coffee. He had arrived earlier but waited for Eliza before going over the scene. The patrolmen who were first to respond ran down the basics for him. He went for a quick look at the body. When Gandy pulled up in the ME wagon, Ike pointed him in the right direction. After standing around watching the crime techs shoot their film, he climbed back into his car to warm up.

Eliza could smell the menthol cough drop in Ike's mouth. She heard him cracking it between his back teeth. His nose was running, and he dabbed at it with a handkerchief. He put the handkerchief back in his pocket and started drumming his fingers against the bottom of the empty paper cup he was still holding in his other hand.

"We got a polar bear?" he said.

Eliza and Gandy were studying the victim.

Facedown. Nude. Shoulder-length brunette hair. Lividity marks discoloring the left side. The body had been moved at least once.

"Okay?" Gandy asked, white teeth flashing.

Eliza said, "Sure. Go ahead."

Ike nodded.

Gandy rolled the body onto its side. They saw it was a naked woman.

"She's really cold. I can't give you a time until we get her back under the lights."

"Don't know how those people take a swim when it's freezing like this," Ike said, continuing the thought he'd been having when he walked up.

"You skinny-dip with a hole in your chest this big?" Gandy asked.

Ike leaned over the assistant ME's shoulder. "Guess I'd sink pretty quick."

"Wonder if she got her money's worth." Eliza nodded at the dead woman's obviously enhanced breasts, which had remained firm despite the circumstances. The detective pressed her latex-covered fingertip against a small tattoo, a black unicorn, printed above the victim's left nipple. No smudging. At least her ink was real.

Ike clucked his tongue. "Why would a young woman want to go and do that?"

"Equal opportunity," Eliza said. "Everybody's got a tattoo these days."

"No, her . . . ah, augmentation." Ike sucked in another cough drop, stuffed his naked hands into his leather jacket.

"You don't get the tit job?" Gandy asked, incredulous.

"Evidently, I don't."

"Really?" Gandy grinned like he was enjoying a joke Ike had missed.

"I'm serious. Always looks like Frankenstein's bride. Word *implant* gives me chills. More science fiction than medicine."

"Yeah, well, other men get chills too," Eliza said.

Ike shrugged.

Gandy continued to inspect the body. "Ligature marks on the arms and ankles. Take a look at her lower back. What would you say those were?" He kept the victim on her side. It was easy because the dead woman was skeletally thin.

Wind grabbed the frigid mist churning over the Rood River's #4 Dam and shoved it right into their faces. Higher up the beach, past the playground, nearer the dunes and in the grasses, the sand was still soft, but under the victim it was as hard-packed as cement. Twisting the body left no impressions.

"Those scars? Somebody's been cuttin' on her pretty good," Ike said. He rubbed two knuckles along his chin. Water droplets sparkled in the day-old, salt-and-pepper stubble. Normally, he kept himself meticulously groomed. Clean-shaven from the neck up, his head too, the only exception was a trim military mustache. But vanity went to the wayside when his beeper chirped predawn and running an electric razor meant waking the whole house. Short on sleep and not enough time for a long, soapy wet shave. He wasn't sure he trusted his hands this morning either, after he looked at them.

Gandy nodded. "I'd say a small pocketknife maybe, or like a fruit knife. Short blade, probably. Or a long blade and he used only the tip. But she would've had to hold pretty still for that. I count five distinct groupings." He pointed with his elbow. "Couple fresh ones down there on her hip. See?"

Ike searched along his collar until he found the lanyard attached to his glasses.

The hip bones were pointed, stretching against the pale skin even in death. On the fleshier side, above the mottled left buttocks, Ike saw the wounds. Like a row of crusty black caterpillars—four slices, roughly vertical and a thumbnail apart. A thicker slash cut diagonally through the bunch, making a crude tally of five. The older scars were like that too. Notches.

Gandy turned the body back on the sand. "Could be those are self-inflicted, given they're superficial and clustered. The stages of healing differ. But they're in weird spots." Gandy pulled his arm around his back. "An itch you can't scratch."

Eliza crouched down level with the dead woman's waist. "How about this? She's a real mess down here. That a knife too?"

"Same as the chest, maybe. Torn up. Probably looking at the forced insertion of a sharp object. We gotta ask Lu to take a peek. But figure the victim didn't do that to herself. And I'd be surprised if she wasn't sexually assaulted prior to the trauma. We'll run a kit for smears. But the river . . ."

"Where's all the blood?" Ike asked. He took a pen from his pocket and jabbed it into the sand.

The pen made a shallow scrape.

"Maybe the cutting was postmortem," Eliza offered.

Ike shook his head. "She didn't tie herself up. Why tie up a dead girl? Unless you're tying her *to* something, a cinder block or what have you, guarantee she stays on the bottom. If that were the case we'd have some rope here. Where's the rope?" He seemed satisfied when no one answered. "You tie her up so you can do what you will." He considered that thought for a moment, then asked, "She didn't drown?"

Gandy raised his shoulders. "We'll check her lungs, but it doesn't look like a drowning. That chest wound is destructive enough to be fatal. Same deal with the amount of bleeding related to the genital area. There's a cut artery in her thigh, not even considering what's internal, so . . . I mean either one or a combo would do it."

"Could somebody have carved her up after she washed in?" Eliza wasn't ready to let go of the idea that the woman had been dead before her flesh was desecrated. *Wishful thinking,* she told herself. But she also wanted to rule out the possibility of two sources for the injuries.

Gandy said, "My feeling is no, the mutilation was proximate to her death. She's practically bled out. Blood loss happened at some other location. Maybe in the river."

Ike squatted and brushed the point of his pen into the victim's black hair. "She hasn't been in the river at all. Hair would be frozen. I don't see a towel. Crime techs pick anything up?"

"Box of pretzels, some cigarette butts. Found a needle in the bushes. Nothing she might've dried her hair with," Gandy said. The corners of his eyes crinkled. "The needle was old, been on the ground for a while. Not promising."

"It's a dump then?" Ike asked.

"Looks like," Gandy said. He shut his bag.

Eliza nodded in agreement. "I don't see any drag marks. He was strong enough to carry her. We'll need to be careful about footprints. But there's nothing nearby except ours. So he swept after himself. He's thinking about us, at least."

Ike said, "I'm with you all on that aspect of the situation."

The side of Eliza's mouth turned downward in mild amusement. "Your approval means so much." She stood up.

"I know. Weight of my experience speaks volumes."

Eliza looked for his smile but didn't find it. Until the last month or two, if someone had asked her, she would've told them her partner was good-tempered and philosophical about his job. But he'd changed. One minute he was cracking jokes, warm and content, the next he'd take your head off at the shoulders. A real bear. Half the time he looked glassy-eyed, like he was verging on a winter slumber. She'd catch him staring off into nothing. Spaced-out. She attributed his grumbling to quitting cigarettes. But he'd kicked at the end of summer. The only difference she noticed then was his clothes smelled better. She couldn't imagine him exercising—but when he lost a few pounds, she was thinking, Okay, good for Ike, he's doing something positive for himself.

But that wasn't it. She was even prepared to blame the bad weather that hit town after the holidays. Ike couldn't let a snowflake go by without complaint. But his moodiness seemed deeper, as if this new outlook might be permanent.

If he was going through a midlife crisis, she wished he'd get through it fast.

So they could move on.

Eliza motioned to the patrol cop. "Okay, Kendicki, tell them to bag her." She snapped off the gloves. Eliza had long elegant fingers;

the nails were buffed round and clear-polished. No wedding ring. She was average height, pushing forty. Her caramel skin had an undertone of gold. Her hair was dark, short. On this chilly morning at the riverside, she wore a burgundy wool beret and matching scarf, an overcoat of camel hair. She'd been a detective for twelve years. Ike was the only cop in the department with a more reliable network of snitches. He'd come to Homicide from the Vice Squad. Eliza made her name collaring midlevel street crew managers over in Gang Crimes.

Partnered for a year, they were solid investigators, as good as any in the city.

Nobody bird-dogged their investigations and that certainly helped.

"We talking to the redhead now?" Ike said.

"Why, you need a date?"

"Jamila's always telling me I work too hard. Go get a hobby."

"Like learning how to walk again?"

Ike laughed and turned up his collar. He was reading a bronze city plaque mounted to a tree trunk on his left. "Kendicki, get tape put up along the Girl Scout Beach here. Follow my finger, okay? That willow there, got it? Okay, from there. And right to the edge of this walk. Make sure nobody messes up anything till Crime Scene sweeps it."

"The Brookies called and said they're sending over two squads. Worried about traffic once the morning rush kicks in. That'll free us up."

"Good man. Suppose rich folks gotta get to work too. But the park belongs to us. Just keep the B-town boys up on the cobblestones where they belong."

"Yes, sir."

Eliza was ready to start walking. The temperature, below freezing overnight, was on the rise. But Eliza couldn't feel it. It was just plain cold. Another storm front headed for the city. The forecast predicted rain changing to freezing rain and snow. Heavy snow expected around dinnertime. While Eliza pondered the weather report, cold drops began to fall. She watched them pock a snowdrift blown against the footing of the tornado slide.

Two attendants from the Medical Examiner's Office rolled a stretcher on the curve of pedestrian trail before wheeling around the playground equipment and onto the beach.

One of them, a twiggy man named Lopes, had worked for the ME as long as Eliza had been a detective. He was unzipping a body bag. The other was an American Indian who wore his hair in a net, a loose braid coiled underneath. Eliza didn't know him. She watched the Indian gaze out at the rushing Rood. The open water was moving fast with snowmelt from the hills. Its path snaked south. Downriver, at a distance from the dam, ice closed in and formed a narrowing channel. The latest precipitation flooded the channel, spilling over the midriver ice, eating at it from above and below and staining the thinned layers cloudy green.

On the opposite shore, a man in a peacoat was walking a Doberman pinscher. The man, who also wore a knit watch cap snug on his head, stopped. Eliza thought she saw binoculars hanging around the man's neck. The man leaned forward, anchoring his elbows on top of a broken concrete abutment.

He was glassing them.

Ike shook his box of cough drops. "Want one? I've got to buy a scarf. This hawk wind's blowing all winter long."

Eliza swiveled at the sound, and glancing over Ike's shoulder, she saw the Indian square himself to the river and raise his hand. It was a slight gesture and Eliza wouldn't have noticed if she hadn't been looking right at him.

Eliza declined Ike's offer.

"Let's find out what Ginger knows." Ike headed for the tunnel.

"Who you waving at?" Eliza asked the attendant.

"What?" The detective's question surprised him. His eyes flicked over to Eliza, then back down to the corpse lying on the sand. Eliza was close enough to read his plastic ID badge. He had it clipped to the sleeve of his navy-blue Nestor County Morgue jacket. His name was Elvis Fat Bear.

"Other side of the river. He a friend of yours?"

"Don't know what you mean." Fat Bear squatted at the dead woman's feet. Lopes had the body bag open. Rain fell inside with a steady *tap-tap-tap*. He was putting paper sacks over the victim's hands.

Eliza looked back across the water and realized her depth perception had been distorted. It was a woman wearing a silver parka walking the dog. She must've been hidden behind the larger silhouette of the peacoat man.

Peacoat was gone.

"We okay to take her?" Lopes asked. He had round tortoiseshell eyeglasses. Raindrops beaded on the lenses. His breath plumed. The rain was freezing. Eliza felt it turning sharp on her cheek. She waited for the other attendant to say something. Fat Bear waited too, head down, his hands around the naked ankles of the dead woman. Eliza didn't answer. Fat Bear hunched his shoulders. Tiny ice drops bounced off his jacket.

"We're good to go, right?" If Lopes thought so he wouldn't have asked again. He used his thumbnail to scale wet ice off the zipper teeth.

Fat Bear looked up at the detective.

Eliza read nothing on his face. He was just a man doing a job in the rain.

"Sure. Get out of this weather."

They lifted the victim into the bag. Eliza approached the water's edge. The woman and her dog were upriver now, following a nature trail into the trees. Eliza peered at the mud. It was smooth except for the frozen footprints of birds. She walked off twenty paces to where a stone retaining wall had been constructed on this side of the water, an answer to the flaking concrete barrier on the Booth City side. She rested her hand on the stones, touched her fingers to the rough mortar gluing them together. Chunks of dirty ice floated past. A kidnapped Nativity lawn ornament—one of the wise men, judging by the purple turban—bobbed in the dam's keeper wave. Eliza tried to imagine how it would feel to plunge beneath the surface. The brutal initial shock. How the cold must burn.

They needed to call the Brooktown area office to see if anybody was missing from the high-rises or brownstones up the street. Had to check the B.C. night patrol logs. Did anybody notice a disabled vehicle pulled to the shoulder by the river park or Figg's Pond? Were the lots chained at dusk? Any reports of unusual activity in the park?

Eliza moved off to join Ike and the redheaded jogger.

The park was quiet now because it was snowing.

"She was naked and not moving."

"You touch her?" Ike asked.

"God no."

"If she was lyin' like we found her, then you couldn't have seen her wounds. So how'd you know she wasn't asleep or passed out?"

"In this cold?" she asked, frowning. "I guess I didn't."

"But you called and said you found a dead body on the beach?"

"She seemed dead. And, I mean, obviously she *is* dead. So what're you getting at?"

"Just your assumption she was dead."

The jogger sipped her water bottle. "She had a crow on her, I think."

"Come again?"

"When I first looked over there—I was just clearing the trees—one of those big crows was hopping on her. Then it flew away. I didn't know what I was seeing. But that's what it was."

"A crow?"

A wisp of red blew across her eyes and she tucked it under her headband. Nodded.

Eliza hadn't said a word since walking up from the river.

"Who's going to sleep through something like that?" the jogger asked her.

Homicide Squad Room

Prints came back quickly with a hit: Delbert Lee Watts.

Ike couldn't believe it—the vic was a man.

He looked again at the crime-scene photos and noticed the

Adam's apple, the square meaty hands. He'd have to give *Doctor* Gandy some grief about this one. There'd be enough to go around. Top it off, Ike had collared the guy no less than five times when he worked Vice details. Solicitation. Public indecency. Possession of a controlled substance. The refrain continued down his sheet. Ike looked at the mug shot inside the folder. Watts had lost about fifty pounds since his last bust eighteen months ago. A long time to stay out of trouble. Where could a transsexual hooker with a cough syrup habit vanish to in a midsized midwestern city? Ike couldn't place the face in the photo. Then he realized he'd probably never seen Watts without makeup and a wig. The file said Watts's street name was Josine.

"Josine." Ike spoke the name out loud, thinking, You can take the Delbert out of the double-wide, but . . . he remembered him now. Josine used to take her johns into the woods. Not around Figg's Pond but downriver and across town on Booth City's east side. Marjorie Broe Woods, or Blow Woods if you asked the locals. Ike wondered if sad-eyed Delbert had picked up a little something extra in the woods one night. Death's blank fin swimming circles in a drop of blood.

The woods were a locus for gay liaisons. Hangout for closeted men who didn't dare enter the bars. Forest haven for anonymous sex. Marketplace where chicken hawks shopped the services of teenaged hustlers who traded their youth for damp bills, then crossed the boulevard and copped rock in the projects.

There were three gay bars within the city limits. The most notorious was an east-side basement club called The Axle. Its interior swallowed light. There must've been a sale on black paint the day before it opened. Spongy floorboards made a man feel as if he might fall through. But fall through to what? Axle air had a warm bleach-water smell like wet mops. The ventilation was whispery, congested. Murderous speakers, real eardrum poppers, were stacked ceiling-high in the four corners. The beat, all kidney-punching bass lines and deep percussive thrums, buzzed your breastbone. Mondays were slow. Tuesdays offered half-priced drafts and an open mike. Wednesdays and Thursdays rotated themes that usually failed to draw a crowd. But if sweat and smoke were crude oil, then on weekends the club was a Texas gusher.

Ascending The Axle's chipped, beer-slick front steps, a patron might notice a bus stop shelter on the other side of the road. Plexiglas etched with gang signs. Crossing the road required some care. Syringes on the sidewalk. Intoxicated drivers of every variety under the moon. Slow-cruising trucks crammed with hill boys looking to mess up a faggot. Cops working undercover. Narco and Vice.

A lit Camel covers the piss smell of the shelter. Nobody sober waits inside unless it's pouring rain. Eye contact means something. No words are incidental. Going for a walk takes you farther each time. A young detective plays the role for a solicitation sting. He looks good in leather. Motorcycle jacket with side laces. Black steer over brown stud. He has the body for bait. Baby face too. This is before he gets married and quits smoking. This is being hungry for action. This is learning on the job.

He still owns the jacket. Never been on a bike in his life.

Beyond the bus stop is a jagged seawall. Only the seawall isn't really a wall but the hundred-year-old stunted trees of Broe Woods, and the sea is the Rood River sliding over Dam #5.

As the scent of decayed leaves rushed up from the well of memory, Ike saw his partner push through the squad room's double doors. "Hey, Eliza, we got a name on the Dead Girl Scout. Delbert Watts."

"Delbert?"

"He's a shemale. You know, a little bit of this, a little bit of that."

"For real?"

Ike was nodding. "Turns out I knew him too."

"You didn't kill him, did you?" Eliza smiled. "Wait. Let me get my coat off before you answer." Her cheeks felt tight from the wind. The squad room smelled like coffee and stale heating. She was already looking for her cup.

"Delbert went by the name Josine. Used to hook in Broe."

"Used to?"

"We haven't picked him up in a year and a half."

"Maybe he got himself clean."

"I think he was sick. Man lost a lot of weight."

"You're saying AIDS?" Eliza asked. Without thinking, she brushed her thumb across the crook of her elbow. That was where her old man liked to shoot until his skin got bicycle-patch tough and his veins shriveled to the circumference of speaker wires. Colleagues thought he wore long-sleeved shirts out of some sense of formality. She'd watch him slide the needle into his ankles, testing—then hunting between his toes—his skinny white leg cranked up in the air and the spike clamped in his jaws. He'd lay there, collapsed on the Naugahyde couch. The basement television bathed him like an indoor moon. Volume knob on the TV had cracked off. So he kept a pair of pliers next to the set. But she never saw him use them. Instead, the sound was always way down and there'd be a Johnny Cash record spinning on the hi-fi turntable. He must've played other albums too, but that was what she always heard in her memory. That big, slow voice resonating like it was coming up from the bottom of a mine shaft. Her father concentrating so hard he missed her slender figure trapped forever in the doorway. Watching.

"Something to check anyway," Ike said. "Pretty much skin and bones when we found him."

Eliza hung her coat on a wall peg. She flipped through her message box. Her desk and Ike's butted together on the far side of the room, in a corner by the coffeemaker. She filled her cup before sitting back in her chair to absorb the new information. "An angry john gets a test, comes back positive. Decides Watts was the likely source . . ."

"Or as good as any."

"He goes to Broe, picks him up again. Maybe they play around a little like old times. All of a sudden playtime's over. Knife's out and he ties him up. And our angry john slices into Watts's junk. Teaches him a lesson. Then he stabs him. Probably does the serious carving after he's dead."

"Just an idea."

"Doesn't explain the old cuts. Or why he's dumped at the river park."

"No better theories going right now," Ike said. He held up his empty hands.

"Don't even know if he had it."

"But Watts was about as high-risk as you can get."

"We should double-check and see if he's still white," she said.

Ike's laugh was triple-wrapped in scratchy smoker's wheeze. Six months since he threw away all his lighters and matchbooks. Ten seconds since he considered walking to the 7-Eleven and buying a pack. He couldn't shop there anymore. Too close to his habit, like having a beer with your old connection; a bad idea you needed to keep out of your head if you didn't want to wake up with the glass pipette in your lap again. Chasing the dragon or, in Ike's case, the camel.

"Any address in his file?" Eliza asked.

"Uh-huh. SRO on the corner of Kingston and Faro. The Limerick."

"I've driven by it. Never been inside."

"Not exactly four-star accommodations. I wouldn't doubt if Delbert was meeting clients there. Working right out of his room. Place is ninety percent alkies, flameouts, and hookers."

"What's the other ten?"

"Vacancies."

Chessman's Bar

But the other ten percent weren't vacancies. Single Room Occupancies were one step above shelters and two up from refrigerator boxes under the bridge. They were former transient hotels. Flophouse Row. Some still offered weekly rates and tickets for soup in St. Bart's basement. The buildings were among the oldest on the riverfront. Booth City had a block of them crowding the piers where the riverboat casinos anchored. A gambler with a good arm could throw his dice and hit an SRO window from any of the decks. The Limerick was full to capacity. Down-and-outers. Disabled people who cashed government checks. Old-timers who had nobody. The functioning mentally ill. Shufflers and nonblinkers. Everybody smoked like Parisians. Ike considered it a miracle all these places hadn't burned to the ground. Carelessness was a way of life down here.

Ike knew a cabby who'd been living in The Limerick for a decade. Wayne Poins. Poins had the money to move out. He talked about leaving. But he never got around to doing it. Poins declared himself a poet. Bard of the underclass. A San Francisco Beat who arrived too late and never quite made it out to the Left Coast. Or out of The Limerick. Even Poins would admit he'd rather warm a bar stool than go about the mundane task of finding a more respectable address. So he learned to sleep through the fights, the wall banging, and the sirens. But Poins had a great memory.

They were early for their appointment with the manager of The Limerick. The man working the desk told them he had a key and they could take a look at Watts's room. The detectives decided to come back in a half hour and talk to the manager. They were in no hurry. They went for a stroll.

Eliza and Ike found Poins throwing darts in a barroom called Chessman's, next door to the hotel. The sign painted over the door showed a chess piece, a black rook with bulging biceps but no face, hoisting a spilling draft into the air. The room was long and narrow with a high ceiling, like a racquetball court. Someone thought it was a good idea to festoon the bar with white Christmas lights, the chasing kind. Ike got the spins after one glance. Zydeco music squeezed joy from the jukebox. The bartender, a squat Latina in her sixties, made them for cops and said nothing. Her liquid brown eyes slipped behind a cloud. Eliza walked right over, asked for a Coke with lemon in Spanish. Ike went directly to the back. This was his contact. He'd take the lead.

Poins was stretched out on a bench. Waiting to take his turn. He had an empty bottle of Michelob resting precariously on his belly while he concentrated on the man throwing, a white guy with blond dreadlocks. Eliza thanked the bartender and followed her partner to the four dartboards in the rear. Only one board was lit. The last dart sailed above the board and stuck in the oak-style paneling. The man hung his head. Poins sat up, handed him his bottle.

He patted him on the shoulder and said, "You'll get it back, friend. I never win twice in a row." His sliding gaze picked Ike out from the shadows. "Ah, is the good detective here to roust us for a bit of gaming?" The cabby's beard was huge and bristly black. Inside it, Ike could see a smile.

"How's the world treating you, Brother Wayne?"

"Like I fucked his sister and told my friends. Join me for a toddy?" Poins stopped when he saw Eliza. He tipped his chin in her direction. "You I don't know."

"Detective Ochoa is my partner. Let's find a table."

The other dart thrower vanished into the men's room. Eliza heard him flushing his stash. The two detectives and the cabby wedged themselves into a sticky wooden booth. Eliza could smell a pizza cooking and wondered where the kitchen was.

Poins waved at the bartender. "Luisa, Irish coffee, *por favor?* Detectives, are you drinking today? No? *Solamente uno*."

"Do you know a tranny hooker named Josine?" Ike asked.

"Ah, cut to the chase, why don't we?" The bar was drafty, and Poins pulled a brown scarf from his hip pocket and wrapped it around his throat. "I do know Josine. She stays at The Limerick, second floor, facing the street. But you knew that already or you wouldn't be here." Poins's coffee arrived in a reindeer mug. He blew at the steam. "What has she done?"

"She's been murdered."

Poins set the mug down. "Oh Christ, did some bashers catch her in the park?"

"What park?" Ike asked.

"I think she was still a regular at Blow Woods. But I hadn't talked to her in the building, oh, in about two months. Light in her window would be on when I came in late. A Chinese paper lantern you can see from the curb. I thought I was just missing her, not crossing paths, our hours mismatched or something. Last time I *did* see her, she was with a date. She brought a few back, you know. More often in the dead of winter. The good-looking gentleman callers she could show off. Repeaters too, ones she was comfortable with, they came up. This guy was blond, had shoulders like a linebacker." Poins spaced his hands out like he was talking about the length of a catfish.

"This was in her room?"

"No. Going up the stairwell. Never saw his face, but young I'd say. Fit, at least. He was taking the stairs two at a time."

Eliza noticed the rings on Poins's hands. He wore silver on each finger. Nine silver rings because his right middle finger was missing.

"Remember ever seeing him before?" Ike asked.

Poins shook his head. "Can't be absolutely sure because all I had was a glimpse from behind and he never turned around. But I'd say no."

"Did Josine have enemies?"

"None she told me about."

"Any problem johns? Guys who got carried away, roughed her up a little?"

"I'm sure that happened from time to time, but . . ."

Eliza slipped a notepad from her overcoat. "Do you recall any names? Anybody who ever really hurt her?"

"We weren't close friends, just acquaintances, building mates. Josine didn't talk shop with me. Our conversations were about weather, music, the neighborhood."

"You knew she worked Broe Woods."

"And she saw me drive my cab. What's the big deal? I gave her a ride to the Woods once in a while. Or I dropped her off at a bar if she was in the mood for a venue change. She was fun to talk to. Made the ride shorter."

"How was Josine's health?"

"What do mean?"

"She sick a lot?" Ike asked.

"Nothing I was aware of. She liked her cough syrup, but in that case she was being, let's say . . . rigorously preventative?"

Eliza wondered about money. "How did Josine pay the bills? She have enough dates to keep the gas on, the phone ringing?"

Poins shook his head. "I'm in the dark on that too, I'm afraid. Seems to me the Woods are pretty lowball. Excuse the pun. But Josine was always flush. I never figured it out. And her cash didn't coincide with long days pounding the pavement either. I think she got checks in the mail. Not Government. Real money."

"So why's she working the Woods?"

"Why are you carrying a shield, Detective Ochoa?"

Eliza stared hard at the cabby. Waited a beat. His eyes came down to the tabletop.

"Maybe she liked the action, Detective." Poins smiled into his coffee. His thumb ring tapped the handle. "But I'm speculating, of course."

"I don't know too many hookers doing it 'cause they like the action, Mr. Poins."

Poins shrugged. His smile was back in place. "That I would not know."

"Delbert get into a lot of beefs with people?" Ike asked.

"Listen, Delbert wouldn't say *Boo!* on Halloween. He was utterly harmless, a quintessential damsel in distress. Auntie Martha across the hall—the lady turned eighty-eight in June—she had to kill his spiders for him. So, no, I can't believe he did anything to provoke someone to the point of murder. Delbert wasn't stupid. The hick kid who just got off the bus was a lifetime ago. He'd been working those woods a long time."

"Delbert wasn't prone to looking for trouble is what you're saying?" Eliza said.

"Oh, he could be bitchy, but that's part of the package, isn't it? The grand charade."

Ike slid out of the booth. He dropped a card on the table. "You call anything comes around doesn't smell right."

Eliza flipped her notebook closed. She had more questions but was willing to hold off if Ike decided the meeting was over. Besides, Poins was starting to irritate her. She didn't do well with male condescension, particularly from slobs with dried egg yolk in their beards. She stood up next to Ike and rebuttoned her coat. Poins's dart comrade had the restroom door cracked, peeking out like a mouse. Eliza took one quick step in his direction and the crack disappeared.

"Where'd you find the poor thing?" Poins asked.

"Figg's Pond," Ike said.

"In the water?"

"No, his body was on the beach."

Poins shook his head in disgust. "Washed up like a godforsaken carp."

The detectives didn't bother to say Delbert never went into the water, that the river never had ahold of him. Instead, they said good-bye.

Poins polished off the Irish coffee and as the doors opened, letting in a slice of brittle winter sunshine, he requested Luisa bring him another.

2

FUNKY, FUNKY SHOES

The Limerick

The manager ended up being a kid in his twenties with a Prince Valiant haircut and a pitiful goatee so wispy Eliza could count the strands. She and the manager were talking. Their shoulders an inch apart as they walked down a narrow upstairs hallway. Ike had fallen behind, his breathing labored after the stairs. He was making enough noise that Eliza turned to check on him. Head hanging into his chest, he glistened with sweat. Like he'd been sprayed with a water bottle, the kind sunbathers used on the beach. Only it wasn't at all warm in the hallway. The air growing noticeably colder the higher they climbed. On this particular floor, it was frigid. Eliza would've guessed a window was left open. But it was too dark.

Ike seemed to be studying the traffic pattern scoured into the faun-colored carpet. His feet were barely moving. He didn't acknowledge her look, but his pace picked up.

"Heat's on the fritz," the kid said.

"That happen a lot?" Eliza asked. Making friendly conversation.

"Only in winter." The kid took a slug of ginseng iced tea. His double-pierced lip clicked against the glass bottle. "So far this year's actually pretty good. Last year was, like, super bad."

Good or bad, whatever was pumping out of the floor vents smelled like scorched metal. The kid was dressed for the job. He had on a zipped-up hoodie with a white thermal showing at the wrists. Earmuffs, ready to go, around his neck. He moved in a cloud of patchouli.

"Here we are. Home sweet home." He produced a key. It was safety-pinned to a circle of teal paper marked *44*.

No number on the door, but Eliza noticed a nail half sunk at eye level. She watched the manager twist the key in a single lock. He pushed the door open a couple inches, and then hesitated.

"My boss says if the tenant's dead, then there's no problem letting you in. Still, this feels like I'm doing you guys a favor here. Maybe next time I call for help, some issue, a dude pulls a shitty number on me, whatever, the car might make it to the scene in less than a half hour, you know?"

"You had a problem?" Eliza asked.

"Yeah, a couple months ago. Dude put this dirty-ass corkscrew up to my eye. The man stunk nasty. Thanksgiving Day. I'm watching the game behind the desk. He took my money, my Tims too. Okay, forty-five minutes afterwards, the cherry top pulls up. Cops were all chest out and crap, like I robbed myself and was bothering them. Sherlocks, I'm thinking, the dude stole my dang boots."

"What did this guy look like?"

"Look like? I told the cops his name. Jimmy Tran. He's Cambodian or Vietnamese. Something like that. I went to high school with him for about a year. Little Tran the Garbage Man, that's what we called him. Totally wasted. No way he recognized me. Almost walks into the wall as he's leaving. But I knew him. Jimmy G-man."

"What is your name?" Ike's soft voice coming at the kid from behind as the three of them crowded the doorway.

"Jared . . . Jared Hoffner."

Ike put a hand on his shoulder. "Brother Jared, we appreciate your spirit of cooperation. I will speak with the watch commander about your troubles."

Hoffner's eyebrows lifted like he was surprised Ike had the ability to speak, or perhaps the surprise came from being touched gently by a policeman. He held the door open and let the detectives enter, careful not to cross over the threshold.

First thing Eliza noticed was warmth lapping around her ankles.

The room, of course, was small. Hardly bigger than a walk-in closet. Twin bed shoved against the wall. Four-drawer dresser. TV on top of the dresser, and a Sony CD Walkman plugged into two pint-sized speakers. Angled into the corner opposite the door was a space heater. Eliza could see the coil flushing orange.

"He's not supposed to have one of those," Hoffner said, showing the eye for detail that preceded his ascent to manager.

"Maybe we let this offense go," Ike said, "considering the man's passed." He slid around Eliza and peered into a second cramped doorway strung with amber and chocolate-brown glass beads. "Had his own toilet and tub," he said. Nodding as if to answer a question no one had asked.

"This is a good unit. We've got a waiting list for the fourth floor and higher." Hoffner had a thought, tilted his head. "Is somebody going to come and get his stuff?"

"Not us," Eliza said. "We'll probably have the crime lab stop by to collect evidence. After they're gone, you're free to clean up and move in somebody new."

"Sounds like more work for me."

"Did Mr. Watts leave any names on file with you?" Ike asked. "Next of kin? Emergency contacts?"

"I'd have to look up his application."

Something like a polite smile lifted Ike's cheeks.

Hoffner screwed the cap onto his empty bottle. "I'll go do that now. If you don't need me here."

"Much thanks, Brother Jared."

With Hoffner heading downstairs to the lobby, Ike and Eliza started to toss Watts's room. Eliza dumped the drawers, one by one, out of the dresser and onto the unmade bed. She refilled each drawer, grabbing handfuls of bras and bikini bottoms, thongs and slippery nightgowns, and stuffed them back into their contact paper-lined homes. Ike emptied the closet, knocking hangers together as he hauled out short dresses, leather skirts, and mini tank tops. When Eliza finished with the dresser she moved to the floor of the closet. Ike switched to the other side of the bed, ducked his head under, and promptly started sneezing.

"Could've used a broom for Christmas," Ike said. He pinched the bridge of his nose, his eyes watering. He sneezed again.

If Eliza learned one positive thing about Josine, it was that she could shop for shoes. How she could afford them was another question.

Ike unfolded his handkerchief, sat on the window ledge, and blew his nose. A Chinese paper lantern, the one Poins had mentioned, hung next to his head. White dragons flew in a red sky inches away from Ike's throbbing left temple. He felt his breath shallowing out so he sat very still. He didn't want to have to fight dizziness or, worse yet, to end up with his ass prone on the floor. A drop of sweat crawled behind his ear. He willed himself to ignore it. Let things be. He needed to settle down.

When they'd come back to The Limerick from visiting Chessman's, Ike had his city eyes wide open. He noticed the millwork in the lobby, a few old sconces lathered in decades of cheap paint, the shadow of a mirror, spiritlike, hovering in the T-shaped hall where fire doors swung shut on twin staircases. This had been a fine place once, a holiday destination rather than a full-stop dead end. The building itself had made the move beyond death to zombification. But from upstairs in Delbert Watts's cubbyhole, it was still quite a view. Ike pushed aside the lantern to take it all in.

The Onyx Bridge was already loaded with rush-hour traffic. Two trains of vehicles chugging in opposite directions. Above them, the city had paid for small Christmas trees to be wired to the lampposts. Although he was too far away, Ike thought he could see their silver and gold orbs flashing. He glanced at the back of his hand and saw the sparks there too. He pulled in a deep lungful of air from the overheated, underattended room.

Don't let me black out in front of my partner. I do not need that right now.

"You okay?"

"Um-hmm."

"Why are your eyes shut?" Eliza asked, dangling a pair of sling-back Ferragamos Ike couldn't possibly see.

"Just thinking. You look out this window here and see St. Bartholomew's stone bell tower at one end of the horizon, riverboats anchored down below. Cushing Points sucking up to the river on the east and the B-town Coastal Towers less than a mile away. It's all there. Heaven and Hell laid out like a medieval map."

"Oh, you're having a moment. Pardon my intrusion."

With his eyes still closed, Ike drew a lazy cross in the air.

"That's sacrilegious."

"I don't know about that. But what you're thinking about doing with those shoes is a sin." The sparks were fading. "Good Catholic girl like you," he said, chuckling. Soft bubbles were popping in his ears. The muscles in his legs twitched.

Eliza's crooked smile flashed at him.

"You find anything under the bed?" he asked.

"Boxes. A big cardboard one and two hatboxes."

Eliza dragged them into the light. The hatboxes were filled with wigs. Mostly black, except for one frizzy blond, and another of wine-colored ringlets. The big box was a trash container. Durex condoms, Prometh w/Codeine VC bottles, Orange Crush soda cans, and six Red Stripe empties. Apparently, Watts ate out or not at all.

"I told you Watts was a syrup-head. Looks like he got his lean on pretty regular." Ike shook the box. Pharmacy labels on the codeine prescription bottles. He counted the names of five local stores. "Must've had a 'script connection," he said, easing himself onto his feet and massaging the side of his neck. "That purple was good to the last drop."

"Poins said the same thing. About liking her syrup."

"Man knows everybody. Hears what they say and what they don't. Tolerating his bullshit is how you pay for it."

"No kidding."

"Lemme poke through the trash. You get on to the bathroom."

An old-fashioned shower curtain ring circled the tub. A pink plastic curtain, spotted with mildew and secured by pink S hooks, splashed sad color into a sadder realm of chipped sea foam tiles. The vanity mirror had an ornate frame of leafy vines but no medicine cabinet behind it. Two silverfish scurried around a chained rubber stopper in the sink. Under the sink Eliza found a plastic makeup caddy and a three-legged stool.

Watts was tall, tall enough to sit on the stool and see himself in the bottom of the mirror. All Eliza could see was the top of her head.

The toilet lid had been left up.

Jamming herself between the toilet and bathtub, Eliza inspected what she had guessed to be a modest trunk standing on its end. The trunk began to hum. Watts had disguised its real function with a lace tablecloth draping over all four sides. A black candle placed on top had, at some earlier point in time, melted into the cotton and spread out like a flattened paw. The trunk was a dorm-sized refrigerator. Eliza opened it.

Contents limited to cans of Orange Crush. About a case's worth stacked on the shelves and lining the door. An electrical cord ran up behind the toilet tank and plugged into an adapter and then the two-holed socket under the mirror. Eliza found a disposable lighter balanced diagonally across a soap dish on the edge of the tub. No soap. But there were ashes and the butts of a dozen extinguished Newports.

When Eliza stood up, she noticed a few inches of water in the tub.

Something else. Plastic bags printed with blue lettering. Knots tied in them. Six knots, six bags. The letters spelling out: CHILLY BEAR ICE CUBES.

"Ike, come in here."

Ike walked backward through the veil of beads. He had his pen inserted about three inches inside one of the Red Stripe bottles. He was holding it horizontally, with his arm away from his body. A swallow of beer sloshed against the curve of the glass. He looked over his shoulder.

Eliza pointed to the tub with her eyes.

Another bag was floating among the slack plastic and melted ice. A Ziploc with a green strip at the top, the kind that people put their leftovers in. Eliza probably had a dozen of them packed in her freezer at home.

The one in Delbert Watts's bathtub held a pound of flesh—a lump of rounded muscle and skin—floating in water, violet and murky.

Ike disappeared. The beads clacked and he was back again without the pen and bottle. He was putting his gloves on.

Eliza could feel her adrenaline rush coming on, could sense Ike's excitement too. He had his lips parted, the tip of his tongue rubbing against his left incisor, something he did when he was concentrating. Or when he was pissed off.

"What sort of ugliness did you get yourself into, Delbert?" Ike asked, using the dead man's given name. He lifted a corner of the Ziploc. The mound slipped around inside the bag. Water trickled into the tub. But the seal on the bag was tight.

The flesh inside looked pearl-gray. It was human—one piece, intact, sliced whole from the body. Cheek of a man's buttocks—skin stippled with light brown hairs, the portion lopped off as neatly as a butcher's roast, although roasts weren't tattooed. Hard to discern in the fluid, the tattoo was nothing so lucky as a name. Rather, it depicted an elaborate symbol—of an interlocking, not quite circular, pattern. Eliza's immediate thought was, It's Celtic.

Ike was about to say something but stopped himself.

She already had her phone out, calling Gandy. He knew she'd ask Gandy to bring Dr. Lu along for the ride.

Josine/Delbert Watts's Room

"Why you need me down here? On Tom's radio they said you don't even have a body. Know how much backlog I got? This weather, I deal with bums dying every night. There's a batch on the street, coming out of Cushing, been knocking those kids like bowling pins. I don't even have the holiday suicides written up yet."

Dr. Lu paused. She put her hand on Ike's shoulder.

"You look like shit."

"I picked up some bug."

"Yeah, maybe you should start smoking again. All your happiness is gone." Lu wore a UC-Berkeley sweatshirt over a black blouse. Her herringbone skirt was too short, too tight. She kept her hair cropped, except for the jet bangs that she combed down to her eyebrows. "Where?" she asked.

Eliza showed her into the bathroom.

She would've sworn that Lu turned around before seeing anything in the water.

"Tom, get the small cooler out of the wagon," the ME said.

Gandy retreated. Hadn't made it past the dresser.

"Your partner is a big-time contaminator. Did you see him playing with this? He can't keep from touching."

Eliza didn't have a chance to reply.

Lu called out to the other room, "Ike, you're lucky I'm so good. I cover all the mistakes. Make you guys look like heroes. Clear everything on the books." She bent over the edge of the tub. In a quieter voice she told Eliza, "He should buy me dinner every Sunday for a month. Not February either."

The forensic pathologist was a head shorter and twenty pounds lighter than the detective. But to Eliza she seemed much bigger. Even when they weren't standing hip-to-hip in a cramped bathroom pondering human remains.

"This is textbook. The killer even put it in a bag. All we need is a label. Know how many detectives are too sloppy to think of doing that?"

Eliza wondered if she was supposed to answer the question.

Lu pressed her chin downward, staring at her own chest. A sprinkle of perspiration shined on her cheekbones. "Tom?"

Eliza moved so Gandy could get in with the cooler.

Ike had left the bedroom. But Eliza could hear his voice coming from the hallway, right outside the door.

"Now this paper is going to make my job a little easier," he said.

Jared Hoffner pointed to the application he'd just passed to Ike. "He left a lot of blanks and I think the references are bogus."

"All right, all right. Still, you did us another favor. The room's considered a crime scene for the time being. We'll tape the door. Keep an eye out and call me if anybody's snooping around." Ike dealt Hoffner a card from his wallet.

"Will do."

"You ever notice anything of interest with Mr. Watts?"

"Naw, Josine was cool. You know she would've of taken offense the way you keep referring to her as a man."

"None intended, Brother Jared."

"Thought you should know about the faux pas, or whatever."

Hoffner padded his way to the stairs. He was snapping his fingers over the backbeat of the broken furnace kicking inside the walls.

Ike showed Eliza the application. There was a lot of white space, but in the middle of the first page—in a section highlighted as mandatory—Watts had spelled out his parents' names in cramped cursive script.

Benton and Lila Watts. A street address in Decatur, Illinois. The area code and first two digits of a phone number were written down and, after second thoughts, scratched out. It was the same dull blue ink as the rest of the answers on the form.

"You gonna be the one?" Eliza asked.

Ike nodded. "Unless they moved or died, I should be able to pull up the Decatur phone book online. That part's simple."

The Limerick

Ike called into the squad room. The street canvass around Figg's Park brought one good lead. A swing shift detective—who the lieutenant assigned to help out, but only after Horner and Ochoa asked—had identified a potential witness. He stopped at an all-night rib shack adjacent to the park and found an ambulance driver pulling a double. The driver thought he remembered a light-colored van parked with its hazards flashing near the park.

"Midnight," the detective said, "or closer to one, one-thirty at the latest. The guy couldn't be exact."

Ike and Eliza agreed to break for dinner and come back to The Limerick in the evening, with hopes of finding more tenants at home watching TV and digesting. Catch them before they were drunk, stoned, or sleepy. Odds were not in their favor.

Afterward, they'd hit Broe Woods and talk to the night crowd. Work the street just like the hustlers do.

Homicide Squad Room

The Wattses *were* in the book. It didn't take a detective to find them. Ike wrote down their number and called, part of him wishing they'd be out. He didn't particularly want to bother good people at their kitchen table, but he did. He heard someone washing dishes and a radio tuned to a weather report.

"Is this Benton Watts?"

"It is."

"This is Detective Ike Horner of the Booth City Police Department. I'm calling in regard to your son, Delbert."

"Is he dead?"

"Yes, I'm sorry to tell you he is. We believe Delbert was the victim of a homicide."

A moment of nothing.

Then the man was talking, his voice muffled, pulling away from the phone. "Lila, why don't you go over to Jeanie's house for a minute. I'll be over shortly. There's been some bad news . . . yes, for Del . . . but I'd like to get the story straight from this gentleman before we talk."

Ike waited.

Benton Watts came back on the line. "Sorry, my wife's going next door to her sister's." Watts cleared his throat. "Do you know what happened?"

"Not yet. We're putting the pieces together. Why, for instance, did you think Delbert was dead when I called?"

"We've been waiting for a call like yours for a long time."

"Delbert was trouble for you?"

"No, I wouldn't say that. He was just one who never found peace with himself."

"Maybe you can tell me something more about your son. Something I can't find looking at evidence."

"Sure, sure. I'll try." There was a pause, and the sound of a chair pulled across a wooden floor. "Del never cared for life here. I haven't heard a word from him since, oh, six years ago it was this last Christmas. We missed the Del we knew. He was a confused soul but he had a kind heart. Mother and I think he felt things, life things that everyone goes through, he felt them too strongly. Del was hurting from the time he was in the cradle. He was my dear boy and you've called to tell me he's gone. I don't know what I can say . . . we'd like to help you, but . . ."

"In Delbert's apartment we found the remains of another person. Can you give us any information about associates of your son or—"

"Del didn't do it. No. Detective Horner, I can assure you of that. I took him to a boxing match at the church gym when he was twelve years old. Del got sick on himself. Popcorn and 7UP everywhere. It was the blood. He never could stomach it."

"Is there anything else you can think of?"

"Not now. Perhaps my wife, her memory's better than mine, but I don't think that's a blessing necessarily. As I said, we'd lost touch with Del. More by his choice than ours."

"Did Delbert drink beer?"

"What an odd question. No, I can't recall him ever having a beer. He was more of a soda drinker. He got caught smoking a marijuana cigarette when he was at the high school. That was years ago."

"Thank you for your time, Mr. Watts. I'm sure you've put a hard day's work in already. And the night's not going to be—"

"I'm laid off."

"Sorry to hear that."

"Happens every winter. I'm in the roofing business."

"Right, of course. It's seasonal."

"Are you folks through with my son, medically?"

Ike gave Benton Watts the number to the County Morgue. He reminded him to call back if he or Lila thought of anything that might help the investigation. Ike dropped the paper with the Wattses' number into Delbert's red file—all Homicide investigation files were denoted by red plastic binders—and he flipped it closed.

Corner of Quarry St. and Pintail Ave.

If home is where a person lives, and not sleeps, then Eliza's childhood home was her mother's kitchen at the restaurant. The kitchen was not so much a place as a flavor. Rice, always rice, steaming up to the discolored tin ceiling panels, and chicken necks boiling for soup stock, onions frying. Oregano. Cinnamon sticks. Beans and lard. Peppers split and seeded on a scarred butcher block.

Her mother slowly rolling a lime under her palm, her other hand automatic, unwatched, choosing a green-handled knife from the magnetic strip screwed into the wall. Escaping from the oven vents, the smell of roasting pork shoulder as strong as a young boxer standing in the corner. Tortilla flour and cornmeal sanded into the pine floor by the busy shoes of two waiters, a dishwasher, and the only cook.

Mamá.

Bone-white plates stacked higher than Mamá's head; each painted in the center with a single marigold, a pattern that her mother had insisted on buying instead of the cheaper plain ones. Her choice, her sweat, and her thriving enterprise: El Cabrito Blanco.

The White Kid Goat.

It was her mother's specialty. A milk-fed kid slaughtered at about one month. They bought theirs from a Swedish farmer, thirty miles west of the city. Her mother smoked *los cabritos* over a barbecue pit in a grassy lot she owned behind the restaurant. When the colder months arrived they covered the pit with a steel grate and used the extra space for parking.

But in the spring and throughout summer it was *cabrito*. Rubbed with oil and sage. Salt and garlic. The smell of burning hickory followed Eliza to school, and later, in the summer, to the YMCA swim class where even the chlorine couldn't kill it in her hair, on her skin. Eliza the child learned to hate the smell, thought the smoke made her skin browner, stranger. Anglo classmates sniffed out her difference. Called it pot. Said her brothers were drug dealers. Her mother sucked off donkeys in a Tijuana tent show. What did they know about her familia?

Eliza pulled around the back, put her parking brake on to keep from slipping backward into the icy alley. The back door to the kitchen was propped open. The escaping heat melted a moon shape into the snow.

Sugar's Java Joint

The light inside the coffeehouse was a good match for the aroma of Jamaican beans brewing behind the counter. Light like old papers, Ike thought, left yellowing in the sun. But there had been no sun to speak of on this day, a twilight darkness descending early and clouds wigging the high-rise rooftops at the city center. The subtleties of changing light gave the impression time was stuck. Sugar's was tucked between the courts building and a health insurance company. Devil and the deep-blue sea, in Ike's opinion. He'd had his fill of aggravation dealing with both lately.

Over the coffeehouse's entrance, a bamboo wind chime played hollow music.

Ike watched her walk in. She propped the door open with her boot just long enough to shake the sleet off her umbrella. Jamila Greene—smooth, dark, and as solid as the walnut door swinging shut behind her—moved with authority. It might have been the rush of chilly outside air that made Ike sit straighter.

Might've been, but wasn't.

He raised two fingers to draw his wife's attention. She smiled and took her time crossing the room. A tall woman with an athletic stride. Oval, silver-rimmed eyeglasses picked up the streaks winding in the crinkled locks on her head. Ike stood up and pulled out a seat for her. She kissed him on the cheek. He took her coat, folded it over the back of the empty third chair at their table. She sat down and leaned her umbrella against the exposed brick wall. Ike noticed the umbrella half-opening like a bat's wing.

"You eat anything?" she asked.

Ike shook his head, took a sip of scorching coffee.

"Can't give up on food, Shang, not wise. Where's your energy going to come from?" Jamila had called him by his old street name, his ball-yard name, though these days she was one of only two people on earth who even knew it.

"I'm not hungry."

"Don't give me that. I'll buy us a couple muffins. Blueberry or cranberry?"

Ike rubbed his chin. "Cranberry." He reached for his wallet, but Jamila was standing, a ten-dollar bill ready in her hand. He hadn't even seen her opening her purse.

Premeditated, he thought. She probably took her money out while she was still on the train. The woman knows me too well. The caffeine made his chest flutter. He told himself it was the caffeine, and he sipped some more.

The Limerick

The cold front was a punch coming late in the round. People stumbled on the sidewalks. Traffic slowed. Steel clouds scraped the horizon. The sky ran empty. No moon, no Milky Way. Tiny snowflakes, like grains of flint, spun from the emptiness. The city had fallen hard.

Fallen through the ice.

Ike found a parking space across the street from the old hotel. He and Eliza readied themselves for the task of knocking on doors.

Their luck came early.

Teo Rossi's hair was carroty red, longish, and limp where it fell against his neck and drooped into his beady, blue thumbtack eyes. His nose turned up at the tip, forever sniffing the air. Two pale damp marks were lips. A heavy pattern of freckles dotted his cheeks, as if his face had gotten jammed in God's printer and been pulled out by the chin.

"Tell her I haven't got her goddamn stereo." He swung the door open wide and waved his arm. "Do you see it? Ask her about my videos. Ask the bitch that and I wonder what she'll say."

"This isn't about a stereo, Mr. Rossi." Eliza stepped into the apartment.

Rossi folded his arms and squeezed his elbows.

He said, "You know I was in the seminary. That was ten years ago, but c'mon. I wouldn't steal. Not even from that bitch, and that wouldn't really be stealing if you knew all the shit I went through with her. The money she spent, which, I shouldn't have to even say, was mine."

"Mr. Rossi, we're here to ask you about your neighbor," Eliza said. "The, ah, the lady who lived right downstairs from you."

"Lived?"

"Yes. She was the apparent victim of a homicide, and we—"

"The drag queen?"

"That's the one."

"She got killed?"

"Yes she did," Ike said.

"I don't know anything about that."

"Did you notice any unusual activity, anything that sticks in your mind from recent weeks? Strange visitors? New people around?" Eliza asked.

"No."

"Okay. Thank you for your time."

Eliza joined Ike in the hallway. Rossi closed his door. Ike was knocking on the next door when Rossi opened his again. He spoke to both of them, but kept his eyes on Eliza.

"You know, she had another girl, if you want to call them girls, living with her for about a week. That was last month. The week of Christmas."

Eliza tried to sound as casual as possible. "Can you give us a description?"

"I never saw the other one. I only heard them talking, singing along to some kind of messed-up rap music."

"But you're sure you never saw her? Or heard anything else?"

"They had some guys, I mean guys who sounded like men, with them a couple times. Partying."

"And were they doing something else you might've heard?" Eliza asked.

Ike hung back in the shadow of the unanswered door.

"Fag stuff," Rossi said.

Eliza turned her head to one side.

"You know, like a gay orgy or something."

"You heard them having sex?"

"No mistake about that. And the one guy, one of the men, he was like busting furniture and hitting the wall."

"But it wasn't a fight?"

"If it was, they made up pretty fast. They all went out together afterward."

"Do you know where they went?"

"No."

"And this other person, who was staying downstairs for that week, are you sure that person was a male and not a female?"

"No. No, I'm not sure."

Broe Woods

Broe Woods was one of the only places in Booth City where, anytime of day or night, a man could find a prostitute, male or female, to service his needs. The city's attitude about prostitution had always been one of containment rather than eradication. But with the burgeoning drug and gang situations, and the budget cuts demanded by the city council, the decision became easier. Create an unofficial arrest-free zone.

It also helped that there were few neighbors. Squirrels and crows didn't care who did what to whom in their proximity. If the arrangement became too obvious or noisy, which it usually did in the summer months, the PD would run a few sweeps, nabbing johns and impounding their cars. Numbers would die down, citizens driving by and not looking for action felt a little safer, and the cycle would start over.

January was definitely not peak season. Johns and whores, like everybody else, moved most of their business indoors when it got cold.

Gia hadn't worked the Woods in a long time. She didn't know what she was doing out there on this night. The city plows were out throwing salt. In forty-five minutes, not a single car even slowed to check her out. She was ready to go home and sleep. She'd make some calls in the morning; find out where Marta was, and Josine. Maybe it wasn't too late to ring up Rocco and ask him if he wanted some special company.

The second time the Chevy rolled by—not slowing down but going slow enough, stuck behind one of the plow trucks—she recognized the driver.

She quickly crossed the street.

There was a package goods store about a block up that was open until four. Gia dropped her head down and walked, thinking about the store lights and not about the cold, or the wind, or the black guy and his partner driving around Blow Woods.

"Fucking cops," she said to herself, "never give a girl a break."

Nestor County Hospital

"Stomachache?"

The patient nodded and rolled onto her side on the examination table, grimacing.

"Have you taken any drugs? Something you got on the street?"

Nurse Patty Martine has to ask a lot of people this question in the middle of the night. Preparing an injection in an adjacent exam area, a doctor glanced through the slit in the curtain. The patient's appearance suggested a possible overdose: age around twenty; hair dyed stiff—spit-curled candied bristles; leather skirt; black fishnet hose; thick-soled platform shoes; claret angora sweater, fitted and soaked through with sweat; glitter makeup. Her forehead gleamed pale as a fish belly.

She had wobbled into the ER alone.

Fell to the floor.

"Kiddo, if you've taken a drug, any drug, we need to know about it, okay?"

"I had a vodka tonic. That's it." Eyes tightening down, lips sealing as if she were bracing for an ocean wave passing over her head.

The wave broke, moved on. "I'm sick."

"Doctor's coming. We've got a crowd in here tonight. Your temp's normal. So is your BP. Remember what you had for dinner? Last time you ate?"

"I skipped dinner. Made myself a fruit salad for lunch. I dunno, about one o'clock. I was fine until a couple hours ago. Then the cramps started. I puked, but it was like water. I quit drinking after the vodka because I didn't feel right. Queasy, you know?"

"Where were you partying?"

"Sarcophagus."

Nurse Patty raised an eyebrow.

"It's a dance club," she said. She was tracing and retracing her own sepia eyebrows with the edge of her pinkie.

"Maybe somebody put something into your drink. Anybody like that you can think of ?" The patient shook her head. "Okay. If you feel like you're gonna throw up again, use this." Nurse Patty handed her a plastic kidney-shaped pan.

The curtains closed, swayed.

The patient, who called herself Reece, stared up at the ER lights and counted to sixty under her breath.

He was with her.

Reece knew that, was convinced of it. As she listened to herself saying numbers, she could hear him breathing. Out of the corner of her eye, she saw the dark stain of him on the wall. He was covered in blood. The Butchered Boy.

Reece swiveled her head around the exam room. Going crazy because no one was there. Nobody was bleeding. Not tonight they weren't.

She counted . . . fifty-eight, fifty-nine, sixty . . . he put his hand on her shoulder. She'd swear it was his touch. Leaning in close, his voice slippery in her ear.

"I promise it's almost over. Not much longer, Reece. Just hold on. You're doing great. He's coming. A bit more and it's finished."

She supposed he meant to soothe her with such words.

Nestor County Hospital ER

"You look tired, Pin. Getting enough sleep?" Reece asked.

"Who told you to call me that name?" The young doctor looked up from Reece's chart.

"A troll I met under the bridge." Reece lifted the edge of her sweater so he could listen to her heart. She wore a black silk bra. Her playful look confused him. Apparently, the cramps had subsided. He pressed his stethoscope to the butterscotch freckles on her chest and listened. The innocent elf with the dilated pupils swung her legs back and forth.

Story time.

"Where's this troll of yours?" he asked. "In the park across the street?"

"Farther off than that by now, I suspect."

Was there a lilt creeping into her voice? "Breathe in and hold." Her lungs sounded clear. "That accent really needs some work. You in the theater?"

"Think I'm pretty enough?" She smiled and shrugged. "There's a lovely compliment in there somewhere." She reached up and touched his cheek with a cool damp fingertip. "Hey, Pin, let's go share a pint. Have ourselves an old-fashioned talk somewhere."

His name tag read: DR. CRISPIN MALONEY. Many people shortened his name to Cris, but only one person had ever called him Pin. Now this girl had used the name twice.

"Do we know one another?" he asked.

"Aye." A nineteenth-century English street urchin's voice. Her eyes were rolling back into her head. She pitched forward. Crispin hugged her around the ribs to keep her from toppling off the examination table. With his face close to the warm crook of her neck, he smelled horses and lager and rain-soaked muddy ground. Crispin pulled back, held her by her shoulders. She was laughing.

"You're high on something, Reece. Tell me what you took."

"I've been to see a man."

"Your dealer?"

"No." She shook him off, waved away his assumption. "A good mate."

"This good mate gave you something?"

" 'At's right, guv'nor. He needs you."

"Who?"

"Your little brother."

Crispin slipped off his glasses. He really did look tired. The circles around his eyes had been there for months. "I don't have a little brother," he said. He spoke as if each word required special effort.

"He said you'd say that."

"Who did?"

The girl bent forward and vomited, filling the pan in her lap. She handed it to the physician and wiped her mouth with her sleeve. He put on his glasses, noted the vomited matter was clear. It had a briny odor like seawater. The girl was steadier. He watched her cheeks flush with blood.

"They're trying to kill me," she said.

"I don't understand what sort of joke you're playing here. I have real patients to get to. You were drinking, yes? Well, hydrate yourself and go to bed. Emergency rooms are not good places for pranks."

"Please," she said.

"Go home and sleep."

The girl lurched off the exam table toward him.

Crispin expected her to get sick again, but instead, an arm shot out and her fingers encircled his wrist. The fierce pressure of her thumbnail hit a nerve bundle at the base of his hand. She rocked back swiftly. Pulling him off balance. So that suddenly she was on the exam table again and he was positioned over the top of her. He felt what he perceived to be her struggling under his weight. He righted himself. She lifted her spindly legs toward the ceiling. Her short skirt rode to her hips with obscene speed. Crispin stared, transfixed at first by the web of her tight mesh stockings, and then by the unmistakable bulge trapped off to one side.

"Do you like my funky, funky shoes?" Reece asked.

Laughing hard enough to bring tears.

3

DETECTIVE MEXICAN MAID

Booth Family Estate

After the initial horrors that assaulted him whenever he woke from deep dreams, Zan started to feel like himself again. Not necessarily a cause for rejoicing, he thought. He oriented himself to time and place. He checked his body for damage.

Home again. Nothing more intimate than one's own bathroom. The bedroom was a setting for illusions, but the bathroom was all about facts. Fact One: Zan had to admit he loved the marble his mother had chosen for the floor. Even as his cheek flattened against the cold slab, even as he peeled himself away and felt the stickiness collecting there. He sat up. A drop of blood wormed its way to the point of his chin. He blinked and opened his mouth. He was trying to decide whether or not to vomit. Fact Two: when he stuck his finger in, nothing happened.

His eyes were reluctant to focus. The world retuned from mute olive to something rosier. He rubbed the heel of his palm against the hard green sea beneath him, tracing bolts of white in the polished stone.

Antarctic ice, he thought.

Wouldn't be so terrible to freeze and have it over with.

The room swam with mist. Wall-length mirrors were fogged. At Zan's back, twin showerheads emptied the last of the hot water tank into a glassed stall. The shower was roomy enough to hold the back field of his high school football team. Zan knew because he'd coaxed them in there once. All very drunk on patois, and very high on Hawaiian. Ever so eager for more.

Fact Three: yes, the blood was his.

He touched the bridge of his nose. Scraped, tender, not broken.

His lip, ah fuck, had split. He tongued his front teeth for evidence of loosening.

Another night survived. Hoo-rah.

Zan recognized his profile outlined in the puddle. He dipped his hand, made a wet dark rainbow. He'd seen worse. Quite.

He mashed bloody handprints into the towels. His mouth tasted like French tobacco and, inexplicably, raisins. But he was so dry. Sahara dry. He touched his jaw. Stiff. The skin felt razor-burned.

Zan stood. He was naked, thin as a jackknife blade. A swimmer's frame comprised of sinew and bone. Narrow and long. He had not one hair on his body, none at all. Wind poured unimpeded through the tall narrow window and swirled around him like a cape. The glass had been knocked out. Nothing glittered on the floor. He shuffled over and tried to close the wood shutters. They didn't budge. Icicles sprouted above the missing pane. Zan's thigh brushed against a layer of frost draping the sill. The shiver running through him was perfectly awful.

Zan put his skull into the hole.

The grounds were in the midst of winter death. A landscape of bleakness and ranks of barren apple trees like giant spiders on their way to the pressing house. The pressing house, his house, was muffled in snow.

He looked down. Glass points twinkled where they'd fallen on a drift.

A patch of hair, made frantic by the gusting winds, was visible among the shards.

Zan knew immediately what had happened.

More and more it seemed he'd be the clown in their circus.

He gazed past the orchard where he could see Cook stealing a smoke before the family's noon meal. The main house was a constant presence—a natural dip in the land being the only separation between the buildings—and it stood as a physical reminder of his so-called punishment. The Putting Out of Zan. His view, from any window except the game room, was of the servants' entrance. Zan thought it showed just how cruel the man who was not his father could be. How unjust.

Maybe that's what he was thinking when he looked out the window last night.

His memory had disconnected after calling for a ride. Electric signals galloped through the soft curls of his brain. Sailor in his disgusting van, a liter of GHB between the seats. Gamma hydroxybutyrate. Bodybuilders enjoyed the benefits of released growth hormone. Date rapists liked the clear-liquid quality. A quick pour made girls silly, sleepy, and wet as snow. Zan smirked. Euphoria and sleep. That's what G was good for. One long swallow erased the board. Most parts, anyway.

Zan guessed the kitchen smells were blowing toward the carriage house. He smelled only snow. Other people had garages. But the Booths had a carriage house. Zan detested their silly aristocratic posturing, their half-assed Anglophilia. He was sure they found his pretensions no less hideous. He didn't care. Neither did they. It was a common refrain.

God, the air was like iron. It made his fillings ache.

The scent of food might've reached as far as the old lane and then bottomed out in the river valley. The road ended abruptly at a pair of concrete towers and a spiked gate. The bars were painted green every spring. Vines wove between them and held on like little fists. At the height of summer, the spikes lay hidden in blooms.

It was a kingdom of few comforts.

Zan remembered Red Cap Gardener burning stacks of leaves in the semidark, the smoke lingering like a shy child. Red Cap never talked. Zan had vague recollections that his English was poor; a Pole or Czech, he'd fled one of those drab, run-down, Eastern Bloc countries. He was dead when Zan returned home from a London visit six years ago. It had been the first time Zan traveled overseas without his mother. The trip overlapped his fourteenth birthday. Thinking about husky old Cap—silent, poking at embers with his rake—made him feel, what? Nostalgia? Sorrow?

But the corral fence drew his attention. Or rather, the horse standing inside its perimeter whinnied. Dappled coat and ears twitching, the Appaloosa stamped its hooves, then waggled its oblong head as a jet of piss smoked the ground. Bits of straw stuck to the beast's belly in pale slashes. The poor horse turned a loose wet eye on the second-story window and snorted.

Zan answered him back in kind.

Specks of snow danced between them. The sunlight faltered. A door closed somewhere downstairs.

Zan breathed the soft odor of apples. The upper rooms were haunted by it.

No, not haunted. He wouldn't allow himself to think of any powers given to the dead. He couldn't afford to. The dead had tried to betray him last night.

The Butchered Boy and Josine.

It might've been them. They convinced him to smash his face through the window.

"Do you want me to get your robe?" the voice behind him asked.

Zan turned to see Mexican Maid, a dark cutout in the frame of the door.

A flicker stirred in his groin. Mexican Maid wore a simple black coat and slacks pulled taut across her gorgeous hips. She'd tied her hair back with a white velvet ribbon. He needed to investigate it with his teeth. But champagne rose volcanic in his throat. He bent in the corner and heaved.

"I'll get you more towels."

Zan nodded. Yes, MM, good call. Fact Five, or was it Four? Oh, screw the facts. He wilted onto the lovely marble. Trembling.

I'm in serious need of a hospital, he thought. The Butchered Boy had urged him to go there in the early hours. Talk to my brother, the Boy said. I'll go with you. Search for some healing. But hadn't they sent him home? He couldn't remember. He had flashes of the tail end of the night. Cuttings. They floated on waves. Floated and then—just when he thought he might have them in the right order—they sank.

He'd piece it all together later. He'd phone Sailor for a pick-me-up-and-get-me-out-of-here. Sleep would suffice for now. He inched away from his mess in the bathroom. He made a tunnel in the blankets strewn on the floor. They said Death was a cousin of sleep. Sleep, until now, had never disappointed.

Zan tried to convey to himself the importance of what he'd observed looking outside his window, the crucial nature. If they weren't careful, the details would undo them. So he simply couldn't forget.

He needed to retrieve Reece's wig from the snowbank. The wig he wore when escaping was paramount.

When he became Reece.

Outside Nestor County Hospital

The ambulance driver was in the parking lot where the girl at the Emergency window said they'd find him. He was trying to light a thin cigar. Not finding success, he leaned tighter against the rear doors of his ambulance.

"Mr. Del Toro?" Ike moved around the bumper and blocked the wind. Del Toro nodded as he pulled in a mouthful of nicotine. Ike gave him a second; the wind stripping smoke from the driver's lips.

"Thanks. You the cops, right?"

"We'd like to know a little more about that van you mentioned to Detective Rogers," Eliza said. She glanced at her open notebook and rattled off the description.

"That's about it. Light creamy color, parked on the street with the hazards on."

"Was this a family type van?" she asked.

"Delivery van. No windows 'cept in front. Beat-up, like I told the other guy. It looked broke down."

"But you didn't see anybody inside or out?"

"Nope."

"Let's go back to something a minute," Ike said. "What makes you say this was a delivery van?"

Del Toro crunched his brow. "What I said about no windows. And being beat to shit like it saw some miles." He was sounding less confident.

"Is that all?"

Del Toro buffed his elbow on the letters written across the ambulance's doors.

"I don't think there was any company name or nothing. My cousin's a plumber and it kind of reminded me of his van."

"No writing?" Eliza asked.

Del Toro shook his head. "I'm driving by, though. Not really staring. But I got a good look. Thing was dirty. Rusted. But I don't remember writing." He flicked ash at a manhole cover. "Hey, it had a rack on top."

"Luggage rack?" Ike asked.

"No. Like my cousin's, he's got his with these big PVC tubes mounted up there. Keeps pipes and stuff in them too long to fit in the back. Van I saw had a couple of the same tubes. Crazy what the mind picks up, huh?"

Eliza wrote: *Plumber's van? 2 Tubes.*

"You've been a great help to us," Ike said.

Del Toro laughed. "Imagine what I'd remember if I slept."

"We've got no tickets and no towing records for any vans in the area on our night. No activity at Figg's Park whatsoever in the last month. Prior to that, it's kids drinking and vagrancy calls. So now we'll run a plate search for commercial vans or trucks picked up in sweeps at Blow Woods. Then go back through arrests the last five years for guys roughing up homosexuals or working girls. See if any are plumbers," Eliza said.

"Related jobs too. Might be other trades use those tubes," Ike said.

Eliza reviewed her notes. "That's thin and it's gonna take forever."

"Thing about forever is . . ."

Ike checked his rearview mirror. A long five seconds. Eliza pumped her foot on the floorboard, the brake she didn't have. Ike's head swiveled around to his right. Watching the curb. He slowed the Chevy, turned into the first lane of an oil-change garage. He didn't pull up, but left the car blocking the sidewalk. He popped his door. Eliza searched outside the passenger window.

"Coming up here," he said. "That's Gia. She worked Blow with Josine. They were picked up together. Acted friendly. Bailed out same time, same dollar. Worth a shot."

Gia walked, unaware, right to the car. She wore a metallic orange parka, jeans, and cowboy boots. Too proud or too worried about her hairdo to flip up her hood; she kept her tousled hair piled high under an assortment of glass dragonflies. A hat might've saved her. Ike would've driven past, talking about *forever.*

Gia saw them now. She had the handles of a plastic sack hooked around her left hand. A purple lighthouse, the logo for a local pharmacy, was prominent on the bag. They'd passed the drugstore three blocks north. Gia dead-stopped, pivoted, and caught a glimpse of the express bus before it clipped the bag from her wrist.

"Shit."

"Hey, hey, Gia, slow down a minute," Ike said. He was clear of the car, cutting her off at the street. "We need to talk, okay? Talk?" He took her arm. Gia's sleeve was wet. Blue dots dripping from her bag: peppermint mouthwash.

"What I do? Almost get me killed, man. I'm comin' home from the store."

"I know. This is only a conversation we're having. Get in the car. Detective Ochoa, we got a napkin or something to wipe her hands?"

"Don't want your motherfuckin' napkin," Gia said, jerking away from Ike's grasp.

"Get in."

Gia's legs were shaking.

"Too cold to argue," Eliza said.

Ike opened Gia's bag with two fingers.

The smashed mouthwash.

Four rolls of toilet paper. Marlboro Lights. Life Savers. Wet blue receipt.

"Police harassment. That's what this is. Can't grab me off the street for nuthin'."

"We're not grabbing you," Ike said.

"Oh, really?"

"You're cooperating," Eliza said.

"See? I'll even hold the door for you." Ike ran his hands. Small of the back, pockets, bootlegs. No weapon.

Car exhaust swirled up in her face. Made Gia sick. The black one pointed to the backseat. The Mexican bitch, all full of herself, ass on the fender and trying for streetwise—bored and hard—eyelids coming half down like she's just past here with whores and fuck-ups. No choice. Gia slid in.

"Aw, this bullshit here is rich," she said.

"You wanna keep it to yourself till we get to the precinct?" Eliza said.

Ike was behind the wheel, gunning it through a yellow going red.

Gia braced her sticky hand against Eliza's seat, pushed. "Don't go bringing your hate up on me."

"What?"

"Your anti-Cubano attitudes." Gia nodded, dragonflies clicking. "Uh-huh. Roll those eyes. Don't the truth sound ugly when you hear it?" She poked a glittery nail at Eliza. "You got a lotta au lait in your café."

Ike cleared his throat. Trying not to laugh.

Eliza resisted the urge to slug him.

Precinct House

The precinct house's oldest neighbor was a Catholic school. Under the same fierce July sun, red-faced Irishmen had poured their foundations. Two buildings constructed together in the age of lead paint and asbestos. Now one turning back before the other to so much sand, water, and lime. The diocese had scheduled St. Bridget's for demolition at the end of the school year. The parish church, rebuilt after a fire in the late seventies, would remain with one full-time priest and a secretary. Parents were given the option of transferring to St. Bartholomew's ten blocks west or attending Thomas Edison on the taxpayers' dime.

The precinct house wasn't going anywhere.

Slow mornings—from an office window positioned high enough that in winter she could view the lake of dirty snowmelt on the school's roof—Eliza would watch the kids lining up at the doors. First bell rang at eight. But children, here and there, almost spectral in the quiet dark, arrived as early as six-thirty. They filled the parking lot until their numbers, like a barrier suddenly breached, exploded with pure energy.

The street became a place where people shouted to be heard.

Last week's snows invited a daily tournament of classmates pushing each other into the deepest, freshest banks. Shrieks and stomping boots followed the action. Bouts flared—chaotic but short-lived. Everyone went on to the next.

Quiet kids sought refuge against the far wall. Impatient, but better at hiding it—they sat on their backpacks, passing time in their heads.

Eliza had been one of those.

Her childhood attention directed itself elsewhere—spying on the blue squads rolling out of the police garage.

Parade of pedestrians bustled on the front steps. Eliza studied faces.

Almost all men: the ones who worked there, the others with chains between their wrists. Lawyers, brothers, fathers, hustlers.

Carrying on the day-to-day business of crime and punishment. She was looking for someone she knew, someone she never found in the crowd or the patrols. He was there. But he was going away.

Twenty years later, Eliza switched sides of the street. Still looking for what she might've missed. The face lighting up, arms opening wide, the voice not hesitating to call out her name. The love she never got. Now when she looked over at the schoolyard, she saw the love she'd never have. The love that said,

Here I am. Where've you been for so long?

Gia kicked Eliza's seat.

Ike dropped the car into Park. Opening his door, he cocked his leg out, in no rush. Slowing it down for Gia. Showing her this visit could take a long time. Maybe give her the idea that cooperating might speed things up.

Their voices really carried, Eliza thought.

The singsong of "Red Rover" hammered off the bricks.

Homicide Unit Interview Rooms

Interview Room 2 had the charm of a train station restroom.

Table bolted to the floor. Three chairs. Handcuff rings screwed to the tabletop.

Gia didn't want to sit down.

"I'm not staying," she said.

The Ochoa bitch said nothing. The one used to be Vice—Horner—hadn't come in with them. Not yet.

"I can smoke, right? No new rule about that?"

Ochoa left her. The door shut, good as locked.

Gia fished in her bag. She lit up. Above her, buzzing fluorescents. The floor in 2 slanted. The doorway was uphill. The brown floor tiles buckled at a spot in the corner like you-didn't-want-to-know-what lived underneath. She looked left, away from the barred windows. Funhouse. Gaze at yourself all twisted in new ways. Gia smoked two. Three.

She gave up. Sat.

The door sprang and Gia almost went over backward.

Horner.

"Be with you in a minute."

"Whatever."

He nodded. "We have this thing we need to resolve."

"So resolve." Gia coughed, not covering up.

The detective, on his way out, held the door a second. Gave her a last glance.

"How about a soda?" she asked.

He turned around, leaned his weight against the door frame. "Coke?"

"You got something diet?"

"Gia, I don't drink soda. I don't know what's in the machine. You want a soda?"

"Yeah, but see if it's diet. I don't need the calories."

"Okay."

If she had to, she'd deal with him. Man had a sweet side. Not shoving her face into his hard-on to prove he's got it. Rare cop.

Ochoa ought to take lessons.

Yeah, she might talk to Horner. Say anything. Only escape this shithole. Room smelled like sweaty ass, too much fear in one place. Nowhere to go, but they had you under their eyes. Gia waved a finger at the mirror.

In case the Ochoa bitch was in there.

Booth Family Estate

Zan had the cell phone to his ear, listening to the raspy sound of Sailor murmuring on the other end.

"In a sec," Zan said. "Got it."

He punched his code into the keypad mounted inside the front door. The gate would be opening. The computer remembered who did the letting in, and the cameras saved a color video image of each passing vehicle. He heard the van accelerate before he broke the connection. Zan wore a black wool turtleneck, leather pants, and a cobalt scarf. He had his Belgian police parka folded tightly over his arm. He felt better.

It was twilight.

By the time he'd gotten to the Reece wig, it was ruined. He left the broken window glass half-buried in the snow. Someone would clean it, without questions, come spring.

He burned the wig in his bedroom fireplace. Flames, blue ones, purple ones, braided and unbraided behind the iron grate. The hairnet turned to white lace and crumbled after a gentle poker twist. He toasted the event with champagne.

And he called Sailor.

The van chewed its way up the lane. Zan spotted Sailor through the filthy windshield—Sailor's left hand, the tattooed fingers, dangling free in the breeze. Zan levered himself into the passenger seat. Sailor U-turned, spewing a mix of mud and slush from the undercarriage. He dug a circular path through the orchard grass, found better traction on the gravel, and headed downhill. They were going to the city. They would be getting high and drunk. They would find other ways to entertain themselves. Diversions.

They might talk about Josine or the Butchered Boy. About their last night together, the four of them, out on the fishing boat. What a bad night it was. The night the Butchered Boy got his name.

Zan couldn't possibly have known how much Sailor just wanted him to be quiet.

Interview Room 2

"You wanna know about her business? Call her."

"She's dead." Ike watched her playing with the pop-top on her Diet Sprite. Shock replaced the obstinacy. The top coming loose, hitting once, and going under the table.

"*Now* you freaking me out."

An hour into it. Gia, until this moment, still playing games. Eliza smoldered.

"I thought you'd help us on this. She was your friend," Ike said.

"I can't help."

Eliza snatched the empty soda can. She shot it over to the wastebasket.

Two points.

"I ain't seen her in a long time. She got a new group she's hangin' with. Rollers. People with money and nice shit. They were takin' care of her. Gonna pay for her operation too."

"Pay for what operation?" Ike asked.

Eliza leaned forward in her chair. "Sex change?"

"Yeah, she talked about going to Thailand. Never gonna happen. But then she's sayin' these people were gonna pay for her to do it right here. Go to California, whatever. And it was real. For her to talk the way she did, it was real."

"Now I don't want to get into your privacy, but . . . ," Ike said.

"Huh?"

"But you haven't had that operation," Ike said.

"Don't need it. I'm good like it is."

"Josine saw herself differently?" Eliza asked.

"Yeah."

Eliza's mind raced to put together a theory. Somebody promises Josine they'll pay for her operation. Somebody she knows and takes time to build a relationship with. This person has the means. A bad temper maybe Josine knows nothing about. She does something to piss him off. Sexual betrayal? She's a street whore. Money? Does she steal? Is there a threat? Whose hunk of flesh is floating in the tub? Whatever the cause, this person reacts. Blows past harm straight to kill. Cuts her down low to make the point clear: *You wanted rid of it.*

"Any names to share with us?" Ike asked.

"Josine didn't tell me."

"You never asked?"

"I asked and she didn't tell me."

"You're lying," Eliza said.

Gia laughed—said, "You'd be the reason if I am."

"We're supposed to believe you worked the streets with Josine, talked intimately with her, got high with her—"

"I don't get high."

"Pardon me. You picked up johns with Josine, didn't score—not even once—you ate together and crashed at her place—"

"Where you get this bullshit?"

"You never stayed with her?"

"No."

"Same guy was pimping you."

"Long time ago. Not recently."

"Forget we mentioned it. Everything else still puts you two close. She steps into a pile of cash. You don't try to find out where it's at?"

"I tried."

"And?"

"She got chilly. Shut me out."

Ike asked, "You heard about her new friends?"

"I heard a lot."

"Okay."

"There was a guy she was seeing. He introduced her to the one liked to spend. The three of them went around. Clubbing. Out for boat rides on Lake Mohegan."

"But no names, no faces."

"That's it."

"Well, you'd better hope they don't think what I think," Eliza said.

"Which is?"

"You know more about them than you do."

The Axle

The bar was deserted. Too early to expect much more. Zan watched the orange starfish flexing on the back of Sailor's hand. Good ink job. The dim surroundings helped. Sailor downed a shot of brandy. Wiped his mouth on the starfish's back.

"How'd you get the fat lip?"

"Stuck my nose where it didn't belong," Zan said.

"Bad habit."

"I collect them."

Sailor smirked. One of many things he did without thinking, without caring who saw. But he had his special worries. Like cops. Sailor worried all the time about cops. A trip back to prison didn't fit his life plan. One of the things they worked on when he lived at the halfway house: forming a life plan. Sticking to it. That was what he'd been doing until this wicked shit flew up around him, around him and Zan.

"Hey, what're we going to do about the detectives?" he asked.

Zan's color changed. He did something Sailor would've thought impossible. He got paler. The whites of his eyes were so watery and red, you expected him to cry blood. He sighed dramatically, overlong, from the soles of his feet.

"I don't know, my good man," Zan said. "We might be lost."

"Fuck that."

"I mean who can be trusted?" Zan asked. "At this point, you and I, we're very, very vulnerable."

Sailor parked his boot on the table corner. He rocked back into a shadow. Like he had no face. Or like a shovel full of dirt spilled, erasing that part of him.

Zan couldn't watch.

"You know, the female looks like somebody we both know," Sailor said.

Zan surveyed the bar. A woman in here? What woman?

"The female?" he asked.

"The two detectives at the park. One's got no dick." A head shook in the soil, a voice spoke from a hole in the ground. "Jesus, what shit are you on? You can't remember who's investigating our fucking case?"

"I remember perfectly. I didn't understand you. You said *female*. If you had said female detective, then I'd know."

"Well?"

Zan, perplexed for a moment, caught on, asked the right question. "Who does the female detective look like?"

The smirk again, unseen this time, but Zan could almost hear it. "Your maid."

"Mexican Maid?"

"Sandra, right?"

"Oh, it's *S* something. But you're saying our detective looks like MM? How funny."

"Older. Still pretty. Your taste, not mine of course."

"That's too funny."

"I thought you'd get a kick out of it."

Zan finished his vodka tonic. The drinks were strong here. Add that to the many reasons they had to keep coming back. It was true he was amused. But he was terrified as well, giddy on terror. He wondered, only briefly, if he should admit to Sailor how stupid he'd been, how absolutely reckless—going to the hospital and talking to the Butchered Boy's brother. The Good Doctor. So concerned. So pained and brave. The way he tried to hide his hurt. His confusion was absolutely charming. How he swallowed it up and did his job. Patching the wounded. No, no. Zan couldn't tell Sailor because Sailor would get angry and then he was no fun. No fun at all.

Zan said, "I think tomorrow we should take a drive in the country. We can piss in some farmer's field. Space to breathe. Blow off this tension."

"Can't." Sailor's face plunged back into the light, among the living.

"Why not?"

"I'm getting buzzed. Had an appointment for a month."

Zan wrinkled his nose. "Another one? Where? What's left of you?"

"Octopus on my right blade." He touched his thumb to a spot over his shoulder.

"More seafood."

"Hey, keeps me happy." Sailor showed him what he meant by happy, his hand floating on invisible waters, bobbing calmly. Corpse hand. He waved for another brandy.

"Well, what about me?"

Sailor shrugged. He wasn't going to try hard. "You could come along and watch."

"A tattoo parlor?"

"You'd like it. Lots of pain, a little blood. Everybody's acting cool. The place I go is the best in the city, the whole state." He rolled up his sleeve so Zan could see the seahorse on his forearm, the black ridges of its back and the unwavering eye.

Zan had seen these things before, yet he played along as if he were truly interested. He really wanted to get away for a day. Maybe going somewhere he'd never been would be a kind of getting away too. "Oh, I suppose we can hang at the parlor," he said, figuring he could balk if the mood struck him. Besides, tomorrow was still distant. "Tonight," he went on, his thoughts tripping lazily into words, "you must get me drunk. And in the morning maybe I'll be adventurous and have them slap a butterfly on my tit." Zan clutched at his flat chest. "Or a shamrock on my ass to remember young Patrick."

It was a mistake to bring him up.

The Butchered Boy. His name was Patrick Maloney.

The dead Irish kid, more man than boy, whom they'd chopped to bits on a summer's night. Mosquitoes smelled the blood, even five miles offshore. The deck of Sailor's boat swarmed with thousands. Under Zan's bare feet the blood felt different, tackier than the lake water they were pouring from buckets as they washed their knives and the rust-specked hatchet. Patrick reduced to bones, to meat. They put him in bags. Zan and Sailor did.

Josine watched them, her face gone to olive. Vomiting Orange Crush and Dimetapp, in fact, over and over into the black water. Coughing like cancer. Swearing softly, slurring. Then quiet as . . . what did his Nanny always say?

Quiet as a church mouse.

Big eyes at half-mast watching them as they tied wires around the bags and then weighted the bags with lead sinkers used for deepwater fishing. Big eyes closing as the boat dipped, dipped, dipped in the darkness. Running with no lights. Butchering by the moon.

"It wasn't our fault," Zan said.

Half truth.

"He brought the junk with him," Sailor said.

They found it when they stripped him, a bag of brown dope—heroin, stuffed in Patrick's underwear. Not for sharing. Or was it the coke that did him? Looked like the coke. Way he dropped and flopped. Like a big salmon. Sailor put a folded towel under his head to keep him from banging too hard.

They were both surprised that Josine started to help. Astonished as she handed them rags from inside a weather-beaten cooler.

"Sailor, you have extra clothes on the boat?" she asked. Her eyes were heavy-lidded. Head cocked to the side like her neck was broken.

"Yeah."

"For the two of you?"

"I think so."

"Take your clothes off. Dump them. Wipe the boat down, whatever. Get dressed."

Zan checked the night sky for helicopters. The coke filled his ears with engine drone. He was listening for them while he listened to Josine. Skinning off his bikini bottoms, he waited for the explosion of searchlights. He waited for the bullhorn voice. He waited for the order not to move. But nothing happened.

Sailor's rib cage pumped in and out like a dog's. He was fatigued from doing most of the cutting. Muscles quivered. He was breathing openmouthed, dying for a drag but his menthols were overboard. He told her he liked the plan. The way she put it. Simply.

Josine, wagging her finger, said, "Wipe it all down. Clean your bodies."

And so Patrick went for his swim.

Zan and Sailor snorted lines from the same bag that killed Patrick, then took turns in the claustrophobic's nightmare of a bathroom.

Alone above, Josine sat on the cooler swinging her foot. She scanned the water. Looking out at the night, maybe for other boats. But knowing her, it was probably the night that captured her attention. Her sleepy little scheme hatching under her in the dark.

The Axle's after-work crowd rumbled down the stairs.

Sailor eyed Zan over the rim of his shot. "Tac wouldn't seem right on you," he said. "Better if I get buzzed by myself."

Zan drew his finger through a wet ring on the table. "So go."

"I will."

Chessman's Bar

When they'd first brought in Gia for questioning, the desk sergeant pulled Ike aside. The sergeant was a dead ringer for Fred Gwynne, the actor who played Herman Munster on the old TV show. He handed Ike an envelope, said, "Fella came here about an hour ago. Said you'd know who he was. Asked me to give this to you."

"Thanks, Tommy."

"Sure thing."

Ike tore the flap. Read the handwritten note.

Interesting people are turning up in the most unusual places.
If I'm not in my room, try Chessman's.

Poins

There were two phone numbers scribbled under the signature. An "H" after the first number, a "C" by the second.

Eliza escorted Gia to the Interview Rooms.

Ike called, got no answer. When he asked the bartender at Chessman's, the woman said Poins hadn't been in, he typically made an appearance about seven.

Ike called his room again.

No pickup.

Hard-cores leaned along the bar, nursing a lot more than drinks. Couple of low-rent working girls sat with a roundtable of guys wearing Carhartts and Red Wings. The same Latina they'd met the other afternoon was pulling drafts. She was as unhappy to see them again. Eliza wondered if she was the owner, if her dislike was more than badge-induced anxiety.

"He's not here," she said before they asked.

"Ginger ale, and a Knob Creek on the rocks," Eliza said.

Without a word, the woman turned her eyes to Ike.

"Ice water."

She went to fill their order.

While they waited, Eliza asked, "How reliable is Poins?"

"Reliable."

"We'll give him fifteen?"

"That's fair."

Their drinks arrived. Eliza dropped a ten on the bar. "Keep it."

The bartender swept up the bill and walked away.

"How's your mom?" Ike asked.

Eliza sipped her whiskey. Drank half the fizzing soda.

"She's good."

"Business good too?"

Eliza nodded. "She wants to put some tables on the roof. Summer seating."

"That'd be nice."

"It really would." Eliza knocked back the rest of the liquor, swirled the ice, and popped a cube in her mouth. She rolled it around with her tongue.

"You still seeing that guy?"

"Which one?"

Ike put his hand to his throat. "Green turtleneck."

"Curtis? No, he and I didn't . . . um, mesh." Eliza tilted her glass, sucked in a thin sharp chip of ice. "Curtis was not for me."

"What'd he do again? His livelihood?"

"Actuary."

"Ah."

Eliza wanted another drink. But the bartender wasn't coming back.

"Let's go see if he came home," she said.

Ike didn't bother to check his watch.

Poins's Room

Top floor. Ike would've expected nothing less from Poins than the highest rung on the shortest ladder. No disappointment here. The hallway smelled very much like cat piss. Somebody, probably the super, had installed fresh lightbulbs but hadn't replaced their plastic covers. No doubt a couple would be missing by morning. But for now the naked effect was too bright, too cruel to the tattered carpet. Ike imagined it didn't spare anyone walking underneath either.

He could hear three TVs blasting through a succession of shut doors. Poins had a corner apartment across from a utility closet.

Ike knocked.

Quiet.

Eliza was jumpy. Sweat on her lip, cinnamon on her breath after a gumball she'd found in the glove compartment.

From a reptilian corner of Ike's consciousness the words: *Gun, gun, get your gun out.*

Eliza slid her back up against the wall. Piece in her grip, but Ike never saw her take it out. Eyes wide. Up on the balls of her feet. Jacked.

Ike, sideways—taking his silhouette away from the shooter—pushed the door and the door swung open slowly, slowly. He crouched, hot palm flush on the wood, his .357 Smith & Wesson pointing into the lit space.

Newspapers spread on the floor. Sunday funnies. Bowl of cat food. Milk.

Shades were drawn, but neon glowing pink at the edges.

Reading lamp in the corner. On.

Book towers, some fallen over, books open like birds' wings.

Empty bed. The closet light on. Pull chain swinging.

"Police!"

Ike—low, fast—took the closet. Nobody.

Eliza took the bathroom. Came out again. Glock muzzle aimed at the floor.

"It's clear," she said.

"Shit."

They met in the middle of the room.

Poins was facedown on a tiger-striped couch salvaged from the curb. His elbows duct-taped behind his back. A plastic bag over his head. Crooked off to the side, unnatural, his eyes stared out into the harsh brightness of the hall. Blood from his nose smeared the inside of the bag. Eyelids cut, swollen blue. Two holes behind his left ear. Small caliber. No exit wounds. The slugs had a chance to rattle around his brainpan.

Eliza put her fingers on his neck. Warm skin.

No pulse.

Ike looked out into the hallway, followed the dead cabby's gaze. The utility closet was open. Brooms, mops, an aluminum bucket on rollers. Open.

He tapped Eliza. Mouthed, *The hall closet.* Her moves were smooth as batter. Ducking into the hall, curled around the door frame to see—no shooter.

Eliza said, "I don't think . . . not the way we came up. Through the lobby?"

"No, the fire escape. There." Ike pointed to the far end of the hallway, a steel door. In a metal box above, red filmy letters: EXIT.

"Definitely."

Push-bar on the door. Eliza used the hinge arm in case there were any prints. Tight. The cold air rushed in like water. The fire escape terrace was empty. Crusty gnarled snow broke free and fell into the dark canyon below. East-west alley. Parallel to the block but narrower than any street. The terrace rang under Ike's shoes, the weight of him shifting. He leaned over the railing.

Crates, city trash cans, Dumpsters—bottles smashed so it was jungle cat's eyes reflecting up at them moonlight, starlight, streetlight.

The alley, as much as they could see of it, empty too.

4

KNIFEPLAY

Bagel Nook

Crispin couldn't shake it. The idea wouldn't let go.

What if Reece did know something about his brother?

He had the day off. Up all night, he was exhausted and not really hungry. He sat by the sandwich shop door. Had to eat or he'd start to see vapor trails. Caffeine can only take a man so far. But he was a true believer in testing the limits. He stared at the veggie cream cheese lumped on a sesame bagel, the large O.J. with its bent rainbow straw. The Nook was popular with hospital staff. An ICU nurse tugged at his elbow as she passed him. Rosy cheeks. Snow dust in her hair. *Was her name Cerise?* He sipped from his second cup—the molten fuel—and kept thinking. Watching as the nurse shed her coat and hunted for an empty hook on the wall. Good and tall. With a cowgirl's bandy legs. A little physical oddity never put him off. Here, it really didn't.

Patrick ran away a year ago. Right after New Year's Eve, like it was his resolution to get lost. He didn't go far; ended up homeless.

Last known residence under the Onyx Bridge. Sleeping on the streets in the city where his family lived.

His family of doctors.

Mother, father, and two older brothers—Crispin, the eldest—they all practiced medicine within a ten-mile radius of Nestor County Hospital. They were good doctors. Progressive. Socially responsible. They volunteered their time and often worked for next to nothing. They cared about the less fortunate. They gave back. Put their knowledge and skills to work in the grimy desperate places where it mattered most. Shelters, low-income clinics, mobile pediatric units. The Maloneys were dedicated to serving the Third World erupting within Booth. Crisis centers, drop-in sites, the night shift at County's ER.

They knew they were good doctors, good people, and Patrick knew that too.

Yet he still walked out on them. He was sixteen.

No fights. No screaming. Most of the time, Patrick acted pretty mellow. Retro stoner cool was his latest thing. School was not, he'd said. But Patrick read a lot. His academic career didn't flame out. No suspensions, no meetings, no dropping grades. He simply decided to leave school . . . and left. It was almost analytical, his systematic withdrawal from his old life.

A precursor.

The hardest part, the most frustrating, was that Patrick didn't say he hated them. He said he wanted to choose another path. That's all. Choose Your Own Adventure, he told them more than once. He made his thought process sound rational. What could the Maloney doctors do?

He wrote them a letter when he left. It was coherent, heartfelt, and exuberant. It gave some detail of Patrick's grand scheme, and reading it the first time, Crispin half wondered if it would work, if they were the fools and if his baby brother had seen something in the world that they'd missed. He felt, what? Envy? Yes, a pang of envy.

On the bottom of the page, Patrick wrote: *Carpe Diem!*

Seeing the words made Crispin wince. Rereading them later was worse.

Crispin knew three things about Patrick. He was handsome. He was a junkie, or had become one a short time after his departure. And he was gay. These were not secrets to anyone in the family. This was Patrick. They loved him.

There was a fourth.

Patrick went missing in August.

Reece's ID was fake, a good fake. Maybe she carried it because she was underage. Could be useful if he wanted to find her. They'd taken Reece into the ER immediately after she collapsed on the floor. She said she was covered under her parents' insurance, but she wasn't carrying any proof. Her clutch purse consisted of two squares of celluloid sewn together with a bootlace. She passed them the license. Crispin looked at a photocopy of it while he drank his coffee.

Reece Golden.

Sex listed as female. Weight as a hundred and five, a twenty-pound lie but who didn't lie at the DMV. There was an address: 5 Fay Street, in Booth. Strange to give a real street in town, Crispin thought.

Unless Reece wasn't from town.

Fay Street dead-ended by the river, where the streets all had women's names—so it might be the ID maker's little joke. Houses down there were mostly trailers converted for year-round living, mobile homes. He began to recite from memory, going north to south: Ann, Beth, Carol, Donna, Elaine.

Fay.

Worth a try, he figured.

The ICU nurse's name was Khari. He remembered it now as he returned, with his untouched bagel and juice in hand, to the counter.

An Arab girl working at the register. She's notable, he thought. Maybe nineteen. His fatigued mind unable to keep from flitting—past to present, sorrow to lust. He'd always been bad when the stress was high. Obsessive about playing the psychosocial games. Picking up women just for the challenge, the distraction it offered, the immediate ego bump. Sport fucking. That's what his last girlfriend had called it. She didn't make it sound like any fun.

Hair swept away from a perfect oval face by a toffee-colored hand. Sentenced to wearing that silly paper hat. He asked her for a to-go tray. Even under the uniform he couldn't help but see her curved back and tight, round bottom. Dancer perhaps? Keeping eye contact with her now that she'd turned to him.

Sloe-eyed, this girl was. Exotic. Tartness mixed with the sweet.

"Refill?"

He handed over the cup. Let his fingers graze her wrist. Barely.

"Cream and sugar?"

"Just the coffee."

He watched as she pressed on the lid with her thumbs. Show me you feel that soft crackling too. Ah yes, right there . . . she gives a warm smile for the road.

He'd come back for her soon.

Ike's House

Shoe print.

Man's casual shoe. Nunn Bush. Size eleven. Comet cleanser spilled and the killer stepped in it while he was hiding inside the utility closet. They had the entire heel and an outline of the shoe's edge. He'd tramped cleanser granules into the hall. No question it was the killer's print.

That's what they had. Ike saw it in his mind's eye—the shoe stepping in blue-green crystals. Grinding. Then gone.

Ike slept on the sofa bed. He did that when he came in late, when he was dirty and dog-tired and didn't want to talk. He woke up to the TV. Fleur's cartoons. Her socked feet padded on the wooden floor. In purple fleece pajamas, a slender figure entered the room, moving to Ike's right and climbing the stacked sofa cushions. She balanced the remote on her knee. Tapped the keys. The TV screen pulsed with color and noise.

"You're not sleeping," she said.

"No," Ike said. "I'm up early like you."

"Oh, that's okay." She switched channels. Two dogs and a pig riding a park bench strung with balloons. She stopped. "Can you make me triangle toast?"

"Sure."

"With syrup."

"French toast?"

She nodded. "But you have to cook it."

Ike lifted the quilt, sat on the edge of the bed in his boxers and tee shirt. The room was cool. Outside, wind moaned through the eaves. He heard icicles clacking as they fell against the house. The shades were pulled.

"In a frying pan," Fleur said. The animals replaced by a talking spaceship.

He picked up last night's clothes and carried them to the laundry room, dropped them in the basket. Found a pair of his Levi's folded beside the dryer.

"One slice?" he asked.

"Two."

"How about bacon?"

"Yeah."

"Think your momma wants bacon?"

"Uh-huh."

"Me too."

Ike plugged in the electric griddle. He got out a bowl and beat four eggs, added a splash of pure vanilla extract. There was a day-old French loaf in the bread box. He saw apple juice in the freezer and mixed up a pitcher. He cut bacon. Dipped bread. Switched the oven on low and put three plates inside to warm. This was how he did things this time around. Given a second chance at family like he had been. A lucky man. The first go had been a disaster. More mistakes than he cared to recount. What he didn't miss of it, he wished he had. A neglected wife and son who decided they were better off without his so-called love. His absences were too many. Disappointment routine. They turned hard against him. Their affection burnt down to angry nubs. They said they wanted him gone.

He was gone.

Giving up on them so easy. It took years to realize they were right. He didn't want to be part of a family.

But with Jamila and Fleur life had changed. He was being careful. He was paying attention. Here and now, he had something he was afraid to lose.

He was also dying for a cigarette. Get back to work. The damned shoe print . . .

Jamila came downstairs as the first pieces of toast browned.

"Umm. Something smells good."

Fleur ran into the kitchen. "We made breakfast for you."

"I see that."

Ike turned to see Jamila's smile. She wore an iridescent robe with Chinese characters painted on the sleeves. Black brushstrokes. Seabirds. Mother and child hugged. He wanted to be loved the way these two loved—Jamila and her blue-eyed daughter. Her Fleur.

But he was thinking about a shoe print.

His beeper chirped in the other room.

He went for it.

Eliza's Apartment

Fresh from the shower, standing in her Jockey bra and underwear by the bedroom mirror, she consciously avoided looking until she had her clothes on. The ugly white pucker at her waistband was a bullet scar. First year out of uniform—it happened a week after her anniversary with the force. Bad hit. Gut shot. She heard one of the paramedics say they were losing her. Nowhere near the street, but in a cornfield.

Finding her took time. Getting to her took more.

She had an opportunity to lie there, bleeding. Thinking. They won't make it. I'm dead. She watched ducks fly by in a V overhead.

She had spotted the farm pond and continued walking inside the fence line. The railroad tracks were to her right, over the fence and built up, so she was in a kind of channel between the corn and the berm. The temperature was hot for early June. Humid. Light rain falling, the tail end of a thunderstorm, as the sun cracked through—molten silver leaking from the clouds—only her arms were spread wide like an angel's and she was lying in the mud on broken cornstalks and an awareness settled down. This was her death. Death and she wasn't sure what to do.

She breathed.

She tried to move and after that tried not to move.

She died.

They brought her back to life in the helicopter. And she died again.

Eliza wondered how it was for Poins. She thought she knew better than most. No point of pride. She wished she knew nothing about it. If possible, she would've given her knowledge back.

You see nobody comes for you. You just go. That's it.

Who wanted to hear that message snatched from the abyss?

Not her mother. Or her brothers. Or her priest.

Poins wouldn't have wanted to know either. After the beating and the bag slipped over his head. Sucking the bloody plastic in and out of his mouth as he panicked. Oxygen deprivation rocketing the fear up into his throat. Did he scream? Nobody in the building reported hearing him if he did. No one heard the shots either. But a small-caliber weapon wouldn't be all that loud. *Pop. Pop.* It's over.

His killer probably knelt on him to minimize the struggle.

Eliza didn't scream when the kid came out of the corn. She felt the hard poke of the barrel jammed into her belly. Wind ripped from her lungs. She saw the kid's face twist up like he'd stepped in dog shit. *Pop. Pop.*

Speared with scalding iron. Heat followed by the acrid, telltale smell of gunpowder. The sound of the kid running away through the corn, his bare feet slapping at the mud. Her weapon, unfired, in her hand—a frivolous afterthought. She let it go. She put her hands on her belly to hold herself in.

The farmer's pond was curved like a guitar and filled with smoky brown water. A ring of scum fuzzed the edges. She remembered yellow jackets flying around her face. These were going to be the last things she saw. She tried to remain there in the moment.

Yellow jackets. Focus your mind and manage the shock, she told herself as she bled out. You're alive in this world, she thought—was thinking—when the darkness grabbed hard and pulled. Dragging her off, body and soul, into the nothing and the never again.

One of the crime techs found a residue of glue around the fire escape doorjamb. Poins's killer had taped the locking mechanism. So he'd been in the buildng earlier. An hour? A day? They didn't know. He put the tape in place and returned without using the lobby. That showed planning. Not a murder, but an execution.

What did Poins see? Who? What was his information?

Eliza dressed in a scarlet blouse, charcoal wool slacks, matching jacket. She bought all her jackets a size too large. Kept her automatic holstered in a shoulder rig under her left arm, Miami-style. Tiny agate earrings: her only jewelry. They never caught the kid. Some low-end drug deal had gone south and he got nervous, dropped two guys on the other team. Happened in the city, but the kid was from out in the sticks. A white kid with a potbelly and pink hairless jowls. They got a tip on his truck. It was parked in front of his grandmother's house. He saw them coming and went out a basement window. Crawled.

They never caught the kid, but they found him. His bottom half lying on its side between the tracks. He'd hid in the fields all day and jumped a freight train that night.

Jumped and missed, apparently.

Eliza told herself for the umpteenth time that she needed to find a new apartment. This place was overpriced. The rooms were too narrow. It offered no view. She might check out the lofts near the Onyx Bridge. She had the money.

There were stars of frost on her living-room windows. A lemony scent of furniture wax combined with the poinsettia standing in a green foil pot on the sideboard. Her purse and keys waited next to the door, on a shelf above a little slate table, where she always put them when she came home. Her coat was hung neatly in the closet. She had no pets to feed. She lived alone and told herself that was fine.

She left a light on.

Double-locked the door after letting herself out.

5 Fay Street

The neighborhood was built on a grid. Like all neighborhoods, some people took better care of their property than others. An old woman in a stocking cap and a housecoat was sprinkling sand from a child's beach bucket onto her stoop, while a pair of androgynous skateboarders jumped a homemade ramp curbside. They each glanced his way.

The house was easy enough to find.

5 Fay Street.

A trailer. No Christmas lights, no wreath on the door. A van parked under an awning. Rack on top. White pipes.

Crispin circled around the block. What was he doing here?

Second time around, the skaters gave him a longer look. The old woman wasn't there anymore. He parked up close behind the van.

Trying to find Reece. Help Patrick.

It took a while for the man to answer his bell. A big guy wearing paint-stained, gray sweatpants. Black flames on the cotton tee stretched across his chest, letters below spelling out: QUAD CITY CHOPPERS.

Crispin nodded, worked on his smile. The guy did not look happy.

Patrick. I'm here for Patrick.

"Can't you read?" the guy asked.

"What?"

The screen shrieked. The guy's meaty hand came out and around. Finger pointed above the doorbell. *No Solicitors.*

"I'm not selling anything."

"Good for you."

"Is Reece around?"

"Pete?" The guy squinted. "Pete's not here."

"No. Reece. Does Reece live here?"

Headshake.

"Sorry to bother you. I'm a . . . you know anybody named Reece?"

The guy scratched his neck. He peered past Crispin, distracted by the smacking of the skater's wheels against the frozen pavement. "Nope."

"Okay. It's just, you know . . . she gave me this address. Your address."

"Man, somebody's jerking your chain."

Crispin backed away. Walked. His hand was on his car. The guy was still waiting there in the doorway. "How about Patrick Maloney?" Crispin called. "You know him?"

"Strike three."

Crispin wasn't sure he understood. Pete, Reece, Patrick. *Strike three.*

"My mistake," he said.

But now the door was closed.

Sailor got the trunk from under his bed. Put it on the bed. Spun the combination locks on the two latches, released them. His collection. Best of the best. The trunk was lined with protective foam. He picked a heavy one. Held it up to the lamp.

Had to be Patrick's brother. Spooky how much they looked alike.

Dead man shows up on your doorstep. What do you do?

Zan, Zan, Zan.

He took a shammy cloth from the trunk and wiped the handle.

Technically, it wasn't a knife. It was a short sword. Replica.

Sailor went to the window. The car was gone.

Zan thought he was bulletproof. Nothing could touch him. Sure Zan talked about worrying, getting caught and the rest, but Sailor saw it was only an act. Drama. Zan was a cold motherfucker. Sailor felt it. When they got into a scene, he'd get hotter and hotter. Feeling the way any person would when you pressed the right buttons in the right order. But not Zan. Zan turned into a block of ice. He had that machine voice coming out of him. The kind of voice that's been bred for generations to push people around and never think twice. Giving orders. *Slap her. Tie the other hand. Tight. Tighter.* He had money too. Despite what he always said. Poor-mouthing. Zan had enough money to get away. He could buy the whole police department. Even if the cops found out what they had done. Money makes you different.

Zan had more money than anybody Sailor ever knew.

Sailor had to be careful. He wasn't going back to prison. He wouldn't let Zan get the upper hand and hurt him again either.

Zan, Zan, Zan.

Quiet was important. Peace. And quiet.

Dead man's brother shows up on your doorstep.

What do you do?

The Morgue

"Shot?"

Dr. Lu pointed to the original wound. With her other hand, she motioned for Ike and Eliza to come closer.

"Yes, Detective Horner. Here. See the splintering of the bone? Not caused by any blade. The bullet, a .22 by the way, traveled on an angle downward into the chest cavity and managed, amazingly, to miss both lungs."

Ike hooked the lanyard with his finger, sliding until he touched the earpiece. He put his glasses on.

The three of them stood there, staring into Delbert Watts's opened chest.

"How do you know it was a .22?" Eliza asked.

Dr. Lu reached for a small clear dish.

"I found it." She rattled the slug around and smiled. Her hair seemed blacker under the morgue lights. Though she wore little makeup, her lips were bright red.

Eliza swallowed dryly. She looked at the chunk of flattened steel.

"Nicked the aorta. The spine stopped it." The ME indicated the precise location. "I think someone else was looking for this inside of Mr. Watts. I think they were not as good as I am."

"The gunshot killed him?" Ike asked.

"That's correct."

"The rest of the wounds, the cutting . . . ?"

"In the chest, as I said, was the result of a search . . . an ill-fated search, for the spent slug. Your shooter—if indeed the shooter and searcher are the same—is not experienced in surgery. However,

I noted some masking of the very fact that this started out as a bullet wound. The killer is not completely stupid."

"And the genital wound?" Eliza asked.

"Postmortem without question." Dr. Lu took back her dish. The detectives said nothing in response. She felt compelled to add more and so she said, "Window dressing."

"We need to find out if the slug matches the two from the Poins shooting," Ike said.

"I've got a box ready to go to Ballistics."

Ike took off his glasses, his gaze bouncing from surface to surface, pinballing around the exam room. It came to rest on Watts's body. The thawed corpse had warmed to room temperature.

B.C.'s morgue inhabited a huge basement. Recirculating flavored air you could taste like well water. That damp feeling. Being alive but underground. Knowledge any light you saw was wired-in, artificial. Rooms built on this level echoed. Monochrome color scheme blended the walls and floor. Beige tile. There were drains under the autopsy tables: a miniature Rome of canals. Ike clamped a hand to his forehead, massaging his temples. He hiccuped. Turned, bumped shoulders with Eliza.

"Out," he said.

He exited through the swinging doors.

Dr. Lu lowered her voice and said, "Your partner's not doing too good. I don't mean a weak stomach either. Tell him. Life's too short."

The detective didn't argue.

STEVEN SIDOR

The Pressing House

Five hundred on the enormous table, another three-fifty and change in his pocket. Two grand in a Ziploc taped inside the toilet tank, strictly for emergencies. Zan was getting low. He counted the cash on the table again. The table wasn't a normal table, but a circle of oak bolted to the old apple pressing mechanism. On it you could serve dinner for Arthur and his knights. Or you could count money. Four-ninety-nine. A crumpled dollar bill on the carpet. He pinched it with his toes. Okay. Five solid. Like he thought.

Time to go to the house and ask for more money.

He hated this shit. Begging.

It wasn't the shame. He had no shame. The effort, that's what got him. Having to ask permission to spend his own inheritance simply put him over the edge.

Adrian Redmon, his oh-so-wise and wicked stepfather, would be at the office. Not necessarily good news. Zan drank champagne from the bottle, the greasy neck rotating in his grasp; a spurt of effervescence bypassed his lips and zipped down his naked chest. The fireplace raged with pinks and purples. Zan rummaged through the pile of comic books. Batman. Spawn. The Punisher. He added them to the conflagration.

So came teals. Avocado. A wisp of chemical-tasting smoke drifted into the room. The heat wouldn't last. Really, he needed to have one of the servants get some wood. His collection was depleted. Seriously.

Copper changing swiftly to midnight-blue.

He crushed his cigarette on the bricked mantel. Shot the butt end at the ashes. In the vintage oval mirror teetering against the wall, he glimpsed himself, full-length, nude. The firelight licked his shaven legs. He thought, *Brazen,* and almost said the word aloud. Except when he was high—which was often these last months—Zan was hyper self-conscious. It was the closest thing he had to a superpower.

His cell phone rang.

He peeked.

Worst number possible. But he had to answer.

"Hello, Uncle." This particular pet name amused Zan beyond all his others.

"Sailor called me just now. Do you know what he said?"

"Haven't a clue."

"He said Patrick's older brother has come around asking questions. At Sailor's house, Zan. Where do you suppose he got the address?"

"The phone book?"

"Don't get fucking smart with me."

"Then I have no idea."

"Well, I have ideas, Zan. Fact is, I'm having one right now."

"Look . . ."

But the line went dead. Just what he needed. Uncle Happy pitching a fit, going mad along with the rest of the gang. Sailor, poor Patrick (dead), and Josine (dead). And when did the madness start?

About the time Uncle Happy came on the scene. No, it was a bit before that.

The bomb under Adrian's Mercedes. That was a marker. A sign. The Mafia, or their equivalent in Booth City, had presumably strapped actual sticks of dynamite under the chassis of Adrian Redmon's S Series in an attempt to, well, kill him off.

Adrian was a developer. Real estate in general, though gated communities and malls in particular made him very rich. Of late, his interest—his all-important and valued *eye*—fell on casinos.

Zan's alleged mother told him exactly when it was happening.

"Adrian's got his eye on a casino," she said. Dina Laurel Booth Tompkins Redmon. She was Adrian Redmon's first wife. He, her second husband, was the founder and president of the Red Moon Group. It was a quaint old story of new money marrying old money to create a greener world.

Money.

Dina had it. Adrian had more. Zan, who was Dina's only child, should've had better access to his share. But he didn't. Lawyers. Fruit of her womb, he was, unfortunately, also a living reminder of her dead first husband, whose suicide put a full-stop end to their marriage. To bury him she wore black. Of course she did. She was stunning too, no doubt. Bowing solemnly at the graveside in the October air, and with the colors of the cemetery trees at their peak—a burning gold rush. Her attire caused a mild scandal. Underneath her furs, beadwork clung from throat to boyish hips. Raising the goblets for a farewell toast? She'd be circulating, people presumed, very soon. The reckless cut of the gown exposed her bare back—and if the years of gossip held true—the kissable ridge of her spine.

Tragedy struck again.

A baby.

Zan would appear in eight months. He was born early—and rather gothically he'd be the first to admit—in sweltering New Orleans. His mother whisked in satin blankets from a Mardi Gras soiree. She treated the hospital staff to her darting, poisonous eyes.

Inconvenient from the get-go, that was Zan's story. She regarded his arrival as she would a chronic infection. He was to be coped with. She would survive him. Dina always had a way of surviving when others didn't. The lady liked to end things on top. Gossip spoke in nastier terms. But how fitting, Zan thought.

Thus, he was forever asking for . . . his paltry money.

He was asking for it the day the Mafia tried to blow up Adrian. Nothing blew up, though. Adrian's driver wanted to put some air in the Mercedes's tires. He discovered a roofing nail buried in Michelin treads. That happened all the time because Adrian the developer loved to be on-site. He kept a hard hat in the trunk, a stiff pair of Red Wings, a Thermos. They drove over a lot of unfinished roads, a lot of nails.

The driver saw the explosives.

"Holy shit," he called out to Zan, who'd been slinking along the wall. "There's a bomb under your father's car."

"A *bomb* bomb?" Zan asked.

They called the cops.

Cops sent the Booth City Bomb Squad.

It was exciting to watch. The BCBS cop dressed in a suit like an old-time deep-sea diver. Zan had taken mescaline with breakfast. He was pleasantly trippy. He kept catching himself holding his breath as he watched the Bomb Cop walk on the ocean's bottom. No fireworks. But not a dud, either. Sophisticated. A wire connected to the ignition and a timer to boot. The bomb would've exploded on the county highway as Adrian and his driver sped along their route to the city. The Bomb Cops were impressed.

Adrian was tall and angular. His complexion was Mediterranean. He played handball twice a week. Who played handball these days?

Adrian had dark features and an intensity that made him difficult to look at. Brooding. He had a disproportionately large head that seemed to grow the further he progressed into middle age. Think of a pint of freshly drawn Guinness. Think Frank Langella as Dracula. He might've been silly if he weren't so serious. Deadly quiet. Polite. Mind always at work. Obsidian chips where most people had eyes. Analytical. Lethal. He smiled like it pained him to do it. His voice never rose in denying Zan's requests. He controlled everything. Zan hated him. Utterly.

After the bomb, Dina suggested—Zan thought rather obviously—upping Adrian's personal security. Hiring bodyguards.

How romantic. Thrilling. You're nobody till somebody wants you dead. His mother seemed absolutely cherry-red with excitement.

Zan met Uncle Happy at a garden party. Springtime. He'd just had a birthday.

Dina was buying a horse. The stable had been vacant for a decade. Her latest desire was fulfillment of a girl's dream. Zan responded to the news by hanging his tongue out. *Blah*. Her dreams always came true. Didn't they? She picked up the Appaloosa at auction. His name was Gelato. He was a gelding. Everyone was invited to meet him.

Uncle Happy had a tuft of white chin whiskers, no mustache. Snow White's dwarf. Chubby like that. Merry. Happy. Here was a man who knew how to whistle a song. He wore a green leather vest. Drank scotch neat. The tip of his round nose was rosy. His teeth were gray, sharp.

"We should get to know one another," he said to Zan.

"Pray tell why?"

He leaned in. Zan wondered if there would be something as strange as a kiss.

"Because you're a fucking mess," Uncle Happy said, and he pressed two capsules into the moist hollow of Zan's palm.

Better than a kiss.

In the tropics of the greenhouse they snorted heavenly cocaine.

"Nothing else up your sleeve?" Zan asked, straightening up.

Uncle Happy rested a paternal hand on his knee. "There are people you need to meet. You swim the same streams, so to speak."

After three A.M. and pupils stretched wide. Down to the final destinations. Uncle Happy leading the way. He provided help on the sidewalk. Missing the curb, falling into Uncle's open arms. Straightening of lapels. Something dispensed from Uncle's pocket pharmacy to iron out the psychic wrinkles. Steel up, we have people to see. The Axle and Sarcophagus. Fading in and out. Here's our man.

Sailor. *Hello, Sailor!*

It seemed so perfect.

The darkness shattered into a snake pit of dancing bodies. A pair broke away and moved along the edge of the dance floor. Beer bottles like cudgels in their fists. Came right over to Sailor and Zan's table. They asked questions without preamble. Where was Uncle? Gone for a stiff one? Again? His hollow leg, you know. Ducking in the john to throw up on his loafers? Probably that. What did he have tonight? Anything good?

Uncle showed up just then. Present and accounted for after all. Descending like a quick terrifying angel to the business of making introductions. Meet Josine and Patrick. Barbarians. Watch out for 'em. Coupla real gamers, like our Sailor. Zan is stepping out a bit tonight. He's a good lamb, boys and girls.

Hellos.

The Fantastic Four.

Before they all went mad together.

The Morgue Steps

Ike was outside bracing his arms against the rails. Hands tingling. It was snowing, gently, the flakes brushing his cheek like eyelashes. Fleur's eyelashes. Jamila's. He was dizzy. His world on a wheel. Blurry. Tilt-a-whirl.

God damn his body for going haywire.

He needed something. Juice. Candy bar.

"You okay?" she asked.

"Light-headed." Ike motioned like he was shooing away a fly. "I've been getting some of that. Missed my breakfast this morning."

"Oh," Eliza said. She didn't know where to go with the conversation.

Ike took care of it for her. Enough was enough. Eliza was his partner. Smart too. She'd put the facts together before long. "I got sugar diabetes."

"You seeing a doctor?"

"Three."

"One holds you down. Other two go through your pockets?"

Ike laughed. "They found problems with my heart. Blockage. Going to need my pipes cleaned."

"When?"

His big shoulders shrugged in the loose-fitting jacket. "Don't know because I haven't gone back. Not since the results came through."

Eliza blinked.

"You have any sweets?" he asked.

"There's a commissary back down there. Vending machines."

"Go buy me a chocolate bar?"

"Sure thing." Eliza hesitated as if she wanted to reach out, put a hand on his shoulder the way Lu had in Josine's apartment. But that wasn't her style, and Ike knew it. Eliza just wasn't the comforting type.

"Don't mean nothing, Ike," she said.

He was sweating in a snowstorm. His face screwed up. "Where'd you hear that?"

A smile beginning as she shrugged, said, "A movie."

"I might've been in that one."

But he was thinking, Girl, you're lying. Daddy was a vet, wasn't he? He must've said it when he came back home. Sitting watching the TV news program flicker. Maybe drinking a cold one, or six, and damn glad to be out. A soldier thing. Ike couldn't remember exactly. But it seemed right. The right age. A war vet who became a cop, like me. Ike knew the rumors.

Change jingled in Eliza's cupped palm. "Wait here."

He sat down on the snowy concrete steps.

"Smoke 'em if you got 'em," he said. Look at me, not too sick to joke.

His head spun.

Doing what he could to keep it light.

Brooktown Main Library

The former policeman sat alone at a long oak table in the Periodicals section of his adopted city's public library. Periodicals was on the ground floor, under a panel of stained-glass windows depicting the Ascent of Man. The former policeman—who had been, in fact, both a detective and a sergeant when he left the force—was reading in a dim splash of harlequin lights. Dim because it was a dark day outside. What light penetrated down through the candy-colored glass came from a streetlamp. Its sensors detected the darkness and ignorantly switched to their nighttime wattage.

He was reading the newspaper, a local, as he did every afternoon. He was like that. Developed his plan and stuck it out. Habitual. Clockwork he was, this former guardian of the people. His name was Terry Duval.

Terry Duval had no one in the world. Not a single person cared whether he lived or died. Well, that was not entirely true. A number of people wished him dead. But it wasn't that easy. Killing off Terry Duval.

Wish in one hand and piss in the other, he'd tell them.

Which fills up first?

See, Terry Duval was a man who didn't need anything from anyone. Or so he thought. And that made him dangerous. He was loyal—to himself. Cautious when the situation merited caution. Daring when least expected. Shrewd. He'd made his life into a maze. Few entered that labyrinth. Those who did discovered why. Survival was the last pleasure Duval had left. He wasn't letting go. It gave him immense joy to see his former rivals, acquaintances, and friends—the whole gang—falling off the charts, winking out, one by one, like dead stars in the vacuum of space.

He put the Obituary pages down. Picked up the Metro.

Here was something.

Below the TOWING CRACKDOWN TO AID SNOW REMOVAL article.

Page three, the very bottom.

Park Murder a Puzzler

> Police detectives have been unable to find any witnesses in the murder of a transsexual prostitute whose body was found on the playground near Figg's Pond earlier this week. The investigation deepened as a search of the victim's residence at the historic Limerick Hotel turned up the partial remains of another individual. Detectives would not reveal specifics about the remains, only that they did not belong to the body discovered in the park. Both deaths are being treated as homicides; their investigations are ongoing. Citizens with information are urged to call the police tip line.

Wasn't that interesting?

He wondered what they found. Exactly which remains? And where? Duval sat back. His chair creaked, and his shoes pushed rhythmically against the library's springy carpeting. He used his detective's imagination. Playing the guessing game. Seeing the shabby quarters in his mind's eye. Unclean bathroom. Blankets lumped on the bed. Smeary window. In the silence of the Periodicals section and in the squalor of the dead hooker's crib simultaneously—he turned and turned—he opened up his five senses and unlocked the experience of the ten thousand or so crime scenes he'd lorded over in his day.

Where, oh, where did they find it?

Cheap furnishings.

He wasn't betting on the treasure being stuffed into a drawer.

Thing about a dirtbag's hovel is: there are only so many hiding places. Say you've got a body part you're . . . keeping. You really don't want it lying around. Even if you're deranged, you think about finding a special home for your little . . .

The bathtub.

He was certain that was where they made their discovery. What a surprise it must've been. Duval twisted in his seat. Pride and anger puffing out his chest. He'd solved it. Kicking himself because the game hadn't been entirely fair. He'd won *and* lost. Fair play wasn't something he admired.

Did these two detectives play fairly?

Out of practice, that was sin. He'd do the penance for it. Someday. But for now he wanted to find whose case this was. Reach out and touch them. He exited to the lobby and punched numbers into the pay phone. The answer he got caused a smile. Maybe this was dumb luck. But wasn't it grand she'd caught this murder? If only he could've been there with her. He would've told her exactly what she now must do.

The River Park

Ike insisted he was feeling better. He wanted to swing by the Watts's dump site, back again to go over the river park. He asked Eliza to drive.

She adjusted the seat so her feet reached the pedals. Ike really *was* sick if he asked her to take the wheel. Right there would've told her something was off. She didn't need him to say another word. Gusting wind rocked the car side to side. Their tires sending a gray wave of slush high over the curb. The snow looked like it wouldn't stop anytime soon. Ike's eyes closed. Head back. His breathing reduced to a soft burr. Two minutes after dropping into the passenger side for the first time in a year and the man was asleep. Eliza shook her head. Ike was a good cop. No question. Best partner she'd ever had. He'd put in his thirty. This diabetes probably meant retirement or a desk assignment. Losing him wasn't something she'd thought about. It had taken the better part of a year for them to get comfortable with each other. Now their partnership might end. What could she do?

She'd miss him.

The car hit a patch of black ice. Fishtail slide. Eliza took her foot off the gas. Steered out. She cut her speed, and a quick look at Ike told her he was still gone. Gone to wherever it is people go when they aren't awake.

He'd seen a pirate ship. He was young and this was Florida—Pensacola. Ike was down on vacation with his mom. His dad trained at Ellyson Field air base to the north, but that was a long time ago. This was vacation. His mom had friends in Florida. Ike wasn't doing as he'd been told. He was swimming in the ocean by himself.

Dusk. After eating his dinner at a taco stand. Watching a sandpiper pick clean a fiddler crab. Bored. He waded into the surf. Out until his feet didn't touch bottom. It was a bad time to be swimming. The beach deserted. His belly full of burritos. If he had a cramp, or if a shark swam up from the deep, what was he going to do?

A shark!

Nothing but a piece of seaweed. Curling around his thigh. Sticking a rough, creepy finger under the edge of his swim trunks. He plucked it away. Flung it into deeper water.

Sunset. The waves going from light to dark instantly. Cotton-ball clouds soaked up oranges and purples. It was something he'd never seen before—these outrageous colors painted in the sky, the horizon a line of jagged black motion.

When Ike spun himself around . . .

That's when he encountered the wooden bow.

Liquid uproar as the ocean kicked its grays over to frothing whiteness.

A ship.

Tall mast. Skull and crossbones flying so high up it hurt his neck to look.

He wasn't scared, because he was supposed to see it.

Ghost ship. Dead men falling on the decks and smoke from a fire or from the cannons . . . smoke poured over the otherwise stilled water. One of the ship's crew, his head swaddled in bandages, raised an arm. Beckoned.

But Ike wasn't scared. He saw what he saw. The bloody hand waving to him. Friendly motions. Pointing to the rope ladder trailing in the water . . .

Eliza nudged his shoulder.

"We're here."

The inch of snow on the windshield made the car's interior seem smaller. Told him they'd been parked there awhile too.

The park trees raised crooked arms to heaven. On some branches, dead fruit hung like shrunken heads. The north side of every kelly-green lamppost wore a soft, white shroud. Easy to believe in ghosts, if a person looked long enough. Wrong mind-set to be in during an investigation, Ike told himself. Blood sugar's playing tricks on you. Screwing with your nerves, your brain. He watched the trees convulse in the wind.

"Get your boots on," he said.

Winter's grip had tightened since their last visit. The jogging path was lost, indistinguishable from the snow-mantled grass, bark, and sand. The storm was burying the playground. And the river—the hardy Rood—had frozen all the way across.

"Why this place?" he asked, as much to himself as his partner.

"Hooker hangout."

"Not for girlie-boys. Nobody's really working this spot since the city started with the riverfront renewal. They cut back all the bushes. Put up them new lights. Hasn't been popular to find a girl here for five years." Ike watched his steps. "And, besides, Broe's where Josine did her business."

"Broe's too busy for a dump."

"Middle of the night? A winter night like this here?"

"He's familiar with the routine," Eliza said. "Knows there's always a chance a patrol car might be driving through, checking for activity."

Ike didn't seem convinced. "It's not the park. What he's trying, maybe, is to get her body into the water."

"But he gets tired of carrying her, or somebody spooks him," Eliza said.

He stopped walking, bent as if he were dropping a body from his shoulder. "How's he got her? Butt naked over his shoulder?"

"Maybe wrapped in a carpet?"

"You ever carry a rolled-up carpet? Down a hill?" But his thoughts remained unfinished, out of focus.

"No fibers either. Maybe he used plastic?" Eliza asked. She had trouble imagining it herself. The ground was slippery. No matter what, it would take time.

Leaves in the trees made papery sounds. Ike had reached a small slope and a knee-deep drift he had no interest in testing. Face-to-face with the iced-over river, he turned up his collar.

"Look." Eliza motioned to the other shore. "Wouldn't it be easier to hide the van on the service road? Then he's got a shorter walk with better cover. He's not in the open like he is here."

"Traffic all hours."

The jade neon of a restaurant's sign glowed spectrally in the fuzz of swirling snow. Above the water on the Booth side, car lights fired head-on as if they were about to dive into the river, then banked left at the last moment. The road hooked, cutting an L through the heart of Booth's Chinatown.

"Right. But he's got to deal with that if he's on either side," Eliza said.

Ike acknowledged the observation with a nod. "He picks this park for a good reason. Because whatever he's doing here, he knows he's taking a big risk. There's got to be a purpose makes it worthwhile. Something that makes sense to him."

"Unless he's crazy."

Ike retreated from the snowy slope—the cold suddenly finding his knee joints, making them ache, making him feel like he'd lived for a hundred years. Time wasted guessing over the unfinished stories left behind by the dead. Sorting through the bones of Booth, covering the same ground Homicide detectives had tromped over since the city was declared a city.

The Lieutenant has rain channeling from the crown of his fedora into the hole. He takes the bewildered patrolman by the elbow and leads him away from the unearthed, mummified skeletons of a mother and child. Tossed among their bones: a crowbar, fox-red with corrosion. What's forcing apart her jaw? That's a pocket Bible. Here this way. Step lightly. The pages long ago exploded in the sandy, well-tended soil. Tomatoes were growing on this patch. Cut down before they went digging. The murderer sits in the backseat of the squad car complaining to no one. Missing the end of his ball game on the radio. He's husband and father to the two in the pit. Was.

Claw on the patrolman's elbow urging him forward and then stops for whiskey. Doesn't offer to share. Poor dental health and dime-store rye blow past the young patrolman's cheeks. The Lieutenant's mouth worked like mouths sometimes do on the senile, the feeble, and the battle-shocked. His clotted eyes keep opening wider and wider as he speaks. He has two faces. One he slips hastily over the other. The top face is for mumbling platitudes, the bullshit that people need to hear when their lives are ruined. But the underneath tells it differently. What he's learned from his time. "The maps lie," he said. "This isn't Booth City. It's Bone City. And you're working in the bone factory. Sure it's a damn shame. They all are. But you stand in there and do the job without looking like the little boy who lost his lollipop. Now pull your shit together. Decide who you are."

"No, he's not crazy." Ike sounded dry, in need of a glass of water. "He's confident. Anything that comes up, he can handle it."

Eliza had to get closer to catch his words.

Ike spoke into the wind, but loudly so she could hear him.

"Man shoots her, but he cuts her up to make it look sexual," he said. "Dumps her remains in a location"—Ike pointed his finger straight down at the ground—"formerly associated with the sex trade. Why the extra effort?"

"He's trying to get us to believe it's a sex-related crime."

"Why's he doing that?"

Eliza blinked away snowflakes. "Because it's not."

"That's all I'm saying."

The chain of a St. Christopher's medal hung around Eliza's neck. Ike noticed it as she looped her scarf around to ward off the hawk wind. A reminder that we're all travelers, he thought. The road is treacherous, our time as journeyers always unknown.

Quick-stepping to the car, he chose the driver's side.

River Road and Fay Street

Crispin couldn't feel his toes. He was afraid if he ran the car's heater too much, somebody would notice him and call the police. He was parked on a hill, across the main drag from the trailer court. Misty Falls. Sounded like a porno queen.

Waiting.

His coffee cup was long empty. Out of necessity, and with a few contortions, he'd refilled it. He was fairly certain no one could see into the car. He had to use his ice scraper every few minutes to keep ice from collecting inside the windshield.

Why did he need to look out? The guy living at 5 Fay Street wasn't going anywhere. Crispin asked himself the question he'd been asking throughout the morning and well into the afternoon. What exactly am I doing here?

Taking the law into my own hands.

It was getting darker. Snowing heavier. Soon he'd have to leave. The snowplows would be running and the street was a posted snow route.

No parking after two inches of snowfall.

It was well past that already. When he'd opened his door to empty his piss, he noticed the snow had deepened to three fingers shy of the curb. If the blizzard kept going until morning, the city would wake up under a foot of white. Crispin rubbed the windshield with his bare hand and watched as a mail carrier's Jeep turned onto Fay.

Through rain, sleet, snow, or dark of night!

He was getting giddy. Wired, tired, and desperate. A lethal combo.

Crispin saw the Jeep round the corner at the same time he saw the van emerge from the trailer court and pull out into traffic. How could he have missed it!

The van's driver sat in darkness, invisible, hidden behind the reflections from the night-lit street. But it had to be the van. The pipes were on top, and when Crispin checked the driveway—no surprises. It was the van.

He turned the ignition key. The wipers shuddered over the glass. Most of the outer surface of the windshield, except his spy hole, was pebbled with ice from the melting snow. He grabbed the scraper and opened the driver's door. He chipped and chiseled and looked up to the see the rear end of the van disappearing. But the scraper was doing its job. There was enough room to peer out, a rectangle of smooth clear glass. He got behind the wheel and shifted into drive.

A pumpkin orange blaze saved him.

Crispin braked; felt his body jerk into his seat—and the blaze in the corner of his eye became a rumble. The city salt truck dropped its plow blade into what felt like his car's trunk. Heart thundering. After the truck passed, the road was empty. But the filthy snow sealed him against the curb securely as a load of wet cement.

A good ER doctor is nothing if not a great improviser. It also helps to have the right tools for the job.

Crispin won on both counts.

He took the shovel and sandbag from his trunk. Dug around the tires. Taking his time because what was the hurry now? He scooped a good amount of sand in the places where it was needed. Let the heater and defrost blast until he needed to unbutton his coat. All the windows were scraped, brushed. New flakes stuck to them—tiny perfect decals—and turned to water.

On the first try, the Saturn rolled out like it was buttered.

Crispin signaled for a right turn. He was staring directly across the intersection into the trailer court. When the idea came, he didn't give himself the chance to debate it. Instead of turning he drove straight. Glided up to 5 Fay Street. A cheap black mailbox mounted on a pole next to the driveway canopy.

Crispin rolled down his window. He flipped the mailbox open and removed the mail from inside. No hesitancy, no second thoughts. Without looking, he dropped everything onto the passenger seat.

He drove away.

CITGO gas station. Riot of blue-tinged light. Crispin parked by the out-of-service air pump. He sorted the stolen mail. Junk, bills, a brown wrapper that felt like a magazine. He saw what he wanted.

The identical name printed on every label.

Evan Spivek. Not Reece Golden.

He tore the brown wrapper. The magazine slid into his lap.

Slick cover. Inside, cheap newsprint pages. Amateurish. Lots of photos. Not illegal as far as Crispin knew. But still.

He noticed he was holding his breath.

He stared at the cover again. The page was cold to the touch. Two people. One kneeling. A leather mask with zippers—the revelation limited to eyes and a raw-looking mouth. The picture snapped close enough you could see sweat on the hooded figure's upper lip, the hairy knuckles of his hand. But the photographer was trying to capture the pink welts and tiny pinpricks of blood on the kneeling man's naked back.

Or perhaps it was the knife.

5

B.C.

Homicide Squad Room

Eliza knew she recognized the guy waiting for them. But from where?

Chessman's. Poins's dart-throwing companion. The mouse hurrying to flush his stash while they chatted with the cabdriver. That's who he was, but wearing a hat this time.

He introduced himself. Marcel Lanier.

"You catch the guy popped Wayne?" he asked. He'd settled, as much as a junkie can settle, into a chair beside the detectives' desks.

"No. Maybe you can shed some light?" Eliza sat closer to him than Ike did, because sometimes that worked. Put the man at ease. He could unburden himself better to a woman. Forget she wore a shield.

Marcel scratched his legs fiercely through his saffron corduroys. He'd trapped his dreads under a crocheted, indigo Rasta hat. The hat looked new, its color vibrant—an odd contrast to the rest of Marcel's street-corner attire. Eliza thought it'd be easy to ignore the man's face under such a beautiful cap. Marcel pivoted, anxious to get back to his pipe. Eliza guessed it took courage to tear his lips away, even for a few hours. Especially to come here. Showing up at the police station was an amazing feat, considering the repercussions were real and word *would* spread about him. No doubt reaching anyone who was paying attention. The neighborhood kept a scorecard. Somebody might be checking Marcel's jersey when he got back on the avenue.

"Wayne went up to Brookie. Told me he thought he saw Josine hanging outside this bar. But she's croaked, right? Can't be Josine."

"She alone? This person he saw?"

"Unaccompanied."

"Who was she?"

"That's what Wayne wanted to know. He tries to have a word with the lady, but she's like . . ." Marcel made a sound like he was letting air out of a balloon.

"Outside the bar . . . what bar was it again?"

"That would be Wickersham's Pub."

"You sure about that, my brother?" Ike asked.

The junkie nodded.

Wickersham's Pub was in Brooktown, outside their jurisdiction. But Eliza and Ike had other reasons for wanting to avoid the place. Eliza's stomach squeezing more than her partner's at the mention of that particular watering hole. She'd buried a bit of personal history there, wanted it to stay buried. She pushed on with her inquiry. "This person was a man dressed like a woman?"

"That's what Wayne said. Dressed like Josine, though, and

nobody else. Clothes he said Josine wore from time to time, and her same style of wig. Gave Wayne the heebie-jeebies."

"But she doesn't tell him who she is? What she's doing dressing like that?"

"They don't converse 'cuz somebody from the bar chased 'em away."

"A customer?" Eliza looked at Ike as she steered the questions in this direction.

"Em-ploy-ee." Fingers grasping behind his head, Marcel twiddled with the drawstring sewn into the rim of his hat. His eyelids fluttered. "The bartender, Wayne said."

"Why'd he do that? Clear them out."

"Don't ask me." Shrug. "Girl was peddling her ass."

"Not outside Wickersham's she wasn't," Ike said.

"Hey, I'm telling you what Wayne told me. You can, like, do a Ripley's, okay? Believe it, or not."

"Say we do believe it. Why should we care?" Eliza asked.

"That bartender up there is an ex-cop. Ex-detective, pardon me. Worked right out of this very precinct. He calls the girl outside Wickersham's by name."

"Josine? He thought she was Josine."

"No. Calls her Reece. Wayne says he tells her, 'Go home, Reece. No more drama for today. Leave before I call the sailors for a ride.' Something, like, to that effect anyway. Now Wayne thought it was . . . exactly what he said was, ' *'Tis passing strange. That* ex-cop knows *this* Reece? Knows her well enough that the Josine getup doesn't throw him?' Wayne was like, '*That bar's got dark glass in the windows and beer signs and a friggin' Christmas tree. Yet the good detective knows her before she turns around*?' Wayne is still speculating when he phones you. Decides that the sailor comment might be like a . . . what-you-call-it . . . a veiled threat. Like she could end up the way Josine did. Floatin'."

"Uh-huh," Ike mumbled. He didn't like any of this. Marcel's story hung together, much like the truth. Where it pointed wasn't helping.

"Wayne gets himself plugged too. He didn't bargain on that shit." Marcel rolled his head, winced as his neck bones cracked. "Tell you what he did say, old Wayne boy. He says, *'I'll give 'em a call but they'll not do much with it.'* So's he right?"

"We're going to catch his killer, Marcel," Eliza said.

"Guaranteed," Ike said.

"My name doesn't get thrown out there? Test the waters if the sharks be hungry?"

"Your name's safe with us," Eliza said. Peripheral vision she sees Ike nodding his head, slowly, like a man who's heard the sermon before.

"I'm cool then." Marcel got to his feet. "Any walkin' money?"

She gave Marcel credit for having guts. Shook him off. *No.*

"Can't hurt to try." Bony fingers slipped inside empty pockets. Pretty blue cap tilting; he fixed it.

Zan's Bathroom

Uncle Happy wasn't very. Though Zan couldn't laugh about it, because he was trying not to swallow any water. Uncle Happy's shoe pressed down, his heel jammed between Zan's shoulder blades. Forcing him deeper into the bowl. Lumps on Zan's forehead where Uncle had slammed him into the lid. This reaction coming after Zan hesitated to lift it, as ordered. That was how their talk began. Now it continued.

"Know what your problem is?"

Submerged, Zan gave no answer. His chin was mashed into the porcelain, and he couldn't have opened his mouth very much if he tried. Couldn't turn his head more than an inch, any direction. The small opening at the base of the bowl where the pipes began—his nose was shoved in there that far, a galaxy bursting before his eyes. The toilet tank was very cold. His flailing hands kept slapping at it.

Thunk thunk thunk thunk thunk thunk

"You're a shit, Zan. Human waste. And waste belongs in a toilet." He let up.

Coughing, shaking all over, Zan extricated himself.

His sweater was soaked; he felt the added weight of it on him as he moved, jerkily, backward—crab-walked, clawing his fingernails into marble but finding no traction, slip-sliding away from the commode, escaping—but there was no escape, only a dry corner where he slumped. He drew his knees up, locked his arms around them. Head down, he suffered through a few lingering spasms.

Uncle approached.

Zan listened to the buckle and fly. He guessed what was about to transpire before sensing the soft patter on his neck, the animal steam as the hollow of his collarbone sizzled and overflowed. Yeasty. The odor of vitamins and boiled coffee clogged his nostrils.

"Little pisser," said Uncle Serpent, adding a gentle, unhinging chuckle to his words.

"Why are you—," Zan began to ask.

"Reward for your shenanigans." Uncle put himself back together. "And to seal my promise. Which is . . . I won't be fixing up after you anymore. Nor will our mutual friend, Mr. Sailor. Understand? We're tired. Of you, and your fucking idiot act as well."

Zan remembered jumping off the high-dive when he was about ten. He hit the water like a railroad spike. He thought he'd die. Never breathe air again. Lost in a chlorinated blue cloud, stretched-out glassy bubbles morphed past his ears. He was feeling that way now. Panic. Absolute panic.

"Total fucking idiot, you are." Uncle Happy wiped his shoes with a bath towel. Face aflame. Wedge of silver hair out of place and he combed it back with a small black comb, the kind they sell in hotel lobbies. He studied his reflection over the sink.

The .38 he sometimes strapped to his ankle?

Zan stole a glance between splayed fingers.

There, underneath Uncle's trouser leg, bulging on his lower calf like a deformity of the bone. Something he hid out of embarrassment. It was on the leg nearest Zan. Reachable. Zan twitched at the possibility, the temptation gaining power—until Uncle decided, every hair reslicked, to step aside. He sat on the edge of the tub.

"Anything you wanted to say?" Uncle asked, smiling.

Touching bottom. Zan pushed off and counted until his next breath. He thought of words, but did not dare. Someday I will damage you, Uncle.

"I'm sorry," he said.

The older man threw him his towel.

Wickersham's Pub

"You want to go?" Ike asked.

Eliza said, "If he's approving the overtime, I'll go."

"Super Mario says clear your cases. The budget's mostly fiction."

"He approved it?" Eliza wasn't buying. Super Mario was the unit supervisor, Lieutenant Mario Ruffalo. He never approved OT unless the case drew public attention or threatened to become political. Dead tranny hooker plus dead cabby poet didn't warrant ink or video. The aldermen at City Hall weren't losing sleep either. If the cost could be shared with another unit, Super Mario might listen. Gang Crimes was an easy target. Ruffalo had a beef with their unit supervisor. Nobody remembered what it was about except Mario. He dogged Eliza for a solid month after she first transferred in. Then he must have decided she was part of the team because his sniping stopped. Overall, he was a decent manager who did the job he'd been given. Part of that job meant keeping an eye on the bottom line.

"We'll submit our time afterward," Ike said.

"Then you know he's not signing off."

"I can always go by myself." Ike with his coat already on, buttoned.

"Lemme call the restaurant and tell them I'll be late." Eliza hit her speed dial. Rey answered. He'd pass the message to Mamá.

"See how this goes. Maybe I'll join you," Ike said.

She clipped the phone to her belt. "Mamá always likes when you visit. She thinks you're a real gentleman. Like Rey."

"Those two going to make it legal?"

Eliza thought, *Not a chance,* said, "Mamá's gun-shy. Restaurant's in her name."

"Does that need to change?"

"Rey's old-fashioned."

"Can't stop the weather," Ike said. He pushed through the doors to the street.

Eliza wasn't sure if he meant Rey's situation or the snow. The steps were icy, salted with a product that resembled tiny foam kernels. Inside the car, under the garage canopy, the two detectives watched a squall blow down the street. Traffic standstill. The street transformed to a white smudge. Ike let the engine warm, shifted into neutral, his foot on the brake. Idling. He touched the pocket inside the lining of his coat. Reflex. His body tricked into looking for cigarettes while his consciousness dealt with other matters. Nicotine Jones knocking on the door. See if anybody's home.

"Wickersham's Pub," he said. "Know what that means?"

Eliza flashed on the Latina pouring drinks at Chessman's.

"Means we'll get served," she said.

Wickersham's was a Brookie cop bar. Everybody who wore blue was familiar, if not intimate, with the establishment. The bar's name had even become code for joint interdepartmental operations. *We got two ongoing Wickershams. Busted that alderman's underage-loving ass in a Wickersham sting last month.* A fair share of B.C. cops drank there regularly. The owner—the bartender from Marcel's story—was an ex-detective from Booth named Terry Duval. Bad rep preceded him. Hothead. Liked to get physical. Word *torture* came up more than once. But never in court. Never on the record. Evidence tickets bearing his signature didn't always match items boxed in the cage. He got flagged, write-ups dropped into his file. Twelve bottles of Dewar's arrived anonymously for the cage crew. Rumors persisted. Duval had intimate knowledge about rental vehicles, big RV units, used for moving coke up from the Gulf. Real weight. Cushing street gangs were the receivers on the Booth end. Maybe Duval set the route up, that was the story. Nothing materialized. His old B.C. partner was doing back-to-backs in the Dexter Pen for a triple execution: two witnesses and their five-year-old, disabled son. Lots of press coverage this time out. Duval was political, in every sense of the word. He called in his markers. Got to retire early, keep his benefits. He stuck close to his home turf. Crossed the river and bought a storefront and a license. Twenty years he was on the job and twenty more evaporated since he left it to serve beer. He had the pub and a small security business that provided guards to city warehouses. But most of his clients were late-night liquor stores. The payroll consisted mainly of off-duty B.C. patrolmen out for extra cash. They worked in uniform, carried their job hardware and attitudes. The city frowned but allowed the practice to continue as long as Duval's employees kept a low profile. He was a troublemaker. But that didn't mean he hired other troublemakers to fill his shifts.

Ike had never been to Wickersham's.

Eliza had, many times, years ago. Didn't look forward to going back.

They parked on a side street. Walked a slippery block to the front door. The atmosphere catered strictly to the nocturnal, no matter where the hands of the clock pointed. A tank of hovering cigarette fumes. All the stools at the bar rail were occupied. Recognizable faces, but most of them not too familiar. Ninety percent Brookie cop turnout this evening. Patrolmen who'd finished up the first shift. Rack suits huddled in one corner, watching the replay of a Super Bowl from the late seventies. Steelers and Cowboys. The detectives were loud. Friendly disagreement. Their glasses held ice cubes, liquors in tan or see-through. The street fighters were drinking beer. No shortage of shot glasses cluttering the bar. Two dozen pairs of cops' eyes checked the new arrivals. It made the hair on Eliza's neck stand up.

Duval wasn't behind the bar.

No free seats at the trough. Ike and Eliza were caught standing. Ike floated a twenty in the general direction of the blonde pulling taps. Gold hoop earrings. Bare midriff. Even though the temperature on the other side of the bricks was in the single digits, nobody was offering her a jacket. Her tip jar could've supported an orphan.

Eliza wanted whiskey. No taste for ginger ale this round.

Ike should've been drinking water. He settled on bottled beer. German.

They took their glassware and headed for a semicircular booth. There were four. Three empty. The design didn't offer much in the way of privacy; they were more like miniature theaters. On the second stage, you could watch the current performance of "Reaching Up the Tipsy Redhead's Blouse."

Eliza regarded the other women. Girlfriends. Nightly rentals. No wives. She was the only female plainclothes cop in the place. Nothing new. But it didn't mean she felt comfortable.

The last time she was inside Wickersham's she'd been underage. But she got served all the same. Duval himself, with full knowledge, neglected to ask her for ID. That would've been an insult considering the circumstances.

"Head out after this drink?" she asked Ike.

He filled his mug. Dabbed a fingertrip in the rising foam.

"Patience," he said.

Eliza was ready to tell him what to do with his patience when the door to the ladies' room swung open and Leah Bloomfield tripped going over the threshold. She banged her hip on the cigarette machine and swore.

"Hey, Leah," Eliza called. Waving her to their table.

Leah's eyes told of an early start, but she'd had plenty of practice by now.

"Ike, you met Leah before?"

"Only observed from afar."

"Here's your chance at a close encounter," Eliza said.

Leah nodded. A fraction too long, too exaggerated. Eliza wondered if maybe Leah had been sipping before the shift change. Not good, if it were true. She had one strike. The review board didn't necessarily allow for three.

"Ochoa ran her mouth in GC. I see you haven't been able to teach her any new tricks." Leah parked herself on the bench next to Eliza, gave her a quick squeeze.

"How's Pedro?" Eliza wanted to know about her replacement in the unit. How he dealt with having Leah for a partner. Leah wasn't for everyone. She was too smart, for one thing. Had degrees in both math and criminal justice. Did a year of graduate school at Brown University before quitting to join the police academy. Why she was chasing bangers in B.C. was a mystery, probably even to Leah. Maybe that's what made the gin so tasty.

"Pedro's Pedro, what can you expect? The guy won't change."

"You spend a lot of time here?" Ike asked.

"That's supposed to be a joke, right?" Leah drummed her

knuckles on the tabletop. The wedding ring was gone, but there was still a pale line. Eliza heard that she and Brendan had tried a last-ditch attempt to salvage their marriage. Two weeks in Antigua. Leah's tan had more staying power. "Let me buy a round, okay? Jeez, I never see you."

Leah beelined to the bar.

"She's been going through a few difficulties," Eliza said, observing as one of the Brookie detectives swooped down. Put his arm around Leah's waist.

"Best keep away from the B-town boys," he said. "They're wannabes, and wannabes are always dangerous."

"That's prejudicial," she said.

"Oh, absolutely."

Leah disentangled herself and negotiated through the pack. Errant auburn curls falling in her eyes, but her hands were putting down their drinks safely. Her gin—*easy on the ice, please*—had a brown lime chunk stranded at the bottom. She didn't seem to notice. Or, if she did, didn't care.

"Owner must be doing well," Ike said. He gestured toward the crowded rail.

"Terry? He's here most weekends. The security thing's got him busy. They're bidding for guard duty on the new riverboat. It'll mean tripling his crew if they win."

"That right?" Ike said. "Good for Terry."

Eliza tried to convince Leah to join them for dinner at her mother's restaurant. Get something solid in her stomach. But Leah was on a kamikaze mission. Eliza hoped she would find a better way to work out the kinks. Brendan was an asshole. Leah deserved more. She really did. That was another problem people had with her. She always made you feel like she'd been cheated. No situation, no relationship gave enough to make her happy. She pushed you. Some cops resented her for it. Pedro, for example. But Leah pushed herself hardest. She thought that's what everyone expected. What they wanted from their colleagues. So she bruised egos and made enemies, especially in her own unit. There were times you could almost see the white-hot glow of Leah's burnout coming on. Eliza had been more cautious. She had no fallback plan. No graduate school diplomas gathering dust in the drawer. Her sense of self was tied completely to being a cop. One among many. Another day, another body to ponder. She worked each case right, paying attention to the details and giving every name in a Homicide red file its due. But Eliza made certain to keep something in reserve. Lately, she wasn't sure why.

Ike shook hands with Eliza's old partner.

"You don't forget now. Tell Terry I said hello."

Leah wouldn't forget. Despite the hours hanging out, she always remembered specifics. Her ability to recall—names, faces, numbers—found refuge somewhere, a calm harbor to ride out the storms.

Walking back, Eliza had a question. "You know Duval?"

"Never had the pleasure," Ike said. A veneer of ice cracked beneath his fingers—the door handle popping under the force of his grip.

Eliza's Bedroom

Phone handset cool against her ear. She wasn't quite conscious, freshly knocked out of REM sleep.

"What?"

"Rise and shine," he said.

Pitch-black except for the streak of starlight slashing her headboard in two. She sat up. Threw off her blankets. Smelled body lotion, her own sleep-time musk and whiskey breath. She was awake.

"Get your blood flowing?" he asked. "Don't insult me by pretending you don't remember my voice."

She did remember. Said nothing.

"Lovely. I've got your attention. I'll be brief. Delbert Watts was murdered because he fucked odd men in the park for money. Overcomplicating things would be a mistake."

She waited to hear if there was more.

"Mad because I forgot your birthday?" he asked.

Laughing. Disconnected.

Eliza made it to the bathroom in time, retched into the toilet. She ran a scalding shower. Stumbled under. Torch-cut the cold sweat off her skin.

She did remember. Said nothing.

Crispin Maloney's Loft

He had vacation coming, a week of it. After calling around, he convinced two other ER docs it was time to repay the shifts he'd covered for them. Seven days starting today to uncover, no matter the outcome, what happened to Patrick. If his search brought no answers, then so be it. His conscience would be clear. Clearer than if he hadn't tried. He told no one. His family would've talked him out of doing it. And he didn't want that. Resolution, he wanted an ounce of fucking resolution.

Spivek's magazine waited for him on the coffee table, next to a hardbound collection of Andy Warhol prints.

"Can I have another towel for my hair?" she asked. Black, unpinned, her hair was shimmering as it swayed above the dimples in the small of her back. He'd been wrong about the dancer part, but that was all. Steam followed her from the bathroom. Funny. He hadn't noticed the shower turning off. Hunching forward, he slipped the magazine between the pages of the Warhol book. Really hoping he wouldn't need to explain.

He leaned over the arm of his chair to kiss the back of her thigh.

"Want coffee?" he asked.

"Oh, please no, the smell makes me gag. My crappy job. How about juice?"

"You can take a look, but I think my supplies are at an all-time low."

"Let's go out."

"No class today?"

"I've got Drawing at two."

He wasn't listening. If Spivek knew Reece and Reece knew Patrick, then the nexus was there. A point of origin. But Spivek might be a dead end. Based on every indication, Reece was a club-drug-addled lunatic. But Crispin had more knowledge than before he'd met them. He was closer to Patrick who was . . .

Gone without a trace. Missing and presumed.

"I said, 'Want to go out?' " She let the towel drop to the floor. "There's a little bakery on Peterson. Wonderful chocolate croissants." She went to the window for a look at the weather.

Hmm.

He picked up the towel by a corner. Hanging from his thumb and forefinger, and then he began whirling it around. It was just wet enough.

"Don't you dare," she said.

"You'll forgive me."

"Snap me and I'll scratch your eyes out."

"Deal." He folded the towel over his arm. "But you'll have to get dressed and go home, I'm afraid. I've got rounds in half an hour." He always tried not to look at them when he did this. "Rain check on the breakfast, okay?"

After she was gone, he outfitted himself in a fleece shirt and jeans and, from the depths of the closet, his mud-caked hiking boots. He shrugged into a goose-down vest. Corduroy fishing cap. He grabbed his gym bag, emptied the contents, and refilled it with what he thought he'd need to do the job.

It was ridiculous, of course.

First he plays Cops.

Now Robbers.

Out the door and he almost forgot Warhol's secret stash.

He stuffed the magazine into his bag.

Minty's Marine Storage

Despite the deep freeze, the boat carpet smelled of mildew. Evan Spivek—Sailor to his friends—unsnapped the canvas boat cover and threw it back. Whooping belch of dead fish and empty beer bottles. He scrambled underneath.

The missing cooler bothered him.

Not right after Patrick died.

But later.

He thought he knew what happened. Knew it now. But he wanted to check again to be sure. Give his babe Josine the benefit of the doubt.

Sailor dug into every compartment. He lifted the trapdoors and yanked the seats from their fittings to get behind. The cooler wasn't that small, the boat not that big.

Clean, like he thought.

He had a feeling before he climbed aboard. Just the shittiest feeling screwing inside him, like a tapeworm. Josine wasn't bluffing. Zan had told him the truth about her and her cheap scheme. He said she'd taken a piece of Patrick that night. Tucked it away while they were doing the dirty work. She'd told Sailor as much, hadn't she? Curling around him that night in bed. He'd thought, She's only joking, of course.

Her pound of flesh.

Death sentence, more like.

Stupid. Thinking the Booths would pay to get it back. Keeping their boy out of trouble. Buying Josine's Thai plane tickets. Hadn't Zan promised her an appointment under the surgeon's knife?

Sailor told her Zan was blowing smoke. She'd gotten her knife all right. Right where she'd asked for it.

Wasn't *his* money good enough? Didn't *he* pay to get her off the cement stroll? Didn't *he* promise to fix her up when they put a little more bread together? Not fast enough I guess, thought Sailor. She sniffs cash on Zan and pulls this stunt. If she'd come to me first, I'd have told her. You can't force people like Zan.

But no. She solos this bright idea.

He has to hear it from Zan. Afterward. When it's too late to do any good.

Zan wouldn't listen to Sailor's excuses. Refused to wait. He went to Uncle Happy with the bad news. Uncle camped in his office at Wickersham's. Doing the bookkeeping, Zan said. Pretending like he was a normal guy and not some creature that would suck the eyes out of a baby if the mood struck him or if there was a dollar in it.

Terry practically had a seizure when he heard the news.

But what Sailor wanted to know was: How could Josine do that to *him*?

They had a special thing. Love? The best Sailor could say was, it was real. Rock solid and you could yell and scream and you could puke all your vilest poison on it but spit on your fist and rub circles and the fucker would shine. Diamond, man.

Sailor kicked a hole in the galley door.

She sold him out!

Sailor slapped himself in the face until his skin caught fire. He bit his knuckles to the bone. This was howling. Being boiled alive. Mainlining hatred. Pure venom surging as he wrapped his arms around his head and kicked, kicked, kicked.

Why did it hurt him?

And why, after all her evil shit, why the fuck was he crying?

Eliza's Car

It was easy to forget that once you drove ten miles outside the city, the rest of Nestor County, and the majority of the state, was rural. Prairie land. Stubble fields where in the summers soybean and corn grew, hardscrabble farms, and between them, tight valleys dotted with small, innocuous homes. Here and there, as you climbed out of the river valley, granite outcroppings soared—totemic, gray, chiseled slabs. Stony crags. The cliffs were popular with jumpers. Kids mostly. Usually zoned on something cheap and lethal. Crack or grain alcohol. Meth. Sometimes they went over in pairs. Eliza even recalled a triple. They shared a whiff of glue before the leap. Crime-scene techs found the crimped tube. Baggie in a boot heel. Saving it for later.

Eliza hadn't been out of Booth for weeks. The landscape never failed to shock. Snow-collapsed barns like sea wrecks on wind-scalded hilltops. She perceived each as a snapshot of destruction—a holocaust of rotted wood and nails.

She had almost *died* on one of these farms. Her blood sucked away by the crumbly, black soil. Manure clod for a pillow. Summer sun getting fatter on one side as if it were about to explode—so close she could've reached and touched it. Silky red washes below her waist, and turning redder by the heartbeat. Knees up. Eliza put the memory away.

She changed lanes, crossed over a bridge.

Small brown sign, white letters: ROOD RIVER.

The Rood ran north to south through most of the state, from the falls on the upper border to the fork at the southeastern tip. But inside the Booth City limits it took a hard left. Like many aspects of B.C., the river was off its usual course. Flowing east/west through the metro area, then veering more or less back to normal a mile after the suburbs started cropping up. Subdivisions and strip malls. Anywhere America.

Booth directions made no sense to downstaters. At a county highway pit stop, the mention of north or south of the Rood would get you a second look. Say it twice and suspicions were confirmed. The rest of the state would have been satisfied if the planet cracked open, swallowed Booth City, and ground her bones. It was that kind of love.

But without B.C. there would be no Dexter Correctional. No lucrative penal contracts for the corporate prison farms, no living wage jobs for the unfortunate, immobile residents of Booth's backwater cousin, Toolsburg.

Eliza spotted the first guard tower. Wouldn't be long now. Fifteen minutes through the gate, maybe another half hour until her meeting. The paint job on the tower roof made it look like terra cotta. Double fence. Concertina wire like outsized, macabre Slinkies. A guard's sky-blue pickup truck patrolled between the fences. The maximum security prison inside the wire was a quarter century old. Two-story building, the layout was simple, like a child's drawing of a star. Three low, cement corridors intersecting at a hub. Guard center at the hub, dividing each corridor into two sections. Six sections, or sectors, total.

Eliza had requested this visit. The prisoner had accepted. Visiting rooms were in the hub. The prisoner was coming from Sector F.

Twenty-four-hour lockdown. The prisoner would get out once a day for a supervised walk indoors. Showers. Never the yard. The prisoner had no cell mates. He had lived here, in this manner, for two decades. It was considered by some to be a miracle—his still being alive. *Miracle* wasn't the right word.

Dexter Correctional Center: Visitation Room

He looked terrible. Aged. His skin was yellow. The jaundice. She knew he'd contracted Hepatitis C, but she didn't know how. Her guesses were bad enough. He wore the state-issue prison blues, a white tee shirt, and a stiff denim jacket, too long in the sleeves. His movements were slow motion, a man trapped in a watery maze. His eyes had lost their fiery cast, turned into the liquid element he walked through. Drowned man. Hanged man. She could see the scar the rope had left around his throat, a pink fold in the sagging yellow melt. He picked up the metal chair, backed it up, and set it down again. Like he was alone in the room and had all the time in the world. Maybe it was true. He couldn't hold her gaze for more than a second. But his eyes were on her. His fingers massaged the bald spot on the top of his head. He cleared his throat. Said nothing. Eliza couldn't speak either. Too many days passed in alternate universes. Too many monsters set loose, howling, in the cramped and silent space. He seemed to realize the deadlock would go on forever if he didn't break it first. He tried to smile. Eliza noticed the dryness cracking his lips.

"So, little Liza," he began, "what brings you to visit your da after twenty years?"

6

LUCKY MARTY

Dexter Correctional Center: Visitation Room

Da. Funny word. Born of baby's babble. Term of endearment. There had been nothing endearing about Martin Gahan. He'd never been a da to his twin sons or to his only daughter.

Eliza Maria Ochoa Gahan. She'd dropped the Gahan when her mother did.

After the sentencing, the divorce, the suicide attempt. During the long horrible period of shame. Her father was *un chota sucio.* Dirty cop. *El perro* capable of executing a child with an I.Q. under fifty. Was that before he fired bullets into the hands of the boy's parents? Before he tapped two into each of their skulls?

"Lucky" Marty Gahan. Or, as he'd been known more formally, Detective Martin Gahan of the Booth City Homicide Unit and partner to Detective Sergeant Terrence Duval. Terrible Terry. But who pulled the trigger? Who fell when the gods of City Hall demanded someone fall?

Lucky Marty. It was Duval who gave him that name.

It was also Duval who promised Eliza—on a sunlit spring afternoon, the back door of Wickersham's propped open to mollify the smell of fresh paint and exchange it for freshly mowed grass as she stared at the purple and yellow tulips drooping their heavy heads in a tin window box with little hearts punched out all around, the alley bricks hosed down and already drying to pink, the hose coiled, dripping in Duval's hand, and beyond the doorway the cries of boys chasing a basketball—Duval who promised her that after she finished her schooling, if she ever applied to the police department, he'd guarantee her application would be accepted. He had the right friends. Friends Marty never had. And didn't he owe something to his old partner? Eliza's mother, well, she wouldn't accept help. But here was an envelope. He dried his hands on his green apron. And other envelopes like it would follow as long as Marty stayed away and stayed quiet. Terry was there to help.

Did she understand?

She understood. They drank a shot of Irish whiskey, toasting the future. Bitter draw. Liquor the same temperature as the long fingers patting her knee. She took the envelope. She'd taken one like it every month until she made detective. Duval always slipped her the cash inside novelty birthday cards—the kind with naked men holding cakes below their waists. When she stopped visiting Wickersham's, the rapid promotions stopped too. Her assignment to Gang Crimes was a genuine surprise. The transfer to Homicide was another. She started to make-believe the years with Duval had never happened. Perhaps he had no influence, she told herself. Maybe she'd done this all on her own. The money? She'd lent some to Mamá for the restaurant. But that loan had been repaid.

The money was . . . she didn't think about it. And she'd stopped taking it. Stopped without a word to Duval. Never went in for the last envelope and that was that. End of story.

Deep in the night, he called to let her know that he'd purchased something with those birthday cards. Her father's past and her own future.

"What brings you to visit?" Da asked her.

Maybe she wanted to see if he still existed.

For such a long time he'd been the exclusive property of her dreams. Waking and sleeping. Memories and the sifted, sour ashes of nightmares.

To see him sitting there made her teeth grind.

She said, "Terry Duval."

And she watched hell rip a hole in his diseased face.

Ike's Desk

Three red files arrayed. Ike chose from the coroner's photos, shuffled them, and flipped them over, one by one, as if he were reading tarot cards.

Cuts on Josine/Delbert Watts's backside
Unidentified male's tattoo
Wayne Poins's swelled, purple eyes
Chest cavity (J/DW)
Serration marks along skin flap (UM)
Skull (WP)
Arms (J/DW)

The shot of Josine's arms highlighted the ligature marks. Ike looked for something else in the red files. Crime Scene photo of Poins with his elbows duct-taped behind his back. He tapped it with his thumb. He picked up the tattoo photo. Eliza had said it might be a Celtic symbol. Red file again. Josine had a tattoo—a unicorn. Ike dug out his phone book. Twenty minutes' worth of calls later, he had a partial answer. He clipped the photos together, slid them into his coat, and walked.

5 Fay Street

Spivek's trailer seemed deserted.

Crispin pried the window with a large flathead screwdriver. Broad daylight but he had a little cover—a propane tank, Spivek's satellite dish, and the Saturn parked under the awning.

The window stuck. He turned his face away and, holding the steel shaft, smashed the glass with the screwdriver handle.

Loud, but not as loud as he had expected.

He pushed in the Venetian blinds.

A bed.

He was careful where he knelt.

Full-blown criminal now, Pin.

He felt the sudden, urgent need to void his bowels. For ten seconds, he stood in the middle of Spivek's invaded home and contemplated using the man's toilet. It was that bad. But the crisis passed.

This guy lived like an animal. Piles of dirty laundry in every corner. The place stunk, overwarm and fishy, like a cat's mouth. A weight bench dominated the far end of the trailer. Three hundred plus loaded on the bar. Dumbbells, iron plates, and collar locks scattered on the floor. Chicken of the Sea cans topping the blue recycle bin.

Crispin slammed through drawers, cabinets. Rifled the two-by-eight shelving.

Junk.

Under the bed, a suitcase. He dragged it out. As far as he could tell, it didn't belong to Patrick. He heaved the case through the broken window, heard it crunch on the snow.

An engine. He waited, screwdriver in hand. The car didn't slow down.

Crispin climbed back through the way he'd come in. His boots left behind wet, gray streaks on the mattress.

He wore gloves. Fingerless. Shit. He wiped the window frame with his sleeve. Felt his shirt snag and tear. Sliver of glass punctured his forearm. He touched the bump on his skin. He was bleeding, his shirt leaking blood. The mounded snow changed from white to white with red craters. He kicked away his footprints—ice clumps striking the trailer's hull—and retrieved the case. Ran.

He started the Saturn. Reversed. His front tire made shrieking contact with an awning pole. The awning leaned. He ignored the stop sign.

No cops down by the river this morning.

If there were, he would've already met them.

Claude's Tattoo Parlor

"Celtic knot, yeah, I didn't do it though. That's Pepe's work."

"Pepe?"

"He's with a client right now."

Claude tipped the scales at one-ten, tops. Flyweight, if Ike remembered his divisions. The piercings, chin up, probably added a quarter pound. Left arm plastered in scarlet monkeys, a conga line, hooking on to each other, hands to tails. They reminded Ike of Fleur's game, the plastic barrel at the bottom of her toy box. Hers didn't have fangs.

More ink, solid black this time, in the crook of Claude's right forearm. Ike couldn't deduce the shape until the tattoo artist straightened his arm to show Ike the bottle.

Keyhole.

"Hey, you ever try this?"

Talisker. The label said it was Scotch. Ten years old.

"Any good?" Ike asked.

"Oh, yeah. I've had better, but this is real decent. Client dropped it off for me."

"Late Christmas present?"

"Exactly." Claude reinserted the bottle into a cardboard canister. "Pepe's finished. That's his lady getting dressed over there."

The woman wore a mahogany velvet tracksuit. She zipped her jacket, lifted a fur shawl from the coat rack next to Pepe's cubicle. Her breeze was scented. Cardamom, star of anise, and Jolly Ranchers.

"Pepe," Claude said. "This guy's a detective from around the block. Horner, right?"

Ike nodded.

The draped cubicle was larger than it looked from the outside. Spartan. The main furnishing was a pink vinyl table that resembled health club equipment. Pepe, antithesis to Claude's Jack Sprat, needed every spare inch of room. He didn't bother to get up. Then Ike saw the wheelchair obscured by the man's poncho-sized shirt.

"Play nice." Claude shut an accordion door, allowing them the illusion of privacy.

"I got sample books, there, on the floor. Or you want a custom?"

"How about like this?" Ike passed him the coroner's color Polaroid, the Celtic knot from the unidentified male's remains. "Claude says it's one of yours."

Pepe inspected, trailing a finger delicately around the circumference of the ringed pattern. He handed the photo back. "What's up with you? You're not here to get inked."

"Never said I was. So's it yours?"

"It's mine," Pepe answered. "And *I* never said it wasn't."

"Person you tattooed there is dead. Chopped up. That scrap is all we've got. Be interesting to know who he was."

"You're shittin' me."

"Not today, my brother. Not today."

The big man shoved the pink table and wheeled out from behind it. His feet, mashed into a pair of green Nikes, scuffled along the floor.

"I keep a record of everybody I touch with my irons."

"Best news I heard all week," Ike said.

Pepe started grabbing up the multicolored binders off the floor.

"You get requests for this type of design?" Ike asked. "Celtic knot?"

"I've done a few. But what you're showing me, that's inked on somebody's ass. I haven't done too many of those." Snaggletooth grin. "You're sure this was a guy?"

Ike considered the question. "Born male. Don't know what he did after that."

"Guy pays for skin art, he usually wants the world to see it. No peek-a-boo games." Pepe thumbed through a binder labeled *Celtic & Tribal.*

Ike waved the photo as if he'd taken it only seconds earlier and was now waiting for the image to dry.

"Most of these are symbolic," Pepe said. "Your knot included."

"What's it stand for?"

"Infinity." Pepe stopped flipping pages. He unsnapped the binder rings, carefully tugged one of his Polaroids from its acetate sleeve. Flipside gave up a name.

Patrick. Followed by another word. *Cash $*.

"I can keep it?" Ike asked.

"Go ahead."

Ike put the matching photos in his pocket. As he did, he touched the corner of a third photograph, Josine's unicorn.

"What do you think?"

Pepe huffed. "That's joint. Scratcher playin' with his hobby gun."

"Crude?"

"Plenty crude." Pepe pedaled backward with his toes. He picked up a washcloth, rubbed the back of his neck. "She get wasted too?" he asked.

Ike glanced down at Josine's breast, the shriveled nipple dead center of the frame. Cockeyed unicorn orbiting. Horn like a swirl of soft-serve ice cream in the middle of its forehead. Chest wound out of sight.

"Very much so."

"It's war, huh?"

Ike wondered how Pepe came to be in his moving chair. What had claimed that part of him? "This thing here wasn't gang-related," Ike said.

"Ain't talking about gangs. Talking life."

Booth's Orchards

Gnarled.

Wizened.

Older than he was—he thrashed and then grew still, hanging with his full weight pulling down, boots not quite reaching the polished crust of snow. Swaying. The tree branch wouldn't break. Zan let it fly. Watched the whip action. Ice jewels sprayed outward. He clapped his gloves together. Doubled over at the waist, breathless, flushed. He probed under his rib cage, on his right side. Sensitivity. His liver in revolt, turning hard and knobby as a candy dish.

Maybe another stint in rehab was the way out. But they'd all be waiting when he got home. There was nowhere. He could, of course, do more of what had made Uncle Happy so eager to inflict pain. He could confess. Not haphazardly to Patrick's brother or Josine's cabdriver friend. No, he could do a proper confession. The station house, or whatever the police called it. He could show up, ask to see Detective Mexican Maid, and then just start talking.

Zan hugged at the tree trunk. He whispered to it until his teeth chattered and his words were lost. Numb-faced. He was thick-lipped and thick-tongued and drooling like a mastiff. He went into his smothering hole of a house because despite everything he had not yet made peace with death. That would come later.

Homicide Squad Room

Ike listened to the honeyed contralto of his partner's voice. At her desk, on the phone, and sounding as if she were about to cross a line and forgo interoffice politeness. The round of re-interviews at The Limerick hadn't gone well if her body language meant anything. Her shoulders hunched forward, elbows anchored to the desktop, free hand grasping her hair—curling it behind her ear. Her hand switched to swinging her empty coffee cup to and fro.

Ike wanted to share his news about his visit to Claude's. But he was patient.

"Yes, a suicide. It predates what we have in our record room, that's why I'm calling. I need the red file on the Leland Tompkins case. A suspicious death ruled suicide. Look, we've been over this five times. What part aren't you getting?"

There, Ike thought. Line crossed. Time to seek cover.

"I'd be happy to come upstairs and find the record myself. Asking you isn't . . ."

Ike leaned over with the coffeepot and filled her moving target.

"By two o'clock? I'm sure we'll both be happier when you do." She dropped the handset into its cradle. Directed the steaming cup to her lips.

He didn't wait for her to regroup. "Any luck at The Limerick?"

"No." The world's best two-letter lie.

"I got us a name to go with our tub victim."

He showed her Pepe's photo. She did what he'd done—she matched it to the one from Crime Scene. No need to walk her through. She turned Pepe's to the white side and read the name marked along the edge.

"How do you like that?" Ike asked.

"I guess it's something."

"You see our friend Jared over at The Limerick?"

Her response was taking too long.

"That's where you went, right?" He probed the soft spot without knowing exactly why. Maybe his internal machine spiked on her deception. Her morning jaunt to the SRO didn't sit right with him. Whatever it was, he sensed decay, and lurking beneath—a live nerve.

"I didn't see him," she said.

"Who did you see?"

When she didn't answer, he told himself to drop the issue. Something, or someone, had rattled her cage.

"At the tattoo parlor," she said, changing the subject. "They remembered our guy?"

"Young. White. Average-looking. Walked in off the street. He only shows the one time. No other skin art on his body the day this Celtic knot goes on. Worthless trying for a sketch, since they're both saying they can't remember his face."

"He's by himself for the session? Nobody's hanging out thumbing through a magazine while he's getting the needle?"

"Alone is what they tell me."

"He has a referral?"

"Claude says Pepe's well known in the area. No one-to-one networking. Pepe, meet Patrick, Patrick, this is Pepe. Nothing like that happened."

"We believe them?" Eliza asked.

Ike gave her nerve one last jab, said, "Do we believe anyone?"

The Alley Behind Claude's Tattoo

"I know they got paper on you. That's why I didn't tell them dick."

"He was just some guy I talked to about finding the best local skin artist. He asked me. I sent him to you, Pepe. I didn't know him."

"It's cool."

"You say it's cool, but you're calling me."

"You're my showcase, man. I've got to keep you circulating."

"Okay."

"Chill. It wasn't about you. Cop was looking for whoever put this Patrick in the wood chipper. Hey, you see that movie? Pregnant lady sheriff and all the snow? Funny shit, that movie."

Silence.

Pepe regretted making the call. Right intentions, but the thing was working backward, blowing Sailor up like a fucking bomb. The man had more cop fear than any of Pepe's other friends. You talk cops and Sailor went ape. It was stupid to get him worried over nothing. Like he'd said, the guy was nobody. Here and gone.

"When we gonna do the mermaid? I drew her up, man. She's ready," Pepe said.

"I don't know."

"Double slot open this Tuesday."

"Sorry for freaking on you, Pep. Somebody trashed my crib. Ripped off my knives. Been a fucking bad day all around."

"They stole your knives?"

"Grabbed the case."

"Might be those skaters, no?"

"It's not the skaters. I know who it was."

"Then go get 'em back."

"I will."

"Tuesday. Name's on my calendar now." Pepe was glad to be heading out of the conversation. No way he wanted Sailor angry with him and more paranoid than before. Pepe wouldn't have said it to his face or to the cops, but Sailor was a scary dude.

"Okay," Sailor said. "Tuesday."

"She's beautiful, man. You'll see. I gave her a nice, fat tail."

Crispin's Loft

There were twelve. The blades wrapped, Crispin couldn't help but think, *lovingly,* in soft, grayish yellow cloths. These were animal hides. Every hair scraped away to swaddle the twelve daggers.

Crispin remembered that movie from the seventies, *The Omen,* where Gregory Peck is given a set of knives and told to murder his demonic son. Atticus the destroyer. The same high sacredness, phony or not, was on display here. The daggers did not appear to be a set. They were individuals, arranged by someone in this special way. Forced into a family. And not by any someone, by Evan Spivek. The case Crispin had found hidden under his bed. It belonged to Spivek. Spivek's knives.

Custom-fit foam inserts.

The trailer's other contents had been, by and large, neglected.

Total impact registered. Taking these knives may have been a big mistake.

Putting them back would be impossible. He tugged at an insert. It wasn't glued. He peeled up a corner, got his fingers underneath, and lifted out the piece.

Photographs.

Not certain if he wanted to look. But knowing he'd be unable to resist.

They were similar to the magazine shots. Spivek, sans a mask, wore blue jeans, a black leather vest, and motorcycle boots. The others were, generally speaking, men. Men dressed as women, wearing fishnet hose, cocktail dresses, and glam wigs. They were made up to look like a menu of fantasies. Whore-of-the-Month Club. Pick a flavor. Oriental. Tex-Mex. Biker. Spivek undressed them. Some had padded bras, others implants. They were skinny little things. That characteristic never wavered. What Spivek did to them went beyond basic whips and chains.

He scraped. He scratched. Pricked and nicked. He sliced. Blood became a lubricant in his sexual arsenal. His partners, though visibly coerced, were playing along. This was consensual. He might've paid them to do it. But a deal had been struck. The photos were taken at different times, different interiors. Somewhere in this city, or nearby, people were keeping dungeons. Getting medieval on each other. Rough-hewn wooden beams, iron cages, O-rings screwed into brickwork. In several photos, there was an obvious audience presence. Sailor performed his parlor tricks. Faces reappeared, the same unclad bodies. Evidence of beer bottles, wineglasses, champagne. Water bottles too. Ice buckets. Stereos and CD towers. The assortment of audio/video equipment in the background was impressive. Obviously, some of these people had money. The gatherings weren't thrown together last-minute. The scenes had an orchestrated quality and a vibe that was, at least in the outermost ring, laid-back and social. Participants knew each other. No strangers here. Or few. Everybody—and every body—engaging in an agreed-upon, mutually shared experience. Getting off together.

Spivek had a favorite partner. Their photos were darker, in terms both of light and theme. An unnameable quality of these photos told of an absence of others. Private sessions. You can watch, but you cannot feel. Not this far in. This far in was a stratum of privacy few couples, committed or otherwise, ever entered.

Intemperate, unpretty needs.

It wasn't the basic mechanics of the acts that shocked Crispin. Variations on a theme, really. But it was the total surrender to power and powerlessness, the double exposure of souls—Spivek's and his lover's—and their stripped-down desires.

Maybe the two weren't completely alone.

Crispin switched on another lamp. He brought the photograph under it.

Like a room turned belly-up, all available light in the shot came from below the waist. Oak floor, stumpy legs of a leather couch, an ashtray with three pewter gargoyles squatting around the rim. Hear no evil. See no evil. Speak no evil. Someone's feet. A spectator. Shadow in the shadows, but no mistaking her.

Reese.

STEVEN SIDOR

El Cabrito Blanco

The lunchtime rush had subsided. Rey blended frozen margaritas for a thirty-something couple munching tortilla chips at a table by the bay window. The woman draped in a parka, but she was smiling. Her companion tipped a crock of homemade red salsa and made eye contact with Rey, lifted the earthen bowl to show it needed refilling.

Eliza had to come here after her visit to Dexter. Time to make her confession, if only a partial one. Mamá was in the kitchen. Her head gliding back and forth in the servers' cutout, like a duck in a shooting gallery.

Here, the sangria was never too sweet. Eliza poured a second glass. Her plate was empty. Napkin folded and returned to the side of her dish. Mamá would be coming to check on her.

Door swing and a flash of umber walls.

Bustle of her apron, too long for her, but she was a short woman. Her body belied her essence. Eliza hadn't half her strength.

She looked tired. It was a permanent feature. She slept four hours a night. Said any more made her feel lazy. Being a teenager in her house had been less than manageable. The twins had baseball, the track, and later, their shop where they built cabinetry for the mansions tucked in the forested hills behind Brooktown. Eliza wasn't so fortunate. She was a reader. Reading, to Mamá, looked a lot like laziness. Eliza ended up in a dusty carrel at the library. But that was history, and who didn't have history with their mother?

"I went to see Martin," Eliza said.

Never a talker, Mamá's reaction remained mysterious. Her face set firm as clay, but Eliza had seen her fall apart too many times to think the cracks were repaired. There would be no more tears. Not for her husband or what he'd done to her and their children. The damage inflicted on past and future dreams. Love turned her on its spit. But she didn't have to acknowledge it.

"So?"

"I think he's dying."

"I hope he does it well this time."

"Mamá, twenty years can—"

"Why are you telling me? You are his daughter, yes? I am not his wife."

"I know."

"He was always a stranger. I didn't recognize him that last day in the courtroom. I could've walked right by him and told you I never saw my husband. That is the truth."

"I needed his help."

"Then you are in a bad position."

Rey breezed past them. Luminescent, fishbowl glasses and salsa balanced on a tray. "Ike and I are investigating three murders. Their killer may be this man who—"

"Martin knows him from inside the prison?"

"From before."

Mamá pulled Eliza's empty plate toward her. She moved the silverware into the middle and covered the dandelion print. Her fingertips circled on the tablecloth, brushed out an unseen wrinkle.

"I want you to let this man go. Do it for me. Let him get away with his crimes. That happens every day and you can't control it. Pretend you can't control this either. Because you can't."

Eliza nodded, looked away, and smiled.

"What's funny?"

"Martin." Eliza chewed a slice of apple tapped from the bottom of her glass. "He told me the same thing."

"Yeah?"

"Yeah. But first he told me a story."

"I don't want to hear it."

"Right, Mamá. But like you said, we're not the same."

"What do you mean?"

"I wanted to hear his story."

"And?"

"I did."

Patrick's Room

Crispin's parents were working. He let himself into the house. Just like you read in the newspapers, they hadn't touched Patrick's room. It was waiting for Patrick when he returned. Like they were. Waiting in the quiet while the dust motes danced. Time suspended. But no one suspends time.

Patrick was dead. He let himself think it, a first, as though it were fact.

The thought made it harder to go through his room. Rescue shifting to recovery. Bringing Patrick back dissolved into finding his body. No closure promised, no hope of satisfaction. But, perhaps, a path opening in the fog of confusion and misinformed guesses. Maybe an answer. If not to why, then to how. A chronology ticking off the origin of their grief. Little consolation. But an answer, something in stone. Grave marker.

Patrick kept no journals. No black book, no calendar. He'd been gone and alive before he'd been gone and . . . vanished.

Matchbooks. Dog-eared souvenirs of family dinners and road trips. Most of the place names weren't local. He'd been too young for the bar scene. Too teenager poor for good restaurants.

Ticket stubs. Movies. Concerts.

Ski lift ticket. Jackson Hole. Maloney reunion of sorts. Crispin had been in residency, on call. He missed the week.

The sheets on the bed were fresh, so Mom had been in here to do that, preparatory to nothing. Crispin flipped the mattress. Harder than he'd intended—a lamp fell over beside the headboard. Not going to get lucky there again, Pin.

An album. He didn't need to look at more pictures. A collection like Spivek's would be secreted away. Crispin couldn't imagine Patrick superimposed in those scenes, but he couldn't imagine him running away, using heroin, or going missing, not until it all happened. The domino line of revelations Patrick had set in motion. But the Maloneys were the ones falling over when they arrived, these bulletins to their disbelief.

The photos were of family.

What were you running from, Pat? Selfish, arrogant little asshole.

Running to. What were you running to?

Did you find it sleeping in your tent in Broe Woods? Copping an eight ball and flexing your biceps? Did that close the gap?

Did you enjoy your adventure?

Crispin sat on the floor. Head against knees.

Broe Woods.

Patrick lived there after getting kicked out of his squat. There and the bridge before going off the radar. That night in the ER,

Reese had said something about calling him Pin. Where did she learn his name? *A troll I met under a bridge.*

Crispin was willing to bet the troll's name was Patrick.

He cleaned up the mess. Shut the bedroom door.

Their parents would never know.

Homicide Squad Room

Clerical delivered the red file to Eliza's in-box: the Leland Tompkins case. She picked it up. It was thin. She opened the flap and saw a sticky note. Part of the file had been erroneously purged and destroyed. Terrific news. She looked inside and found two-thirds of the pages were blank sheets. Wonderful.

Underneath the red file was the crime tech supplemental report on the fingerprints dotting Josine's apartment. Lift a dead log in Broe Woods. What crawls away from the sunlight? Here was a list of the city's invertebrates. Three deserved further checking.

Gia. So she lied. She'd been there swilling cough syrup and soda, her thumb on the crystal display of the Walkman, three greasy digits on one of the bootleg CDs.

The other two made Eliza's pulse tick faster. She pulled their histories from the database. Dug a little deeper.

Evan Spivek. The Red Stripe drinker. Depending on when Josine took out her trash, Spivek was in her room approximate to the date of the murder. A good lawyer would tear that apart. But Spivek hadn't been able to afford representation for his last run-in. Assigned a public defender. Spivek served his time at Dexter. Providing alcohol to a minor and sexual assault of the same aforementioned youth.

A boy of fourteen. The charge boiled down to statutory rape. The kid didn't want to press charges; his parents did. Spivek hadn't helped himself by resisting arrest and separating the shoulder of one of the responding officers. He'd been inside before, a short stay. But, better yet, an aggravated assault with a knife. The victim was a male prostitute. Congratulations, Mr. Spivek. You've upgraded your status to prime suspect in a series of related homicides. Three corpses, or two and a partial, are hollering out your name.

The final computer hit raised Eliza's eyebrows.

Alexander Temple Booth III. Juvie record. But the prosecutor decided to charge him as an adult, so the files were open. Party boy. A girl claimed he'd drugged her at a Halloween kegger in the Booth Orchards. Young Alexander sliced away her gypsy costume with a pair of hedge clippers and shot a video. Eliza pulled the tape from evidence. Watched it. She agreed with the court. The tape was inconclusive. The girl was in it, chugging Goldschlager and awake if not lucid. The final minutes featured her naked backside and the cameraman's slack member. She's going, going, gone—passed out. This happened indoors. She lost consciousness, drooling face-down on a haystack of leather coats. Alexander got a close-up of that. But didn't touch her. He went back outside. Seemed more interested in recording himself evacuating into the hollow of a tree.

No time served. Probation and court-ordered drug treatment. Current address confirmed Eliza's suspicions. Mansion on the hill. City founders, no less. Homeboy Supreme.

She was tempted to give up. Go for Spivek and Spivek alone.

But Lucky Marty's story from this morning featured a Booth name—mentioned it repeatedly side by side with Terry Duval's. It was the reason she needed to read about the Leland Tompkins suicide. She didn't believe her father. Didn't believe *in* him, either. But she wanted to rule out everything he'd said. His take on Duval and the Booths.

If she wanted a connection between Spivek and the Booth family, Eliza had it. There in black and white was a printout of Spivek's employment sheet. His current job was seasonal, running a fishing charter on Lake Mohegan. No problem there. His name was on the charter license. But Spivek didn't own the boat. The boat was listed as property of RMG, the marina operator. Red Moon Group cut his checks. And Red Moon's president was the newsworthy Adrian Redmon, Alexander's stepfather. Maybe it wasn't straight, but there was a line. Point A to Point B.

Eliza didn't want a line. She wanted a triangle.

Where was her third point? Where was Terrible Terry?

The phone on her desk broke her thoughts, the strands fluttering loose. Leah Bloomfield's voice, asking about setting up a lunch date. Or what about a ladies' night on the town? Eliza tried to sidetrack her, valiant effort but a hopeless cause. They chose a Saturday in February, Valentine's Day weekend, the night before the calendar holiday. Neither detective had a better offer pending.

"Tell Ike that Terry won the riverboat contract," Leah said. "Owner decided to change the name, though. Red Moon Casino sounded too Indian. They want a nautical theme. They're running a contest. What do you think of *The Bounty*?"

Eliza thanked her for calling.

Spivek—Booths—Duval.

Triangle.

Belli's Butcher Shop

Ike tried the door. Locked. He shielded his eyes from the glare. Scudding cloud cover muffled the sunlight. The world turned blue. The steel security gates over the door and windows were folded away. The butcher shop's sign flipped to OPEN, and there was a light on, in the back, deep in the shop, behind the counter. Ike used his shoe to lift the mail slot on the ancient oak and glass door. He could smell the coffee percolating. He rapped his knuckles on the chilled glass.

"Mr. Belli?"

A figure moved, came slowly to the door. The white butcher's apron dyed in the same cool tones of the day. Hands worked the locks.

The man looked about seventy, but Ike's calculations put his age at closer to ninety.

"Detective Horner, good afternoon. Not so cold as last week, eh?"

"It's been a long winter."

"She's not done with us yet," Mr. Belli said. He swung the door wide so Ike could step into the shop. He locked it again behind him. "Come, I get you your cup."

Ike smelled the sawdust now, felt the shavings mash softly under his soles. He smelled the olives marinating in their old wooden casks. The refrigerated display cases were pretty empty. How many customers did he have these days?

A dozen regulars? Probably less.

In the back room, past the block counters, the hanging saws, and the silver door to the freezer, Belli had a card table. Two kitchen chairs. The only thing on the table was a Zenith radio.

Belli pointed to the chairs. "Sit, sit."

He picked up a hand towel and used it to remove the percolator from the burner. The little stove, like a child's play set, was lodged in the corner. He filled their cups, shuffled to the table, and joined Ike in sitting.

"Best part of the day," Belli said.

Ike said nothing. He blew into his cup.

The butcher reached into his pocket and produced a black cigarillo. This was the only part Ike disliked. Belli lit the tobacco. The cigarillo looked and smelled, as far as Ike was concerned, like a skinny dog's turd.

The men had known each other over forty years.

Ike's mother had been working the night shift at the hospital. Part of her rotation at the time, but she liked it. She would eventually make the hours permanent. Work nights until the day she died. But she started that summer. Ike—twelve years old, restless, and unwilling to admit how scared he felt sleeping and waking alone in their silent, only-the-Frigidaire-humming-to-keep-you-company apartment. The four rooms grew larger during the night. He forced himself to stay in bed, under the sheets, ignoring the dark, but listening to the ocean of the night street slurring words below his window. By morning the walls were closing again and he needed to bust out. Ike got an idea. He would take the bushel of baseballs he'd collected from Edwards Park—the right field foul line ran parallel to thick woods and a lagoon—and he'd drag them down the block, to a vacant lot he knew. Long time ago, kids spray-painted a strike zone on the lot's chain-link fence.

He did it. Walked there with the bushel bouncing against his kneecaps. Stood up on the concrete buckle they called a pitcher's mound. Dropped his basket. Started hurling balls at the fence.

Across the street—Belli, in the enclave to his shop, smoking his day's first.

Called out, "Hey, you got a wristwatch?"

"No. Why you ask me that?"

" 'Cause it's six o'clock in the A.M., ballplayer."

"So?"

"People not gonna like you making racket. *Shang. Shang. Shang.* They gotta get up, go to work. You come in. Have a cup of coffee. The buses start running, then you go back to throwing the ball."

The name stuck. The daily coffee breaks did too.

It was a cliché, but Mrs. Belli was always trying to feed him. Salami, cappacola, smoked ham sliced off the bone. Cheeses she cut with a wire. They stared at each other a lot. Not quite sure of Mr. Belli's breakfast arrangement.

Mrs. Belli was twenty years in the ground. But it was ten years before that when the changes came. The change between Mrs. Belli and the world, between Mr. Belli and Ike.

It was a simple stickup.

Empty the register, now. Do it fast.

Mr. Belli is at a supplier, hoping to arrange an earlier stop on their delivery route.

Put it in the bag. Everything.

Two guys.

How you like this fuckin' dago shit, huh? From the old country and crap . . .

Man, go stay by the door.

Two guns.

You tell her get that shit from under the tray? They always hidin' sumpthin'.

Okay, that's good. You keep quiet and we're gone.

She puttin' the evil eye on us, or what?

Let's go.

Hey, bug-eyed bitch. What you lookin' at?

They are out the door when he reaches back and fires a bullet into Mrs. Belli. Shoulder wound. An in-and-out. She doesn't die. But she doesn't return to the shop. She's the ghost who inhabits the flat above. Her footsteps, her figure stirs behind the lace curtains. She's upstairs when Ike visits. Never talks to him again.

Ike's a cop already when this goes down. He doesn't work Robbery. His beat is in Cushing Point. Mr. Belli rages, pleads. Find these guys. They do. Ike has no hand in it. It's Robbery that gets them, matches the gun, and puts the pen in their hands, urges them to sign the confessions. The guys go to Dexter. Mr. Belli is happy. He's happy with Ike and his brethren. Ike goes from being Shang to Officer Horner. Later, Belli's the first civilian to call him *Detective* Horner. Through all of it, Ike sees Mr. Belli shifting emotions, wearing them for a day or two, like masks—the stickup guys wore masks—only Mr. Belli lives in his masks while he's got them on. When they go on, that's him. Like they're tied to the bone. When they come off, he's somebody else. He's Mr. Belli again. But through all of it, the mask Ike never sees is Fear. He thinks maybe it's because Mr. Belli wears that one when he sleeps.

And Mrs. Belli . . . she never comes downstairs.

Ike's Stoop

First full-on afternoon sun in a month. Harsh bolting light filed the ends off anything metal. Glacial views. Not a blade of grass showed on the block. The snow pack made Ike squint. No sunglasses, instant headache. But feeling lucky to find a spot this side of the street. He'd be inside in a minute. Jamila and Fleur home for lunch. He was bringing them a carton of black olive tapenade and a loaf of crusty bread. Whole ride from Belli's he's thinking, Don't let me end up old and alone. Out of the car, the air braced him. Even the pink behind his eyelids seemed bleached.

"We have not," the man said.

Ike hadn't seen him. Trying to open wider, he only pinched tears. Blinking. Trying again. No more than slits, and fighting for that. Reflex: Ike's right hand going up under the coat for his slide holster. Middle digit tensed on the trigger guard. Goddamn glare was worse than night.

"Pardon me?" he said.

"Met before. You were under the impression we had. I'd remember. With a face like yours."

White man. Gray beard. No hat. Gore-Tex jacket buttoned to the throat, but his arms hanging limp at his sides. Gloves empty.

"You must've been occupied," the man said. "Rousing piss bums and ticketing speeders. When I retired, I mean. Long time ago. Ice Age."

Ike said, "I read about you in the papers."

"Any cop worth his salt doesn't read the goddamn papers. Even you should've learned that, Ike. I can call you Ike, can't I? Old friends like us."

Fleur at the window. She must've been watching for Ike's car. Saw him park. Her arm snuggled around her Keisha doll. Eating a Nutter Butter. She had the bitten cookie in her fingers. Frowning at the appearance of this strange man with Ike.

Terry Duval waved to her. "Nice to see the sensitive toys they make for kids nowadays."

Ike happy Fleur wasn't waving back.

Duval thumbed a droplet from his nose. Sniffed. He went into his pocket.

Ike ready to throw if need be.

Handkerchief. Blowing his nose. "Nasty bug. I'd love to be rid of it. You keep your girl inside. Can't be too careful."

"You want to have a conversation?"

Duval laughed, a cloudy bark. "I thought we were."

"I meant a sit-down."

"Sit-down? Sounds serious. I may bring my lawyer."

"Do what makes you comfortable."

"Already have."

Duval showed him his broad back, walking away, the cop swagger never lost. He climbed behind the wheel of a white Ford Explorer. Ike standing on the sidewalk until the Ford pulled away, and doing one last thing: committing the plate number.

5 Fay Street

When Ike got back, he didn't say a word to Eliza about his encounter with Duval. The timing was wrong. She was juiced up about the Spivek lead. Ready to go out and grab the perv now.

Maybe Ike didn't want to admit he'd been blindsided a few steps from his front door. Duval was only picking up the gauntlet, showing Ike that his were made of steel and intimidation wouldn't go unanswered. But Ike had flushed him. That counted for something.

The trailer looked abandoned. Had Spivek already skipped? Ike did a perimeter walk. Given what Eliza had told him, he was eager to haul Spivek in. Scare him. Sweat his butt at the precinct for a few hours. Let the man remember what it was like to be cuffed and ordered around. Make him feel the need to barter, to ask permission for each freedom.

Rear window boarded. The work seemed fresh. Screw points piercing outward through the vinyl casement. Sawdust clung in the grooves, no sign of rusting. The board looked new, not weathered. An apricot-colored knot dead center, slit vertically like a cat's eye. Enough to give Ike the sensation of being watched.

They had no search warrant. Questionable on what little they had.

Print on a beer bottle and Spivek's priors.

No blood in Josine's apartment. Nobody killed there. The tub contents were hard evidence of a crime. But whose crime?

"Want to go to the marina and come back?" Eliza asked.

She stepped around the corner, onto the carport. The awning above her creaking like it might give after another snowfall. Before heading to Fay Street, they called the harbormaster. Spivek was still on the payroll, doing odd jobs, janitor duties until the ice went out. It was sporadic, unscheduled, but he turned up every other Friday for his money.

"What do *you* think?"

"I think we should check, see if he's pushing his broom."

"Uh-huh." His standard nonanswer answer, because he didn't like it when she rushed him. Eliza glanced down at the asphalt, her toe spanning a tributary in the delta of cracks.

"There a reason to stick around?" she asked.

"Nope."

She started walking down the driveway. He considered for a second if she was actually going to wait for him in the car.

"Spivek has a driver's license but no vehicle registered in his name?"

"You got it," he said.

She pointed at the crescents slashed in the driveway ice. "Whose truck is this?"

Crispin's Saturn

He knew Spivek had lied about knowing Reese, and by the time he got to the trailer, he'd convinced himself that he lied about Patrick too. I'll offer him a trade. Knives and photos for telling me where Patrick is. What happened to my brother?

Spivek wasn't home.

Crispin was waiting for a break in traffic so he could turn when he noticed the cops. They were using his old spot. He turned. Now they were following him. He'd taken three rights, brought them with him in a big circle. Hanging there, two cars back.

The fourth turn was the trigger. They hit him with the siren. One of those cherry domes tossed up on the dashboard. He resisted the urge to start a chase, instead, pulled off on a side street. Curbed.

An older black guy and a woman. They had their guns drawn. The black guy creeping up on his bumper. The woman aiming at his head through the back window.

Were they insane? He hadn't done anything wrong.

Hey, Pin. Try breaking and entering. Burglary?

The black cop was shouting.

Do as you're told, Pin. Hands in plain sight.

He was out of the car. In the cold. Face hitting the street. Cuffed. Jerked to his feet, then facedown again, on the warm filthy hood of his car. The black cop was asking questions, but Crispin couldn't speak.

Finally, "I'm a doctor."

They were behind him. Up close. Pulling out his pockets. Taking inventory.

The woman, silent during the exchange until this moment, tilted her face to look into his eyes.

"It's not him," she said.

7

BONE FROM A BLACK CAT

Interview Room 3

Now they had this doctor sweating blood. Scared shitless. Trying to sell them on the story he'd been checking up on Spivek, following up an ER visit. House call? Eliza broke him down using only the tone of her voice. He backtracked. Admitted he didn't know how to talk to them. He asked for a lawyer. Ike told him he could walk away anytime he wanted. They were only asking for a little cooperation. Simple questions. And he wanted to cooperate. Let them leave his car on the street. A promise from Ike that he'd get a ride back, when they finished, seemed to calm him down.

Crime Scene called to tell them they'd completed the hair and fiber from Josine's apartment. Nothing matched fibers on her body because she'd been whistle clean. Nails clipped. They collected from bathroom traps and drains.

Point of interest in the tub pipes.

"Fish scales?" Ike asked, not sure he'd heard right.

"Yep. We sent the sample out. They confirmed it. Chinook salmon."

"I'll be damned."

Spivek looked guiltier by the second. But they didn't have him. They had his doctor friend. Eliza guessed drugs, and that made sense. Hours of nothing, then they pull this whole nasty bird's net out of the airshaft. Twigs, strings, feathers. Woven but messy. Dr. Maloney was jittery. Maybe he knew where the bird had flown.

Eliza thrilled at the evidence update. She had blood in her eye and didn't want to leave Maloney alone for too long. He might just figure out how disadvantaged they were. Ike kept his mouth shut, tried to look bored, casual, whatever would put Maloney at ease.

"Evan Spivek was not a patient of yours?" she asked.

"No."

"No he wasn't or no he was?"

"Wasn't."

"Okay."

"But I did go to his house to follow up on a patient who visited the ER."

"Professional or personal? Your follow-up."

"Personal. I wanted to find this patient."

"Why?"

"We had, you know, connected. I wanted to see if it would go anywhere."

"We're talking about a woman?"

"Yes."

"You do this a lot?" Eliza asked. Ready for another run at the doctor's defenses.

"I . . . this was highly unusual for me."

So is being interrogated, Ike thought. Doctors like answering questions about as much as cops.

"Onetime thing?" she asked. Smiled, letting him know it was okay. Ladies make you act crazy. Your behavior falls within the range of normal. We aren't talking about crimes. The way he looked at her. He wasn't afraid of women. No sir.

Maloney held up his index finger.

"Let's be frank, Doctor," Eliza said. "Pursuing a female patient to her home, to what you believe to be her home, for the purpose of striking up a sexual relationship is borderline unethical. I'm sure the administrators at Nestor County would agree. At the very least, you're crossing doctor-patient boundaries. What kind of a creep are you?"

"This wasn't about sex. You're twisting what I said. I never—"

"I think it was about sex, Mr. Maloney. I think you became obsessed with a female patient and you stalked her to this house. I think we caught you doing something you knew was wrong. You're in real danger here. Detective Horner and I are going to feel obligated to inform your bosses of this excursion."

Maloney's hands flew from his lap. Eliza and Ike both startled.

"It was not about sex. I went there looking for somebody."

"You told us that."

"Not my patient. Somebody else."

Eliza shot a glance at Ike, raised her eyebrows, her shoulders lifted in a shrug.

Where was he going with this?

Maloney let out a long breath. He was giving up. Next would be the truth.

"I went to the trailer today because . . . because Spivek . . ." He said these words, hesitating, not finding the language for what had to be spoken. Fighting with the story inside him. He sat back, chin to chest. When he came up, his jaw was flexed, muscles bulging like he was biting into a rubber ball.

He said, "Spivek might know where Patrick is."

Patrick, Eliza thought, the name on the back of our tattoo photo. The tattoo put on ice in Josine's bathtub. Here we go. For whatever reason, Spivek and Josine murder this Patrick. Do it together. Then Spivek quiets Josine. Understandable. At least on the surface, the pieces were starting to match up.

Ike was looking over at her. She nodded.

"Who's Patrick?" Ike asked.

"I've kind of lost track of him." Tears fell. He used his sleeve. Wiped his nose. Did a thorough job, after being pushed somewhere past shame. "He's my little brother."

Eliza, guessing correctly, asked, "Runaway?"

"Sort of."

"There's an item we need you to take a look at."

"Something belonging to Patrick?"

"You tell us."

Homicide Squad Room, Interview Room 1

"What's not to like?" Eliza asked.

Interview 1 had no mirrors, no mikes. This was as close to

private as they we're going to get without leaving the building. The doctor was still in 3, composing himself. Drinking a cup of cold water.

"That suitcase of knives for one thing," Ike said. "I don't want to arrest him for B and E, but I don't like us finding the thing in his possession. Messy doesn't begin to describe the chain of evidence. We'll end up losing it. Now, in the trailer and under Spivek's bed? Different story. That's where I want to find it," Ike said. He held her gaze, made a steeple of his fingers.

"That's where Patrick told his brother that Spivek kept it. Or did I hear him wrong?"

"No, you heard him. Same as I did," Ike said.

"Let's go remind the doctor about what he told us. Review the facts. Then he can write his statement. You do the affidavit. See the judge. I'll bring Maloney back to his car and follow him home. He's shaky. I'll walk him up. Well-being check."

What they had proposed was clearly illegal, no wiggle room, no stretch would make it fit any definition of police procedures. But that wouldn't stop them from doing it. One thing would. "Only if he's in his right mind," Ike said. "We go ahead, he can't say anything stupid."

"He's not stupid. He's upset. Place he's at, who wouldn't be? He's going to listen to this option and take it. The alternative is we've got him by the balls on a felony and the guy who butchered his brother waves good-bye. Slides back into the muck."

Four people would know. Spivek and Maloney, Ike and Eliza. Spivek's word was worthless in court. He hadn't called in the burglary; he would likely be on the hook for multiple murder charges. Maloney was the weak spot. But they'd stick him with the two-prong fork of his brother's death and the break-in. It could work. Was it wrong? This wasn't philosophy class; this was Booth City.

"We'll need a cheek swab before he leaves. Hope for a DNA match."

"He's not hoping what we're hoping," she said.

"All his cards are on the table, played out. Man says he wants the truth."

"Not this truth."

"You don't get to pick and choose," Ike said.

"He didn't know about any tattoo," Eliza reminded him.

"Think there's a chance it's not Patrick?" he asked.

"Slim," Eliza said. "I get my butt tattooed, I'm not broadcasting it to my family. This feels right to me."

"Me too."

"One last thing," Eliza said. "You ever see Spivek's truck?"

"His van? Sure."

The tech capped the swab and left the room. Crispin had the urge to drink something and wash the taste out of his mouth. He found a roll of Life Savers in his pocket. Butter Rum. He worked one loose.

"White and beat-up?" Eliza asked. "Pipes mounted on top?"

Crispin nodded, asked, "How long have you been after him?"

"Welcome to Day One."

"We get lucky, there's no Day Two," Ike said.

5 Fay Street

About the size of a day planner, but it wasn't. Ike tugged the zipper around the kit's edge. They looked like dental tools. The door took less than a minute.

No light, no movement.

He took two steps in. The defeated door, at his back, remained open. But the screen creaked shut, wood bumped against wood. Blue streetlight followed him, overtook him like a phantom.

The empty twin mattress. Scrambled bedding, a folded jacket he must've used for a pillow. Pair of black Doc Martens tucked under the foot of the bed frame.

Ike turned as if he were about to speak, throw words over his shoulder.

Spivek tackled him.

He had a pipe, one of the unloaded dumbbells, in his fist. He pushed off on Ike's back, sat up so he could start beating him. An easy target, pinned to the floor. The head would go first. No missing it.

"Don't," Eliza said. "I will shoot you, so fucking don't." She touched the Glock to the top of Spivek's spine.

Blowing hard out his nose. The raised pipe halted midair.

"Drop your weapon," she said. "Now."

The piece of black steel fell—a thud—gouging the vinyl linoleum.

"Stand." She pressed the gun into his neck bones. "Listen to me, you'd better come up *slow-ly*."

Spivek climbed off her partner's prone body. He swayed. His

sense of balance screwed up because his hands were locked on his scalp, arms chicken-winged.

Ike rolled over, got to his knees.

"You okay?" she asked.

"Yeah."

Spivek felt the gun leave his skin.

Lights flipped on. Buzz. The gun returned, this time between his blades, urging him over to the wall.

"Grab it," she said.

Spread-eagle. But she kicked his feet out farther. Some set of rocks she's got on her, he thought. Corner of his eye, Spivek saw her. Saw what she had under her arm too. He recognized it immediately.

"That's mine," he said.

"We're glad you agree," Ike said. He moved in and cuffed him.

Booth Main House

She was a petite woman, the lady who dismissed the maid. Sporting black Ralph Lauren jeans and an untucked flannel shirt that matched the oak planks of the foyer. Her sleeves were rolled back once, and a string of garnets hung at her throat. Some certain boldness revealed itself there, considering time had loosened the flesh under her chin, but her strong jaw helped on that front. Eliza noticed her no-nonsense hair—a boyish cut to the deeply brown bangs—and she suspected a pricey color job. Hands and wrists free of jewelry. The only remarkable trace of makeup was plum lipstick. A shade too dark, Eliza thought, but darker tones suited her. Her large eyes were nearly black. Pupils and irises melded. The looked-upon felt intensity even when none was intended. Eliza doubted Dina Booth was oblivious to the power embedded in her every glance. Yet with simple politeness and a wave of her small-boned hand, she had welcomed them to follow her into the downstairs library. The heels of her girl-sized boots clicked like a dry-fired pistol until they reached Persian carpet.

"Sorry for the noise," Mrs. Booth said. She was pointing to the ceiling. A lone hammer banged away somewhere above them.

Ike had his cap in his hand, rotating. "Renovations?" he asked.

"A grand old lady like ours is always in need of repairs. I shouldn't complain. I love it. New projects lurk behind each door. Keeps me busy." She opened a drawer. Both hands disappeared inside, produced a scratched, dulled gold case and a figurine—a bull's head. She thumbed the bull's nose and a flame shot up between his horns.

"Care to sit?" She nudged the tip of her cigarette at a conversation nook, four leather chairs cornering a knee-high sculpture made of blued wire filigrees.

Eliza sat across from her. The chair sighed. Ike put himself at Dina Booth's left hand. The move split her visual duties. If his choice annoyed her, she was good at hiding signs of displeasure.

She said, "Zan will be coming up to the house on the hour. You wanted to speak with me first? Before his arrival?"

"We're trying to get some background information on a couple of your son's friends," Eliza said.

"I probably know nothing about them."

"Anything you can contribute would be useful," Ike said. Get her head swiveling early. Do what he could to keep her off balance.

Most people, when they got nervous, talked too much. That was Ike's experience.

"My son is disturbed," she said. "I know how that sounds coming from my mouth. But it's true. He's a drunk and an addict. We've done everything under the sun to get him treatment, but he is not treatable. Not in his current incarnation, anyway. If this involves his junkie friends, well, so be it. Lock them up. If I thought locking up Zan would help him, I'd give you the keys. He wouldn't be fazed, though. Prison is no threat. The concept amuses him."

"These friends of his were murdered," Eliza said.

"Jesus, he's really sunk to the bottom feeders, hasn't he? Drug dealers? We're talking about drug dealers?"

"No. Though drugs may have played a role."

"These men were engaged in what we would call the sex trade," Ike said. "One was, for certain now, a transsexual prostitute. The other boy—he was younger than Zan, a runaway, only seventeen—he may have been selling himself on the street as well. To buy drugs? That's not unlikely."

"You're aware, then, that my son is bisexual?"

"We were not," Eliza said.

"Oh." She tapped ash into a crystal ring. "He started off liking girls. We thought—Adrian and I—well, we were actually relieved that something normal piqued his interest. But it didn't last. He went through a very busy period of boys and girls together. That would've been senior year. The time we had to go to court with him. That girl? She was a con artist. Her parents came to us with a settlement offer. Can you imagine? They're accusing

Zan of violating their daughter, then they flat out ask for a payoff. Shameful."

"He didn't do it?"

"Remarkably, no. Zan doesn't need to drug his conquests. Not that I would rule it out on principle. You must understand that Zan's thing is wickedness. The more wicked, the better. He's far from harmless. But his harm is directed. Acutely. At me. And at Adrian, of course. He's trying to hurt us. That's the constant."

"Why?"

"If I could answer that, I'd have saved a lot on psychiatrist's bills."

"Do you recall meeting either of these people?" Eliza passed photos of Josine and Patrick Maloney to Dina.

"Never. These are the murder victims?"

"Yes."

"I don't recognize them. Zan may. He dresses like a woman sometimes. I can see him through my window. Parading around in the most godawful outfits. Punk, S-and-M chic, I suppose. Hideous. Wait until you meet him. I'm sure he'll make quite the impression."

"Are you aware of his comings and goings?" Eliza asked.

"I gave up the spy game years ago, Detective Ochoa. I don't keep track of him. He's here when he needs to be, gone when he wants to be. This is the arrangement we've settled into. I won't glorify it by saying it's a compromise. It's not. Zan pilots his own craft. If it weren't for the terms of his trust fund, he would've blown us off by now."

"What are those terms?" Eliza asked.

"I sign all the disbursements until he turns twenty-one. But Adrian handles the money. Zan is too exasperating for me. He hates Adrian. But Adrian has a natural authority and Zan will push only so far. With me, he can . . . his creative side really holds forth."

"The money in the trust . . ."

"From my first husband. He's deceased."

"How was Zan's relationship with his biological father?"

"They had no relationship. I was pregnant when my husband killed himself."

"That must have been difficult," Eliza said.

Dina said nothing. She crossed her legs and kicked the air, back and forth.

"When we passed the gates, I noticed a security camera," Ike said. "Are the videos removed and logged on a regular schedule?"

"You'd have to ask Adrian. He deals with the security people. Our camera was vandalized several times."

"Your security measures are—"

"How much longer is this going to take?"

"As long as you'd like. We can wait for Zan—"

"You don't have to wait. I'll have Sandra retrieve him."

He discarded the eyeliner pencil. *Black Velvet*. Picked up the applicator wand, pinched it with his twitchy fingers, and scraped the hardened, dusty reservoir of eye shadow. Reminding him of the cakes of watercolor paint he swabbed his brush into at the last rehab facility. Healing through creative play. Oh, how it had cured his ills.

In his current project he went for postmortem. Vampiric. Dead alive.

Rocky Raccoon, at least. Dina would appreciate the effort. A nostalgic stab into the recesses of her heyday, her wild youth burgeoning at the ass end of Sixties London, the beginning of an age—Aquarius?—and the death of another, of propriety. Grandfather had said so. She'd been away at school. On loan like a book that comes back with more pages between the covers. She'd fucked her brains out. Zan was positive. Where else did he get that hot lump of coal charring his pelvic girdle? Sweet mother, thank you for this, your genetic token. He reached down, gave himself a stroke through his leather pants.

He shook a blond wig from the box, the brassiest. Because she'd been blond then too. Pre-childbirth, pre-Zan. The time when she'd actually felt happiness, she'd told him, her retelling offered more than once. More like once a year.

Darling, you were the death of me.

So you say.

Here comes Death walking, Mother.

The top of the mirror frame crowned him with a laurel of wooden rosettes. A quiver swam in the glass reflected over his shoulder—someone in the orchard.

Mexican Maid bundled in a long coat, taking the path to his door, and she had a black man with her. He watched them. Holy shit, Sailor was right. She was a dead ringer for MM.

Send in the cops. Oh, never mind, they're already here.

Booth Precinct Holding Cells

This was how it was going to be. Terry laying it all on him. His cop friends busting into the trailer like commandos. Terry making certain he didn't have the van tonight. Fucking setup. Spivek wondered what else Terry had done. He sat on his bunk, hands balled into fists. Light through the bars throwing shadows over his body, shadows he swore he'd never live to see again. But here he was. Here he was.

Not about to talk because he'd only damage his case. That's what he told himself. Keep your mouth shut. Never bad advice. Inside or out. Why should he let them pile this shit on his head? He didn't call a lawyer. He called Terry. Denials, of course. A promise of a helping hand. Thanks, but no thanks, Ter. You've done enough. The call was a heads-up. Spivek wasn't a fool. He didn't plan to talk about Terry to the cops sent to nail his ass. No, he did something smarter. He gave them Zan.

Let's see how you deal with that, Terry.

The Pressing House

Eliza didn't like it. Ike telling her to go soft, talk to the mother. Play it cool. They'd serve the rich boy up. When they got to the smaller outbuilding, Zan's house, that's when they shifted. No easy does it. They arrested him. He made a half-assed run, and they put him on the ground. Read him his rights. Told him he murdered Patrick Maloney and Delbert Watts.

The wig fell off in the struggle. His shaved head gleamed. Snow making streaky black tears out of his Halloween getup. The boy, to his credit, didn't scream or fuss once they had him hog-tied.

He got quiet.

Racer's

The bar was like bars should be—dark and rumbling with an undercurrent of life. Bursts of laughter, the snick of lighters, and the constant rhythm of glass touching wood. You had to listen for those sounds inside Racer's, unless it was early or between sets. Racer's was a live music joint, the oldest of its kind in the city. Ike supposed you could call it a honky-tonk, but that label didn't fit. The crowd was half black, half white. The memorabilia on the walls spoke redneck. Checkered flags, the crumpled purple door from a Mustang, snapshots of white men drinking champagne from the bottle, though Bud probably tasted better in the pits and garages, the hot gasoline-stinking tracks where these men drove their machines. Some pictures were blurs of primary colors, the speed impossible to capture or fully erase.

The neighborhood around Racer's was all black. Ike had grown up three blocks east. When he was young, he'd stayed away. Racer's was off-limits. Bikes parked out front, a shiny row of Harleys and Buells. Men wearing leathers, bandanas, and walrus mustaches, stares that said you'd better not even try, boy. But times changed. Ike knew as much. He wasn't sure what terrified him more, change or stagnation. On a personal level, he was missing the man he used to be. The man who didn't walk around fearing death daily, whether by the gun or the surgeon's knife.

The man who didn't get ambushed on his front stoop, or speared in the dark by a hopped-up con who had a need for slicing up street meat.

Maybe change was good for the world but bad for the people who lived in it.

In the dark.

Spivek's trailer.

Ike's heart pounded. The hitch in his chest sputtering every few seconds like an engine about to go out. Up off the floor. His legs turned elastic.

Now he leaned for the lights of the vending machine and bought a pack of Camels.

At the bar, he ordered a gin.

The chalkboard told him the name of tonight's act. Big Bill Lomak. But Ike already knew who was playing. That's why he was here. *Flavors surely do change,* he thought. The music piping in was pure Delta, and from the hills too. That fuzzy trance groove. The white folks sitting around the tables didn't seem scared. Refried hippies and goddamn leather-jacketed yuppies. Maybe they weren't hearing what he was hearing.

Big Bill was white. Ike would've pegged him as a cracker. The smoky drawl. Oily cowboy hat and a thick, gray braid swinging between his shoulders when he got himself waist-deep into a tune, chewing the guts of his harp and blowing spit into the stage lights. The band hadn't come on yet. But Ike had seen them before. He'd even met Bill after one of the gigs. The man seemed decent. Coked to the eyeballs, and unclean from fingernails to gums—but decent. Polite. Ike had locked up a lot of Bills.

He found a seat in back. A corner. *Little Ike Horner sat in his corner, drinking his liquor dry*. The gin was good. The Camel was fantastic. Ike blew smoke. It looked grainy against the wall. Like if he put his hand out, there'd be sand in the creases of his palm. If this was his last time, then that was okay. He'd take it and not feel sorry. He wasn't a bad man. And he was a damn good cop. Nobody should feel pity for him when he was gone. He'd had his gravy too.

The stage lights pulsed.

The drummer sat down, waved his sticks at somebody in the audience.

Bass player and guitar player plugged in, checked their amps. The mikes were working. Everybody waited for Big Bill.

The impossible happened—the room got darker.

Big Bill ambled out into the only light. Sly cracker's smile and two fingers pulling on the front of his hat, he had the fat chunk of steel in his other hand. The band started gathering steam and Bill put the steel to his mouth.

By the fourth gin, Ike was feeling the hitch again. His head floating. The vibrations in his chair not all caused by the music. Bill looked like he'd run through a rainstorm. He'd sung about his mojo, his black cat bone. This white man's voodoo worked overtime. Dirty white blues. He had to catch his breath, duck backstage to chop and vacuum up his lines. The band's job to keep everybody interested. When he came around the amps, newly jacked, he introduced them.

"On the drums here, man's been with me for a looooong time . . . Roy DeBeers."

People clapped. Roy's buddies at the front row table whooped.

"Odell Kersey plays the beat strong." Big Bill took his hat off, pointed the brim at the bass player, a rotund black man who could've been twenty-five, or fifty.

"And let me tell you something, folks. We've got a rising star on our hands. I don't know how long I can keep him under my wing." Bill mopped coke sweat with the tail of his shirt, snatched a tequila off a cruising waitress's tray. Laughter as he killed it, handed back the empty shot. "He's just a baby. Look at those smooth cheeks, ladies." Bill's hat dropped to the floor and he lifted it with the toe of his boot. He settled it back on his skull, tapped it down. "He's also the evilest guitar player from here to . . . Sterling Horner."

Big Bill told the crowd there were CDs for sale in the lobby. But Racer's had no lobby, just a card table beside the pay phone, next to the john.

Ike watched his son.

Sterling ignored the applause, turned sideways to switch guitars. He wouldn't let them see if he was smiling. But Ike guessed he wasn't. Young man was too serious for his age. Shy in public. Uncomfortable with praise, though it had been building for more than a year. He wanted back into a song. To show them Big Bill didn't lie.

The last number was a slow burn. Ike had his chance to leave, but he didn't. If Sterling recognized him, the moment passed without acknowledgment.

Ike's body liked where it was, didn't look forward to moving.

He had to agree.

The house lights came on, and Sterling headed for the steps. He had to stop to shake a few hands. A bottle of beer offered. Ike watched him scanning the room, real casual, but it told Ike he'd been seen. Sterling's eyes finding his. The surprise evident—*you still here, huh.*

The hand rose high enough for Ike to glimpse.

Be with you in a minute.

Taking care of business first.

Half a pack down, Ike fished for another butt. Shaking it out. Used the bar matches. Contemplated what one more gin would do. He'd be walking this off as it was. Jamila, if he woke her, she'd know his shape without a word. Silence at breakfast—he could expect that. This night would not pass unnoticed. She'd give him twenty-four and then bite into him. Love. Hers was fierce, ruthless. More than he could say of his legal marriage to Corinne, Sterling's mother. They'd been mutually mistaken. But Ike had been the destructive one. He broke everything about their union six ways. He wasn't proud. Sterling was old enough to remember the end. That hurt. Their relationship still not right to this day. Other obstacles were involved. Ike preferred not to think about them. Jamila read Sterling better; they got along fine. It was Ike who was the problem. He wouldn't deny it. But Sterling didn't give an inch. Father and son minted on the same coin.

"Buy you one?"

"I shouldn't," Ike said.

"Shouldn't have had the first, either."

"True."

He accepted the chilly glass. Sterling poured his beer into a mug, sipped.

"You sounded good tonight," Ike said.

"Thanks. What are you celebrating?"

"Came to hear you play." Ike showed the offense taken.

"I know why you came. I'm asking what you're celebrating."

Ike stared at his son's hands, wondered, where did the talent come from? Ike had none. Corinne couldn't even play a record without screwing it up. So how did this boy come into existence? He looked and saw the reason for the rattling in his glass—down to ice again. "Eliza and I collared a couple of bad guys. The usual."

"They kill somebody?"

"Most definitely."

Sterling nodded. The beer had gone instantly flat in his mug, a greasy smear on the side he hadn't touched. "Let me give you a ride home."

"Don't need one."

"Really?" Sterling had the attitude, ready as a razor. But Ike was in no mood for bloodletting. He let him know the offer was acceptable.

"I'll get my coat," his son said. "Odell's packing up tonight, anyway."

"Find me out front."

The air didn't help. Ike was dizzy, cold to the bone. The semiwarm interior of Sterling's Jeep brought some relief. Light traffic—the stalwart nighthawks out trolling—as Sterling pulled the Wrangler away from the curb. He sped through the side streets. Darkened house fronts swept the windows. Ike, dog-tired and drunk, let the silence be.

Hand on his shoulder. "Hey, here's where you get out."

Ike straightened himself in the bucket seat. Juniper berries on his tongue and Sterling reaching across for the door. Ike tried to get up, felt the tightness across his chest.

"Got to take that off," Sterling said. Pointed to the seat belt.

Ike thumbed the release.

"Too old for this shit?" Sterling asked.

"You'll be there soon enough."

"Have your keys?"

Ike dangled his key ring at eye level. He pressed his palms against the soft sides of the Wrangler. "Now I want to ask you a question."

"Go ahead."

"You and your housemate ever hang at The Axle?"

"Since when you care to hear about us?"

"Just answer."

"Talking to me like I'm a—"

"Watch yourself. 'S all I'm trying to say." Ike took his hands off the Jeep, wiped the street grime from them on his pants. "Careful drivin' home. Get some sleep."

"Night, old man." The smile was Corinne's, best thing about her Ike remembered.

"G'night."

The Wrangler left him. He leaned away from the exhaust fumes—a cruiserweight backing against the ropes. But there weren't any ropes holding him up. He teetered. Wanted a cigarette. Dug for them.

Planning to sit on the steps and smoke his nightcap.

Couldn't be the wind, because there was no wind down at street level. Not tonight. The screen door was propped. Ike drew it back, arm's length, saw a cube on the threshold. Cardboard that lost its color in the moonlight. He picked it up. No weight to the thing. Florist's box, the kind for corsages. He pressed the flap, found an edge.

White lily.

Or it had been before. Cut to pieces. Loose petals bunched in a corner and the empty stem, curved like a skinny green talon, taped down.

Check Fleur. Jamila.

Heavy footfalls, his shoulder smacked the wall. Can a man fall up the stairs?

"Ike?"

He skipped their bedroom. Looked in on Fleur. Sleeping under a ladybug print bedspread. Her face untouched by worry, the way only a child can sleep. Keisha posed on Fleur's desk, a blanket across her lap. Ike backpedaled.

From the hall he said, "It's just me."

Perfumed sheets. No nightlight here. But Jamila's frown visible in the dimness. She wasn't waiting until tomorrow.

"What're you doing to yourself, Shang?"

The forgotten Camel sandwiched between his lips. "Last one."

"Slow suicide. You've said as much."

"And like all suicides, best carried out alone." The anger in him sparked, landing on the wrong people. The close by, the dear.

She rolled over, took the comforter with her.

In the skylight above Jamila's head, Ike watched the white moon disappear. Clouds slid to cover it quickly—gloved gray hands.

Foggy.

Weatherman said it was supposed to be warmer today. Jamila kicked the hall rug to stuff the draft at the bottom of the door. Dishwater light overflowed from the den. Ike slept down among the dead. She looked at him, took in her lover—fully dressed, jackknifed in his sad, tan recliner. Ike's sagging jaw, his silence, and his hands folded over his little belly. His pistol rested between his knees. Her mind tripped on the craziest idea, just for a second. Then he stirred.

Opened a bloodshot eye.

Dexter Correctional Center

His daily hour spent out of the cell. Now back again. The scent of Irish Spring like a bad joke rubbed into his sallow skin. His chin soft, silver whiskers carried down the drain and into a sewer pipe, but then where? Out of here. The world he'd never see again. Martin stuck his finger into a corner of his towel and dried behind his ears. Like Ma taught him. Ma, so dead and gone she was like Jesus in his memory, a legend, a nice story to tuck you into bed with at night. *Sorry, Ma, for the blaspheming. If you can hear me, I'm sorry for it all. Don't know if that's better or worse.* Either way, they wouldn't be meeting. In this world or the next.

Martin stared at his open cell door.

His feet were clumsy, slow in the shower flip-flops. Two inmates. Coming down the corridor. Excitement stretched their faces like rubber masks. Anticipating the deed. Aryan boys, bare arms sleeved in tattoos. Eagles, dragons, iron crosses. Shamrocks.

He had a homemade shiv inside his radio.

Martin fumbled with the catch, tore the batteries out. They banged on the floor and rolled around.

His doorway filled.

The taller inmate had a rope of knotted bedsheets. The end—he held it up for Martin to contemplate—was tied into a hangman's noose. Pendulum motions.

Martin went for the short man's neck. A roundhouse. Lunged point first, praying for an artery, something that would spout blood. Maybe freeze them. Give him a chance to make the corridor, the camera. But the guard had to have been paid. *Hadn't he?* This pair didn't wander in on their own. Not without protest.

It didn't matter. The short man snatched his wrist. Bent. He kicked the fallen blade under Martin's bed and buried his knee in Martin's scrotum.

The tall man slipped the noose over his head, gave it a jerk.

They struggled to get him backward against the bars of his open door.

The tall man looped the bedsheet rope over a crossbar. Martin pulled to his toes, hands clawing at his throat. Believing and not believing.

"Get him higher," the short man said. He hit Martin with a hook to the kidney.

"Can't."

Another hook. Then another. Another.

"Hold on," said the short man.

Martin choked. His thoughts were not about his ex-wife, his sons, or Eliza. He was concentrating on screwing his thumb into the short man's eye. He was too close now for punching. The man hugged him. Panting hotly, his face crushed into Martin's chest, his spittle and moist, tearful left eye wetting the inside of Martin's shirt.

Head forced between two bars, an ear ground raw. The short man, who was also the wider of the two, wrapped his legs through the bars, crossed his ankles, and dropped. The weight of them, Martin and the short man, was enough.

8

LEFT HAND OF THE SUN

Interview Room 2

"I watch a lot of cop shows on TV."

"That right?"

"I want a lawyer."

"Doesn't make your situation look too good."

"We're watching the same shows, I see."

Zan hadn't slept down in the holding cells. It showed. Some new friend busted his mouth for him. He was sucking a lower lip big as a walnut. And he'd called for his counsel the day before. Ike was aware. Counsel hadn't appeared yet. The Booths operated in strange ways. When the uniforms put Zan in the cruiser—two stand-by patrols rolling up to the estate after Ike called them in—Dina watched the arrest from a second-story window. Her son trussed, shirtfront dragging in the snow, his face purple, and not a peep from Mom.

"Spivek told us some interesting stories about you," Ike said.

"Sailor's got an imagination. That's his problem."

"So you know him?"

"I told you last night that I know him."

"You know Patrick Maloney?"

"Patrick's dead." Zan's eyes darted. "But, yes, I knew him. Bit of a junkie, that boy. Had the greedy part down cold."

"You a junkie too?"

"More or less."

"Which is it?"

"More."

If Spivek had told them the truth, then Zan bought the bag of coke they shared—Spivek, Zan, Patrick, and Josine—the night Patrick died. Bobbing and snorting out on placid Mohegan, riding Spivek's charter fishing boat. They'd have the boat, the *Oh Mickey!,* impounded as evidence soon enough.

How Spivek relayed it, Zan went crazy.

Afterward, together, they chopped up the body. Fed him to the turtles. But Zan could turn it around, point his finger at Spivek. Their only witness, Josine, was dead. The whole thing might go either way, like a lot of dope shit. Whatever transpired on the *Oh Mickey!* was going to remain vague. Ike wanted to know who capped Josine and Wayne. And why. Whose shoe print was in the janitor's closet? Spivek wore a size thirteen. Zan, an eight and a half. Ike had the glass slipper ready for Terry Duval's foot. But he needed a reason.

"Sailor said what exactly? I killed Patrick?"

"He said that."

"I don't believe you."

"Said the four of you got high together. You stabbed Patrick."

"Why'd I do it?"

"You saying you did it?"

"No, I'm asking. What did Sailor say? As to my motive?"

"He said you're insane."

"Ah." Zan winced, touched a finger to his lip.

"Need some ice for your mouth?"

"You should ask Sailor about ice. And coolers. Ask him about coolers."

"We have a photograph of the three of you."

"Sailor, me, and Patrick?" Genuine surprise registered.

Ike shook his head. "Sailor humping Josine, and you in the background watching." Ike dropped the photo on the scarred table.

Zan said, "Sailor learned how to use the self-timer. A real achievement."

"How about when you two killed Josine? Any picture-taking?"

"Sly, Detective, very sly." Zan shut his right eye and poked his finger at Ike.

"She made you nervous?"

"Hardly."

"A payoff, then? She asked for hush money?" Ike asked.

"You were cold. Now you're warm."

Knock at the door.

Homicide Unit

Eliza recognized Adrian Redmon from the About Town section of the newspaper. His fashion choices didn't speak real-estate mogul. Khakis and a cream button-down, a plaid hunting jacket with no bulk to it. He looked more like a catalogue model in his last year of work. Weathered, but well kept. She half expected a Labrador to trot up to him with a duck in its mouth. But his only companion was a tailored Gray Suit matching him stride for stride—criminal defense attorney Shelly Zeller.

She sent word in to Ike. He wouldn't have much time.

Timing had worked against them once already this morning. With Spivek and Zan Booth temporarily boxed up, Eliza wanted another heart-to-heart with Gia. So she pulled a dawn raid on Gia's apartment, swooping down with two patrols backing her up. She wasn't worried about a shoot-out. Her concern being Gia might run. They had leverage on her for lying and impeding the progress of a felony prosecution. Gia's antennae would be out. All they hoped to get was corroboration of Spivek's version of events. Not eyewitness testimony. But Gia skipped before they arrived. Couple nights ago, her neighbor said. Hauled everything away in garbage bags. Even the roach traps were missing.

Eliza was pondering Gia's quick exit when she saw her mother. The end of the hallway where Adrian Redmon had passed by a moment ago—now Mamá stood there, talking to the squad's receptionist. She never visited Eliza at work. Never before today. Eliza pushed off the corner of her desk. Felt ice up inside.

Body language tells more than most people think. Cops know this. Seeing her mother's dry but stony eyes should've given something away. Purse on her shoulder pulled front and center with both hands. Clutched to her midsection, shielding vital organs from frontal attack. These are instinctive, animalistic postures. But Eliza wasn't able to process her mother's attitude. Her suddenly showing up at the squad lit too many lines in Eliza's brain. Emotions engaged at too high a speed. She couldn't make it make sense.

Mamá saw her coming. Thrust words in her path.

"Martin hanged himself this morning," she said. "They phoned me."

Eliza said nothing. She caught the wall with an outstretched arm. Made it look natural, like a regular cop with sore feet just leaning.

"I won't bury him," her mother said.

"No one expects you to."

"They did at Dexter. That's why they called."

"Funerals services for inmates without families are provided," Eliza said, "by the prison." Hearing herself and knowing exactly how she sounded. Quoting verbatim from the DOC manual. Flipping to autopilot.

Her mother said, "You went to visit him. Now this."

Eliza spiraled down inside herself and fought the panic. Guilt shoved panic aside and began to pummel her. It was physical. She felt the blows landing.

Her mother wanted no explanation. Offered two things instead: a statement of fact and a suggestion. "He was your father. Put him to rest."

Red File

CASE NUMBER 80-117-772

SUPPLEMENTARY REPORT

(SUMMARY)

Decedent is a Caucasian male, approx. forty years of age, identified as Anthony Leland Tompkins by spouse, Dina Booth Tompkins.

Body of decedent at the time of our (Dets. Martin Gahan and Terrence Duval, Hom. Div. BCPD) response to the scene was located in the bathroom (partitioned shower stall) of the master bath in conjunction with the master bedroom, and having two doors opening upon the master bedroom and secondary bedroom (guest bedroom) as described by decedent's spouse and home staff (Henrietta Washington and Wilfred Jenks). Decedent was lying on his back. Unclothed. Body position was lower half on the floor of bathroom, with legs adjacent to master bedroom doorway and upper torso inside the stall. Blood, tissue, and body matter were present in stall area and immediate area surrounding. Water in shower stall running and turned off by Det. Duval. Measurements and sketches of crime scene recorded by Det. Gahan. Pellet damage to tile noted. Pellets and tile fragmentations collected. Appearance of significant trauma to the head/neck from a single gunshot wound is apparent and consistent with close range firing of the weapon (Ithaca .410 double gun) discovered beside body. Weapon collected into evidecne. Witnesses (Mrs. Booth, Mrs. Washington, and Mr. Jenks) reported hearing one gunshot alerting them to the upstairs north hall of residence. Door to master bedroom suite was locked, but door to secondary bedroom had faulty locking mechanism (door lock would not properly engage from warping of wood around lock housing). Witnesses gained entry from secondary bedroom and found decedent nonresponsive prior to calling for ambulance and police assistance. No sign of struggle or forcible entry. Investigation of residence beyond room containing body of decedent yielded no additional evidence of criminal activity. Witness Dina Booth states that her husband had been despondent over failed business ventures and inability to stop excessive drinking. Decedent had been under doctor's care for alcoholism. Visit to drying-out facility had been discussed but not followed up upon in last three months. Bouts of drinking heavily over recent weeks reported by Mrs. Booth and house staff members. All witnesses deny suicidal threats made by decedent at any time. Evidence collected and inventoried by Det. Gahan and Det. Duval. Cause of death is as yet undetermined pending medical autopsy.

[signed] *Det. Martin Gahan*

Eliza read it again. This shred from the useless file. This incomplete, poorly written record of the past. She touched her father's signature.

She made her call to Dexter.

Nestor County ER

A Cub Scout banquet was responsible for an old-fashioned food poisoning. Parents and their sons were filling up the waiting room.

Patrick was dead.

Crispin hadn't breathed a word to his family, not until the tests came back from the police lab. But he was feeling the edge of certainty now. He'd sunk from the high of his criminal foray, his tangle with Booth Homicide, his discovery and subsequent agreement at a cover-up.

Detective Ochoa's grim advice cemented into his memory.

"You'll lie technically. Do it for your brother. Spivek's scum."

He didn't dare to question her judgment. Patrick had pulled

him this far into the whirlpool. He had to save himself. He had a duty to get his own back from Spivek.

So why did it feel like failure?

The boy on the bed didn't look like Patrick. He was Hispanic. His stomach hurt and his mouth, inside and out, showed signs of dehydration. They'd narrowed it down to the green beans or the chicken. Another twenty-four hours and he'd be past the worst of it. Supportive care in the meantime was all they could offer.

He'd looked Spivek in the eye and no alarm bells rang. His brother's murderer, and blankness was the calling card. Bad liar. Spivek's lame attempt to throw him off. But it might have been nothing. The better part of him telling him to write off the encounter. The nagging in his mind could've easily been mistaken, a symptom of his grief.

Detective Ochoa told him they got lucky.

The boy on the bed would need to ride this one out. He was unlucky and lucky in the same instant. Crispin understood that.

They told him what happened. She did most of the talking. Spivek hacked up Patrick's body. He might've done the deed alone or had an accomplice. The crime itself remained murky. They might tie loose ends together. Eventually.

He covered the boy's hand with his.

Left him lying there without pulling the curtain.

Homicide Unit Squad Room

"Now is not the best time," Eliza said.

"For me either," he said.

"I'm sorry for your loss, Dr. Maloney. But can we discuss this later?"

"I'm at work too, you know," he said. "Could we meet somewhere?"

"Look, Dr. Mal—"

"It's okay to call me Crispin."

Shelly Zeller had gotten up from the bench, whispered to Redmon, and was making straight for her desk. She flipped her hand, palm out—a stop sign. He blew through it. "You free for dinner?" she asked into the phone. "There's a restaurant on the corner of Pintail and Quarry, El Cabrito Blanco. Let's get together at, say, seven?"

"Okay, but—"

"See you at seven. Bye."

Zeller rested his briefcase on the edge of the desk. A pebbly smile.

Eliza put the phone back in its cradle. "Mr. Zeller, I'm sure your client must be very eager to speak with you."

"Precisely my thoughts, Detective Ochoa."

"Of course." Her peripheral vision picked up the messenger she'd sent back to Ike, and close behind him—Ike cutting the corner. "Here comes my partner now."

Ike had kept the florist's box a secret. He and Jamila would need to talk about the threat. But that conversation would open the door leading to the state of his job, his health, and last night's slip along the personal demons front. He knew his responsibilities, but the prospect of discussion had no appeal. If Duval were going to try something, he would've done it unannounced. The box was meant to shove Ike back a few yards, give Duval his running room. Jamila would be teaching through the morning. Fleur went to preschool. Ike asked for a patrol car to pay a visit. Plain sight—like he was gunning speeders in the school zone.

Ike made a call, not to Jamila's number.

"Hello?"

"Is this Terry?"

"Who's asking?"

"Terry, Ike Horner, from over at the precinct. Thought I'd give you an update on what we're looking at here."

"Speak of the devil."

"You discussing me?"

"I was."

"We've got them in custody."

"Who's that now?"

"Spivek and Zan Booth."

"I'm not familiar with Mr. Spivek."

"He works for you guys over at the marina."

"As you know, Ike, I'm a barman. Not much of a sailor."

"This sailor says he knows you."

"Isn't that the queerest thing?"

"Hey, Terry, just between us cops. Are you slipping it to both them boys?"

The stone dropped and dropped in a bottomless well.

Anger can make a man patient. Ike waited. The breathing told him Duval hadn't broken the connection. "This is a courtesy here, my calling you. I won't take up any more of your valuable time."

Ike hung up.

Ballard College

It was easy to forget that Booth City was a college town. Ballard College had been built into the city's steepest hillside. The dorms staggered in a rough U-shape, surrounding the class halls and administration buildings. A gymnasium anchored the low point, on the river. A person deposited onto the middle of campus might mistake the grounds for a patch of relocated Eastern Seaboard, but surrounded by some of the cheapest, most run-down housing in the state. No sea here, just eggy-smelling, brown and gold river. At least winter had thrown a lid over the top. Summer day? No wind? You'd think there was sulfur mining going on. The miners must enjoy killing fish too. And drinking cheap beer. The half-crushed empties toppled amid flat, weathered fish bones.

Ike parked in the visitors' lot.

Alumni Recitation Hall.

The English Department offices tucked up in a corner on the ground floor.

Ike found Jamila's office. Her office mate, Anton—a Romanian with bad skin and a deeply ingrained sense of irony—wasn't home. The office smelled like Captain Black, a can of it sitting on Anton's desk. Ike hung his jacket, sat in a student's chair. You could've run a strip of tape down the middle of the office, that's how they'd divided it. North and South. Jamila's half was lived-in. Anton's was lived-under. Enough loose papers to start an inferno. He'd built himself a castle of books. On his wall, he tacked a poster of Alice and her looking glass. The brown fan of a water stain ran haphazard from her feet to the baseboard. Ike caught a quick movement. His first thought was *city rat.*

The toe of a burgundy slipper brushed along a desk leg.

"Ike Horner, how's it going?"

"Not bad. Didn't see you way up in there."

"I saw you, though."

"How'd you get in?"

"Underground passage."

If Ike didn't know him, he would've thought the man meant every word.

Anton pulled a stack of journals inside his walls. His face tracked with darkened furrows digging into his cheese-slab cheeks. "A poet was murdered. Would you have any information? His name was Wayne Poins."

"My case. How'd you know Poins?"

"Poetry slams," Anton said. "Last Thursday of every month over at the Aquarium Bar on Fifth. He was of the Bukowski tribe. I am not as conversant with the gutter. But that's not necessarily of my own choosing."

"Was he any good?"

Ike listened as Anton wheeled his office chair in a semicircle, opened a drawer, and rummaged. The bowl of Anton's Savinelli fired up and a flag of smoke fluttered over the castle walls.

"Who am I to say?" He passed a bar napkin through his book-lined hatch. "One of his haikus. Not a strict five-seven-five syllabic measure, but freer forms do prevail." Ink scrawl. It was the same handwriting as the note Poins left for Ike at the precinct. The blue letters bled out, fuzzy.

Lime and liquor moon,
Left hand of the Sun, salts the web.
Bit, bitter, bitten.

"Is it supposed to be sad?" Ike said.

"What poem isn't?" Anton asked. The question was rhetorical. "Nailing people through the heart. Wayne told me that's what he wanted for his poems." He took the napkin and reset the brick-work of journals. "You know he died on a Friday. I saw him the night before. He didn't read. But he was there."

"What time was he at the bar?"

"Ten? Eleven? I think he was waiting for someone. He was wired. Eyeing the door. He kept getting up to use the john." The professor tapped the side of his nose.

"Poins was alone?"

"When I saw him he was."

Classes were letting out. The long hallway erupted with noise. Voices, doors banging against rubber stops, and footsteps. Anton spoke with the pipe bit clenched in his teeth.

Ike could barely hear him.

"But," the Romanian said, "he left with a woman."

If Jamila could've grabbed Ike by the shoulders and shook him, she would have done it. But they were over the bridge and into Brooktown. A short jog on the four-lane highway, then jump across the Rood again where the avenue emptied a hundred yards from her daughter's preschool. A long-cut. They missed the B.C. lights this way.

"Fleur and I are not going to stay with Sterling and David."

"It's only an idea."

"A bad idea."

"Then I'll ask him to pack a bag. Room in with us for a week or two."

"What does that solve?" she asked.

"Doesn't solve anything. He's an extra set of eyes and ears."

"You're telling me we need a bodyguard?"

Ike didn't answer. He scanned for the patrol, missed seeing it, and swore under his breath. Found it—slow-rolling the fence around the playground. He cranked his window. Pulled along the opposite curbside of the traffic flow, no traffic here anyhow, so he could exchange words with the driver.

Ike sent the cruiser home to the precinct.

"Be honest with me, Shang. How serious is this?" Jamila asked.

"Serious enough."

"I don't like the thought of running scared."

"Nobody's asking you to."

Jamila found Fleur's classroom window. Paper snowflakes taped to the glass. Hers was the red one, higher than the others. The teacher said she asked to stand on a chair to put it up. They were early. When Ike turned the engine off, the kids were still singing. Sitting on the floor and so the room looked empty. Like they were waiting for nobody.

She said, "I want out of this."

"I do too."

"I'm talking about a permanent change."

"Leave the job?"

"Yes."

"Uh-huh."

"How old was your father when he had his heart attack?"

Ike flashed on the last photo of him. Kneeling next to a U.S. Marine helicopter.

"Man was *thirty-two,*" she said. "You put twenty on top of that already."

"I know my age, thank you."

"Well, then know that I don't want you on borrowed time. Your mother walked around in mourning for over half her life. That's not my path. And I won't walk it."

Ike rubbed his forehead. "I can't go now."

"Then when?"

"Not now."

Jamila exited the car. Her daughter coming to her, down the steps.

El Cabrito Blanco

They didn't need to order anything.

Rey brought them two plates of enchiladas in green sauce, a bowl of steaming yellow rice to share. Two ice-cold bottles of Dos Equis. Crispin had the look of a man at sea with his thoughts. The arrival of food was a surprise. His color improved slightly. Eliza asked if he was hungry. He took a half second to answer.

"Starving. I should wash up, though." He excused himself, went to the restroom.

Rey materialized at her side. *"Quien es el rubio?"*

"Nobody, Rey. She send you out here?"

"No."

"C'mon, Rey. You gonna lie to a cop?"

"Why you ask, if you know the answer?"

"Valid point."

"So who is he?"

"It's work-related. He's a doctor over at County. His brother was murdered."

"Oh, a doctor. She's gonna like to hear that."

"Don't you tell her anything."

"She's my boss, *mi hija*. I got no choice."

"Out of my sight, Rey."

Crispin returned, paying no attention to Rey's retreat.

She guessed he must've splashed some cold water on his face. A spot faded above his shirt pocket. Clean lines combed through his wavy hair.

He moved his silverware. Casual tone, but the subject wasn't. "What if it's not him? Patrick never had any tattoos." Lifting his fork, and his eyes followed it.

"You believe it's not him, or you want to believe it's not him?"

"No, I think it's him."

"So do we," Eliza said. "Makes you feel any better, we're sticking our necks out on this, same as you. Maybe more."

"I appreciate the effort."

Did she hear sarcasm, or was it resignation?

A short, brown-haired woman set a plate of warm tortillas on their table and a small dish of braised pork. Crispin could smell onions, cumin, and something else—sweet and citrus. The woman looked him up and down, pinched her lips. Happy.

When she was gone, Eliza said, "She thinks you're my date."

"Why should she care?"

"She's my mother."

Crispin glanced over his shoulder, but the kitchen doors were closing. "You might've said something to me."

"Why?"

"I would've introduced myself."

"Why?"

"Because that's the polite thing to do."

Eliza shrugged.

"Is he your father?" Crispin nodded at Rey, who was poised behind the register pretending to count the day's receipts.

"No. That's Rey. My father killed himself this morning."

"What?"

Eliza was chewing, shaking her head slowly. She rolled a tortilla around a spoonful of pork. "He was nobody special."

"That's pretty cold."

"You didn't know him. Neither did I. He destroyed our family. Whatever we have is despite him. Far as I'm concerned, he's been dead for a long time."

Crispin took a pull from the Dos Equis. Then another.

He asked, "Ever take it off?"

"What?"

"This hard shell of yours."

"No."

"That's too bad."

Eliza drank her beer. Watching him. She wondered if he meant the comment as a general observation or if he had a more personal interest. It might have pleased her to know he was asking himself the same question.

"Why are we here?" she asked.

"You mean in a cosmic sense?"

She put down her beer. "Why did you call me?"

"Every day I'd wake up, thinking maybe it's the day Patrick shows up. Since we did this thing with Spivek? I've been dreaming about Patrick. Not nightmares. Dreams. Never happened before. I don't believe it's a message from the spiritual world or anything. But I think you got the wrong guy. Spivek didn't kill him."

"He's dirty on this. You saw the knives and pictures. What else you need?"

"Did he admit killing him?"

"He didn't confess. But he's not the type who would." Eliza decided against her better judgment to tell him more. "Spivek implicated another party. They were probably in it together. Your brother . . . I mean no offense here, but you know he was living close to the edge. Dangerous territory. You work the streets; you get what the street serves up. I think he fell victim to a thrill-kill. That said, this other party—"

"What other party?"

"Seems to be saying that your brother OD'd. Bad junk was swirling around. They're selling it in Cushing now. We've seen the numbers climb."

"Patrick died months ago. Isn't that what you told me?"

"First batch hit last summer. Second started around Christmas. Typically, the street product gets cuts down—way, way down. But some empty skull didn't do his job right. The purity was too high. Your brother was using heroin?"

"That's what we'd heard."

"The bad product was Asian heroin. So, okay, it fits. But they were snorting coke on the boat. Different animal. Now let's say your Patrick's got his own private stash he's not sharing *and* he starts hitting their bag . . ."

"It could've been accidental. A heroin-*plus* overdose."

"I don't think that's what we're looking at in this case. But yes."

"Why wouldn't Spivek say it was an overdose? He's going to be charged with murder. Why not give himself an out?"

"Good question."

"You said there were related cases?"

"Two we know about. Our theory is they're connected."

"Is Reece the other party?"

"I shouldn't be talking to you about an ongoing investigation." She saw the protest coming. She cut him off. "It's Reece. His real name is Zan Booth."

Crispin's wheels turned. Booth City. Those Booths?

Eliza helped him. "That's his family."

He braced his arms on the table, at sea again and riding out. How could he be prepared? After the first serious rush kicked your legs horizontal, the rest sucked you out deeper and deeper. Land became your fantasy—a piece of solid ground you dig your heels into. You weren't drowning, not yet, but you weren't swimming either. Welcome to the rip current of fear. The shock never wore off.

Eliza felt it. Cold-burning along her scarred belly.

She said, "Test comes back, I'll call. Until then, you have to do the toughest part."

She didn't need to tell him what it was.

You wait.

5 Fay Street

Beautiful B.C. morning. Warm wind huffing like a diesel from the west, and everything drenched with trickling snowmelt. The blacktop was blacker, smelled like oil as he crossed streets. Coming home from the bus stop.

He paused to watch the white contrails of a passenger jet screaming silently high above, keying the blue gloss sky. Temps would crack the fifty-degree mark before noon. Spring—what a con game—was not blowing on the breeze. The air had a taste of metal. Swamp gas mixing up from the river. Fair skies fooled some people. Change in the jet stream lent false hopes.

He knew better.

Sailor slogged through the mush behind his trailer.

Zan had bonded out. A hundred K on the mil-do set by the judge. DNA a positive match on the Patrick Maloney remains. The Butchered Boy claimed at long last. Josine's fucked-up money grab hounded them, still barking and chasing. The state presented for a murder. No hard evidence connecting Zan and Sailor to Josine or the cabdriver.

Because those were Terry's deeds and Terry wouldn't let himself get touched.

Reason enough to worry.

Sailor came around to the front. He scraped the clay from his boots. Big X of police tape. He ripped through. Snappy jerk as the wind snatched it—the yellow snake undulated down the street, lifted on an updraft, and carried over his neighbor's unit.

River-bound.

Inside was a shambles. He expected as much, but seeing it was worse. His hands trembled. Anger looped hotly around his neck. Fingerprint powder, cop grime was everywhere. They'd get Josine's prints and Zan's. Patrick had crashed with him for a weekend—so him too. Nothing Sailor could do about that now. His shit was dumped on the floor. Drawers left hanging open. Royal fuck-you from Booth's finest. The space under his bed called out—violation. What did he have left to lose?

The surprise came in court. Zan's team was cleared and in the parking lot or home by the time they led Sailor to the table. Sailor's PD saw the negatives piling up. Going through the motions. Time-waster for everybody involved. He'd sat through these shows before. Knew the ending.

Bail matched Zan's. The prosecutor jumped up like he had a scorpion in his boxers. Sailor got another feeling. Like the feeling he got when he went on the *Oh Mickey!* to look for the cooler. This was a setup. Terry and the Booths held the softy judge on a leash. Might have been worse. Bottom line, the same result. He'd wait it out in the cells.

Only somebody posted the money and he was free to go.

He didn't have to ask who was shilling.

Not a whisper the whole time he was in custody. He guessed they'd reach out for him tonight. It would be Terry, maybe with a handout, certainly with a plan.

Sailor knew what was coming.

He had to call the Indian.

Stupid to use his own phone. But where was he going to go on foot? He had no vehicle. Terry made sure of that. The van was likely parked at the marina. Good and clean, no doubt. Terry would feed them some bullshit about how Chariot Security maintained the marina fleet. Fleet—oh, that was bullshit too, because at the marina it was just the van, rusting away hauling around wet crap off the docks. Sailor was willing to bet Terry washed the fucker out himself, with bleach water and a fucking blowtorch, before the cops got around to impounding it. It was stupid to pick up his phone. But he did it because what the fuck did it matter at this point. Really. What the fuck did it matter.

Get to the end of your rope. Tie a knot.

Everybody swings, sooner or later.

Everybody.

9

MASKS

Homicide Squad Room

Eliza waited until the end of her shift, but as promised, she called him. If she got his machine, that would've been easier. This way she heard the impact—the cruel, hard rebound her words made over his silence.

"Crispin, you okay?"

No comment.

"I'm really sorry it played out this way. But this is what we were expecting, right?"

He was gone.

Did it sound like a sob there at the end?

She had the dial tone buzzing in her ear.

Thought about calling the parents, but she couldn't take that step. It wasn't right for anybody else to bring the news. He had to shoulder it.

Keep out, she told herself.

Couldn't take her own advice. Didn't need to write down his address because she'd been there. *Well-being check.* Paid a visit to pick up Sailor's suitcase and set the trap. Now she was going again, for real—the truth that proves the lie.

Crispin's Loft

He had his keys, a jacket on when he answered the door.

"I can't sit here," he said.

"You got anybody? Friends maybe you can call?"

"I'm not ready."

"Hey, c'mon, let me inside a minute. We'll talk."

"I told you . . ."

Red-eyed. His voice was huskier than she remembered. He stepped into the hall. She backed up, gave him room to lock the door. He dropped his keys, tried again.

He turned. Showed her his profile—stubbly jaw, a commalike scar outside the corner of his eye, a tiny stud earring.

"So where you going?" she asked.

He brushed past her.

"I get there," he said over his shoulder, "then I'll know."

Her eyes followed his retreat. He passed through the diffused rays falling from a skylight. Dust motes dancing. He wasn't going to turn around again.

"Wait up," she said.

Throwbackland

Thing about B.C. is, you're never far from a drink if you need one. This place was nothing to brag about. Old-timers would've called it a hole-in-the-wall. Locals gone to seed, ongoing personal tragedies, desperation you could taste. If it had a name, you couldn't tell from outside, or once you went in, for that matter. A stand-alone mausoleum, cinder block painted tan. The windows were glass block. Weepy since the melt started. *No frills* would've been overstating the interior decor. There was an electric waterfall clock. Crispin sat left of it, at a table. Eliza didn't want to take her jacket off. But the thermostat was busted or somebody liked it cranked to tropical heat wave. Nobody welcomed them.

Eliza went for the drinks.

Lady on the stick was friendly as a padlock, her hairdo twisted up tight with a pencil. Maybe she was taking blood-thinners. Her fingers brushed Eliza's, transferred a shiver. The pair of drafts exchanged for a five-dollar bill. She sucked back under the TV.

First round, they sat quiet.

After the second, he talked about the ER, the Cub Scout on the gurney. His voice lost its edge. He had a baby face, a soft easy smile he used naturally, even in his grief, like some people use their hands—to help the words along.

"Up for another?" he asked.

Eliza understood his situation. He had a terrible new power. Lifting his finger was all it would take to set a black fire raging around his family. He'd poured the gas, balled up the newspapers. The lighter was in his hand. But he was working on his courage. Backing into it, slowly.

We're both on burial duty, she thought.

If she had a single good memory of Martin, it wasn't making itself known. Speak ill of the dead. I hated you, Marty. There, I said it. I'm not like you either. Thanks for the last story to remember you by. Thanks for the mindfuck on your way out the door.

Whose pain was greater? Crispin's, she would've insisted, no question. He had somebody to lose. And lost. She had an emptiness that grew emptier. Grief works on a sliding scale. You pay what you can. Marty would've liked an Irish wake, so she'd make this pitiful last gesture. Raise a toast. At least the boy was a Paddy. Cheers, Da.

Leah was calling her.

Eliza saw the number, realized. *Valentine's Day is tomorrow. Girls' night out tonight.*

You'd think the bar would've had at least a single red paper heart taped somewhere, even on the dartboard. The date would've registered when she walked in. She would've had a chance to pull out. Explain. But no, this was Throwbackland, a no-time zone. The world banished. It was too late for Eliza to return Leah's call. Leah was tough on her best day. But stood up?

Eliza turned off her cell phone, her pager. Strictly not cool. She'd be the first to bitch if the tables were turned. But she couldn't talk to Leah now. She didn't have the energy. Her skills weren't there. Matching drinks with Crispin was her good deed for the month. She would turn on again later, after Leah had a chance to fizzle.

She told herself an hour should do the trick.

Eliza's Apartment

He won't go back to his place. She can drive, but she'd blow way over .08 and she doesn't want to take the wheel. Walking is an option. B.C. is small enough. Her apartment is reachable in an hour. But the walk might sober them up.

They hail a taxi.

She rests her hand on his upper thigh. Feels him jump.

Inside her apartment, she avoids the light switch. Doesn't want to risk breaking the mood, the spell, whatever's happening. Candles. She picks a tall votive, St. Jude etched on the glass. She kept it in the cupboard for power outages.

Pray for us.

Eliza has a great black leather couch.

They sink a little. They don't bother with music.

He finds the scar with his tongue.

"What's this?"

"Bullet wound."

"Really?"

She watches his face, the screwy smile. He isn't sure if she's telling him the truth. His eyes are aqua and glazy. St. Jude shrunken at the irises. Crispin's hair mussed from her fingers.

"You got anything?" he asks. He props up crookedly on his elbow.

"Anything?"

"You know."

She considers what he's asking. One way to take it is to be

insulted; the other is that he's trying to be responsible. She gives him the benefit of the doubt.

"I can't get pregnant."

"The pill?"

She doesn't respond.

He's doing what he was doing before the questions. Gets his palms under her.

"I'm not on the pill." She grabs herself behind her knees. Pulls back. Feels herself being drawn apart. He's helping with that.

His brow scrunches up and he's holding eye contact. Trying to figure out what she meant by her comment. After all the booze he's a little slow. Then it must click for him because his face, what she can see, smooths over. He goes cross-eyed for a second, gazing at the coin of scar tissue under his nose. Traveling the slope of bone with his tongue. He is persistent. Paying attention to the scar because he understands what it means.

Eliza feels a warm elasticity snaring her lower spine. Cinching, relaxing. She raises her hips and rubs her slickness against his upper chest without a word or self-conscious thought. There are demarcations of pleasure. She is approaching one.

He breaks away—smack—wet skin releasing from a wet mouth. He climbs up to kiss her. His tongue is a peach stone caught in her teeth. Sliding.

"Don't talk," she says. "Where you were . . . was fine."

"Was I here?"

"I said don't talk." Her breathing changes, sounds like paper tearing.

He doesn't ask again.

Belli's Butcher Shop

"Retire? I don't understand retire. You need your work," Belli said.

Ike emptied the last drops from the coffeepot.

Belli was busy, cutting through muscle and bone.

"Without work, what are you?" Belli asked.

Ike couldn't think of an answer.

"See?" Belli laid out a steak on the waxy paper. "You don't know. I don't either."

The saw in Belli's hand looked too big, like he needed help to keep it steady. He stopped sawing, turned to Ike. Ike noticed a gully in the old man's neck where he'd missed with the razor, maybe more than once, the whiskers growing in thick as hog bristles.

"Day I don't open the shop is the day you gotta bust the door down. You'll find me leaking into the mattress in the bedroom. But I won't be there. I'll be gone. Like Jesus."

Ike knew the man was right. The day wasn't far off.

"You got health problems, you fix them. But fix them so you can work more, not stop working." Belli was breathing hard through his mouth, the dry sound interrupted with a cackle. "Besides, I don't need you across the street throwing baseballs against the fence. Isn't that the truth?"

"Evidently."

"Okay," Belli said. He finished his last cut. Tore a long strip from the roll of tape that had been resting at his elbow.

"Here," he said.

Ike took the package in both hands.

"Happy Valentine's Day."

Ike drove back to the house to put the steaks in the freezer. He had time. Jamila would be gone, taking Fleur to her school. An hour until he'd meet with Eliza to plan the day. His world dropped into a lower, smoother gear. Take away the speed and nothing looked as dangerous. The numbness in his hands, the dizzy spells, and the tight chest—he'd adapt. Wasn't adaptation a daily attempt at happiness?

Visiting Belli always settled him. Gave him a chance to focus.

The taxi, a maroon Crown Vic, idled curbside. Didn't need much focusing to see it parked there in front of his house. The driver had the trunk open. He stared as Ike pulled close, double-parked, and effectively pinned the cab in place. The driver was tall. Ramrod back. Not likely a part of Duval's crowd. A primal sense of warning flashed and died. Another replaced it. Ike glanced into the trunk. Three suitcases neatly stowed.

"What is this?" the driver asked him. He was a Sikh and wore a blue turban, a full salt-and-pepper beard. His eyes filled with quiet alarm.

Ike showed his shield. "Police business."

"You request to see my city license?"

"Ain't about you. Sit tight."

He didn't get halfway up the walk. Jamila came through the front door with her carry-on bag. Fleur followed on her heels.

"I'm not leaving you, Ike."

"Oh?"

He stepped aside so they could pass. Fleur caught acting shy because the driver was a stranger. Her sidelong gaze signaling Ike to the man's presence. The driver held the door for them. Jamila took Fleur by the hand and helped her into the taxi.

"But I am leaving here. We're flying to Jerome's."

Jerome was her brother. He lived in Corpus Christi with his wife and five boys. Owned a shrimp boat. Ike met him twice, liked him.

"Okay. But stealing away behind my back. It doesn't feel right." He leaned into the cloying sweetness of the taxi's air-freshener. Vanilla. Jamila clicked Fleur's seat belt. She twisted back around, her hand came toward him and paused midair. Closed fist. He saw the pink flesh under her clear-polished thumbnail. Bracelet of jade cubes he gave her for her birthday. Stone ring and black gel watchband. She was waiting for him to open his hand. He did. She dropped a rifle cartridge into his palm.

"I found that in Fleur's backpack."

Ike recognized the 7mm Remington Magnum. It was a popular load with hunters. Used for deer, mostly. None of these facts were important. "Does she know?" he asked.

Jamila's lips made a hard line. She shook her head. No.

"Good," he said.

Then, "I'm sorry."

Jamila pulled the door closed.

He wasn't going to talk through the glass. Wouldn't act the fool.

The driver asked her if he should go. He reminded her their way was blocked.

Ike motioned: *Roll the damn window down.*

She looked at him, deciding.

His pager vibrated on his hip. He tapped the display button, switching his eyes off hers long enough to read the number. Habit.

That was enough. The window came down, but not for a goodbye kiss. She said, "Our plane takes off"—checked her watch—"in forty minutes."

"You got my number, you need me."

"Move your car."

"We're flying on a big airplane!" Fleur shouted.

"Be careful, baby girl. Have fun."

Jamila said, "You be careful too, Shang."

Window up.

He moved his car so they wouldn't be late.

Unincorporated Nestor County

Perfect spot.

Middle of nowhere.

Ike parked at the development's north entrance. Switched on his hazards.

blink blink blink

He decided to go in on foot. Radioed ahead. Asked them not to shoot him. There'd be a traffic jam at the site. He'd rather walk it. Less hassle getting out when he finished. He needed to clear his head beforehand. Jamila and Fleur taking a flight. He picked up the call buzzing on his hip. Bodies. We need you here to take a look. Only a quarter mile, they said. But hurry. They were waiting.

Ike lit a Camel. He took a long drag. Ground the butt in the car's ashtray.

The shooters must have come out of nowhere too. Or out of the fog. He'd gone twenty paces and the orange blinks were hazy.

Ten more, they vanished. This was a river valley. Under the right conditions—no wind, high dew point—the fog would settle, make visibility a matter of feet. Lights weren't much help. Ike should have hated it. He didn't. It was like being there and not being there. Waltzing into somebody else's dream. Unreal.

This dream had a carnival.

Shapes turned solid.

What he could make out was this.

The occupants knew them. Must have. No alarm bells.

Dark—was it blue or black?—a dark *blue* Lincoln Navigator parked with its engine still running, sputtering though, sucking on fumes. Squads blocked entry into the unpaved cul-de-sac. Four black-and-whites formed a double arrow to the crime. Their cherries lashed red whips at the walls of fog and beyond the surrounding clay fields. An ambulance's crisp white flash added to the spectacle. The ME wagon had its lonely blue bubble revolving. Perfect.

The color scheme wasn't lost on him. He'd noticed it before.

Press van lurked, nudging slowly up the road. They saw him pass. Piled out the back. Spotlight opening, tagging along like a curious, lewd eye stuck to his backside. Here's your American Heartland horror story lit pretty for the cameras.

He ignored them. Crossed under the tape.

Looking for Eliza. He didn't see her among the group. It was the B.C. first string out on the turf for this call. Gandy was there. But so was Lu—deep inside the hood of her black down parka. Ike heard the reedy music of her voice. Whatever she said made Gandy nod along.

Denis Bitman, Booth's senior crime technician, was a big man, narrow in the shoulders and hips, slouchy—slow to move and methodical once he did. He lifted a hand, acknowledged Ike. Guarding the virgin scene with his two assistants. If they wanted, they could've linked arms and sung a chorus of "Kumbaya." Normally Bitman was a prick to deal with. But lately he'd been winding down. He'd filed for his retirement. Less than a month until Hawaiian shirts, cigars, and hugs all around. His joy was running old Lionel trains in his basement. It was no secret. People have their passions and their limits. Bitman knew his. These days he'd rather be watching his tables. He felt no particular urge to go crawling on his hands and knees in the aftermath of a triple homicide. But orders had issued from the mountaintop. And the mountain moved. Bitman had timed his departure about right. You can't predict when one will go flying off the rails.

Nothing unusual, the fact Ike arrived first. But he'd been delayed. Crossed town to get here. The precinct and Eliza's apartment were closer. So where was she?

He walked up to the reason for the impromptu light show.

The two men in the front seat of the SUV were wearing their jackets unbuttoned, had their guns holstered. The driver's door was open to the gravel street. The crime-scene techs wouldn't be able to pour any decent footprint casts. The rocks were too loosely packed. Everything looked like a print. Or didn't. No way they'd be able to match the shoe that stepped inside Poins's utility closet.

Ike went closer.

Regan Strawberry, the driver—an ex-cop from a B.C. tactical unit whom half the team recognized—was touching the steering wheel with his left palm. His right hand nestled in his crotch as if to ward off a kick. Bullet holes puckered his throat and forehead. The look on his face was more annoyed than alarmed, like he had a bug in his ear.

Ike walked around to the other side of the Navigator.

"You declare them?" he asked Lu.

She nodded.

He reached in and checked the coat of the passenger. Trifold wallet. License told who he was; *what* he was, was a mess. Salazar Luna. Hugely fat. His immensity relaxed by death. His head, topped by a brown Kangol cap, was knocked back like a Pez dispenser. He had no nose. Ground round where his chin and throat used to be. His gold wire-rimmed eyeglasses dangled from a plump fleshy ear. Whoever was wielding the shotgun had probably used his open mouth as a target. The glass in his window was gone. The upward angle of the blast suggested the shooter was kneeling on the ground, or letting fly from the hip. Here again, the gravel wasn't helping. Ike looked down and saw two small, shallow indentations in the rocks. They might've been nothing.

Okay. The weapon gets put against the glass. Sliding around maybe? Triggerman's feeling nervous? Tilts and then . . . *BOOM*. Some of the load missed Luna and blew saltshaker holes through the roof. Hey, maybe they were looking at a kiddie hitman.

Put out an APB on shorties with shotguns.

The man sitting in the backseat had definitely reacted. His body was hunched over, crouching, like he'd been trying to burrow under the bench seat. A sheaf of papers, amazingly free of bloodstains, lay fanned on the wheat leather, next to the rearview of a hundred-dollar haircut.

Gunfire ruined Adrian Redmon's duck-hunting jacket. Ike

could see chunks of white spine. He counted eight entry wounds, all torso shots. From the same weapon, likely, that did Strawberry. The interior stank of gunpowder, as if someone had tossed a belt of firecrackers on the dashboard, then run away.

Ike opened the passenger-side rear door. He balanced his foot on the rocker panel and lifted himself up for a better look. The shifting weight dropped Luna's cap. It fell and blew out onto the sloppy gravel.

"Bag that," Ike said.

One of the crime techs was already closing in. Bitman.

poc poc poc

Somebody was shooting at them. Shattering of glass. Yelling. Bitman shouldered him; moved so quick Ike's first thought was the guy's hit. But the tech was squirming under the Navigator.

Ike dove headfirst into the backseat.

"Chinese fire drill," Bitman said later, recalling the event in court.

No one able to tell the direction of the shots fired.

Fast hands responded in the patrol cars. Radio commands: Down. Stay down. Get down and stay down. Lie flat.

poc poc poc poc poc poc

"Muzzle flashes. Three o'clock." Gandy pointed into the color-swept field.

There was a volley of return fire. But they couldn't see a target. Their own lights were blinding them and giving the shooter an advantage—something to aim for.

Ike sprawled across the backseat of the Navigator, Adrian Redmon's corpse underneath him. The earthy, salty smell was pervasive—and the damp warmth sticking through his clothes. Ike tried slowing his breathing. He bit his lips, fought the rippling nausea. The dead man's leg had gotten twisted; an ankle pushed into Ike's privates. Through the open door, he had Gandy. He forced himself to concentrate on Gandy's profile.

The assistant ME contorted for a better view of the sniper's position.

"Picked a good spot," he said.

Ike tucked his knees, braced himself against the seat. The windshield hadn't been damaged. He rose on his haunches for a quick look. Air spurted from Redmon. Ike was kneeling on his rib cage the same way the killer had probably knelt on Poins. Taking a control position. Just like the sniper.

Uphill, and the hill was slop.

The only sure footing was a gravel cul-de-sac identical to where the Navigator was parked, but northeast—second leaf on a clover. The hill rested in-between. They couldn't move on him. Not until a SWAT team arrived.

Ike looked again, noticed the hill was darker than the clay and not part of the original landscape. More like a mound. The topsoil was studded with rock. But the mound had been there awhile. The melting snow exposed streaks of pale yellow grass, remnants of growth. As far as Ike could see, the shooter hadn't left an out.

"He's moving," Gandy said.

Ike climbed off Redmon and started running. He was going in the opposite direction of the others. They were already getting their shoes stuck. His legs pumped as he came down the first cul-de-sac and ran up the next.

Shooter was there. Ike saw a head bobbing low, something not right with the perspective. Shooter was getting smaller. Ike realized: There's a ditch behind him we can't see. He was in and through the mud. Not just a ditch—drainage canal. Solid concrete, and Shooter was making good use of the footing. Ike drew his .357.

"Stop! Police!"

Shooter didn't slow down. Big splashes. He was kicking up brown water. Moving with a purpose. Dark overalls and boots, nothing more Ike could identify. Getting smaller again. And quickly. Had he fallen?

There was a road overpass directly ahead. A tunnel.

Ike was going too fast to stop. He felt the frozen grip of the canal water switch from his ankles to his thighs. Seizing him around the waist. The depth dropped three feet and leveled. A moment of buoyancy surprised him and then the unbelievable cold.

Shooter was wearing hip waders.

Ike's gun hand waved over his head. His legs . . . he couldn't tell if they were doing what his brain asked. He caught himself pitching forward. Balance lost, twisting sideways as he went face-down into the pool. Came up coughing. Seeing gold stars. Gold stars on brown water. He wiped his eyes. Watched Shooter disappear into the tunnel mouth. If he turned around, Ike was dead. Sitting duck. Ike did his best. Fired off a defensive round. Blue sparks. His bullet must've pinged the corrugated metal inside the tunnel.

The tunnel was darkness.

Shooter climbed out the other end. Ike saw the half circle of gray light appear.

They were with him in the canal now. Young bloods from the patrol units were the first to reach him, racing in their socks. Being cautious, not sure if he was really playing for the good guys. Drawing down on him as he crawled blindly toward them. He was telling them about Shooter. They saw the blood on his jacket, Redmon's blood. But they didn't know that. They were telling him to throw his gun away. He wasn't doing it.

Ike put his left hand down, like sticking his fist into a cooler for the last beer and keeping it there, because he needed to and wasn't sure why. Damn cold water. Fumbling around. His vision screwed to the size of a pinpoint. Ears stuffed with cotton. He knew he was losing consciousness. Shutting down. He didn't want to drown in ditchwater. Didn't want to give Shooter the satisfaction.

He sensed the thing before he touched it—a chunk of solid warmth. He concentrated. The water, though not very deep, was turbulent. The object skittered along in the flow. His cold-crippled fingers made a cage.

"That's Detective Horner."

"Paramedics!"

"We got an officer down!"

"Hold on."

Cops on either side of him, arms under his, trying to lift him out of the foul water.

"Right here," Ike said. He could see gradations returning in the light, different shapes—of men, water, concrete slabs. "I got his piece."

Nestor County Hospital

"Lost him where?"

Eliza sat on the bed, both her feet on the floor. "Keogh Park. South end. Early this morning." Ike was alert and looking much better. She would've gladly traded places. Could've used his blanket to climb under.

"Another park?"

"Yeah. I think Sailor's admitting he's our boy. Rubbing our noses in it."

"Who had the detail?"

"Dallas and Hernandez."

"What'd they say?"

"Suspect's on a trail. Then he takes off into the bushes. They pursued. But, you know, they'd given him some cushion. He knew they were there. Some couple riding bikes gets between them. He booked."

"How's he get to the park?"

"Bus."

"Afterward he didn't boost a set of wheels?"

"Nothing's come across. But he's not hoofing it to meet Redmon. Maybe he knows there's a ride waiting. Same driver picks him up at the tunnel. That's why we missed."

"We're watching the trailer?"

She nodded. "Closing the barn door . . ."

"I know."

His clothing had been stuffed in a hospital-issue tote, the kind with a snapping handle. An info capsule printed at the upper corner. Patient's name, room, and bed. He pawed around inside.

Squinting without his specs. He took out his shoes—the ruined mocha-brown wingtips; not exactly cop shoes, Eliza thought—and he placed them carefully on the blanket. She saw worry crossing his face and told him what she'd locked in the car—his wallet, badge, and sidearm. He sat back. Sighed. She thought he looked twenty years older, just in that moment, as if she were crystal-balling his future; it broke her heart.

"Hey, sorry I wasn't there," she said.

"Forget it. Your landlord let you in?"

Eliza nodded. "Last time I go for a run without my phone and a spare key."

Ike wasn't comfortable. He folded his pillow, readjusted the strap on the oxygen tubes. His arm stung where they'd taped him, above the wrist.

Eliza said, "I tried to reach Jamila. Let her know you were okay. Get you some clean clothes."

"She went on a trip."

"That's what the college people told me." Eliza waited to hear if there was more to the story. She didn't want to push. Pushing him wouldn't yield anything. Maybe the less she knew, the better.

"I'll call my son," he said. "Thanks for the effort."

Subject closed. Eliza appreciated his need to keep matters private. They had that in common. Tight-lipped. Good quality in a cop, especially a partner. Last thing you wanted was to get sucked into a soap opera, hearing the minutiae of day-to-day tribulations outside the job. Everybody screwed up. Ike was no exception. She was happy to listen if he needed that, happier to let it go.

He shook his head. "Time frame's too close together. Spivek couldn't set this up, shed the tail, and catch a ride to the development.

Then he and an associate pop Redmon and the bodyguards? I don't buy it. Where do the waders come from? The weapons? Location was hashed out before the fact and he doesn't have the opportunity. Or the smarts."

"We keep the theory it's two gunmen?"

"Right."

"But not Spivek and Booth?"

"Strange way to thank Redmon for bail money."

"Maybe the situation's complicated."

"I like simple," Ike said. "That wasn't a chance meeting what happened this morning in the valley. That was a hit. Somebody planned it."

"In the canal, he almost screws up."

"Almost makes all the difference."

"He's not just getting lucky."

"Whoever did this thought about it for a long time. Worked his scheme forward and backward. He's sold on it. But what stands out is he's too aggressive. Trying to force us to look this one way. But me, now I'm looking the other."

Terry Duval set up executions. Eliza's father played triggerman, and then circled the drain for a couple decades. Duval's murders were history but not ancient history. Proof was out there if you hunted for it, not courtroom evidence, but street knowledge. Street knowledge. The same thing kept you alive, day-in day-out.

"Any word on Zan Booth?" he asked.

"Nothing after our first pass. We're shaking the trees."

Machine to Ike's left spit a paper scroll into a tray. Graphing the electrical mountains under his sternum. No flats. He wasn't boarding the death ship today. Nurse on rounds checked his pulse, swept up his heart's ticker tape. Filipina, a grip swift and firm, like a seabird's. Ebony eyes. Her touch sent a weak current into him. He was comforted and, to his surprise, mildly aroused.

Dehydrated, that's all. Haven't come down from my morning shot of adrenaline.

Unusual thoughts masqueraded as rational. He'd been here before, and he was on the lookout this time. Sorting interference from all quarters. Crazy ideas didn't need sharing. Little snips of panic. His mind knocked out of joint, fuzzy. Unreliable. Racing one minute, paralyzed the next. Sweat peppered his gown. White gunk collected in the corners of his lizard mouth. He wiped his lips with a damp paper towel. In his mind's eye, a dark aura accumulated like a thunderhead. The air charged up with ions. Post-action jitters—Ike had them in bunches. No pain. This was coasting. He'd level soon. His logic wanted back on the streets. They had the momentum.

Strike was coming.

Ike wanted it to be theirs.

His emergency visit had been played out. Five more minutes, he'd pull the needle and sign the papers. Let it all just be. As long as he could walk away, he was good.

Sign posted: CELL PHONE USE PROHIBITED.

Eliza caught the incoming call on the half ring. Over to the window, and she lowered her voice. The nurse's sharp look was a quick penalty. She'd make it brief.

"Where they taking him? ETA? Thanks, cowboy."

"What's up?"

"Dallas says they found Zan Booth. He's an OD. Touch and go. They're bringing him to St. Leonard's."

St. Leonard's was closer to the Booth estate.

"He was at the family residence?"

"Yep. Anonymous call told us where to find him."

"How come we couldn't turn him up?"

"Dallas says he was . . . hidden."

"Hidden?"

"In the old apple press."

"I'll be."

10

BAD DREAM

St. Leonard's ICU

Reece is stuck on a loop. It's doesn't occur to her that she might be dead. Or hooked—arm, lungs, cock, heart, brain—to machinery in St. Leonard's ICU. But she knows she's not alone. She can smell Josine's orange and Prometh breath . . . the musk emanating from Patrick's sleeping bag—he lugged that smelly green roll everywhere.

Uncle Happy's shaving cream. Smearing his neck, cheeks, and narrow upper lip. Anointing them. It was something cheap, very bottom shelf. Barbasol Lemon-Lime. He'd shaved for the occasion. Trimmed his chin whiskers to a shovel's blade.

A freshly barbered Uncle Happy has come to pay a visit. Knocking on the pressing house door, his image wavering, mercurial in the leaded panels. His viperous shadow staying put for the moment, slumbering on the floor. He's smiling. Neither Uncle Serpent nor Terrible Terry Duval. But never showing his true self.

It's Uncle Happy Time Again! Hooray!

Bearing gifts.

"Welcome home. Aren't you my prettiest girl?" Uncle drops his packages, headlocks her, snatches away the burnt, curly-haired wig so he can stroke his knuckles over the peach fuzz that grew while she rotted in her cell. They're spinning around in front of the fireplace. Almost dancing. Reece's skirt whips like a black flag. She loses her heels. Kicking the grate with her bare feet perturbs the flames. (Mexican Maid delivered the fresh birch logs.) Reece feels his embrace evolve. Sweeping her in. Tight. Holding for too long. A metal button on Uncle's jacket scratches her jaw. An arm dips under her chin and stops her air. Uncle's knee finds the small of her back. Forcing her to stretch. She tries struggling, but the fight's over.

Until Uncle lets her go. He regards her with a leer. Not-so-secret loathing spurred his violence. Funny, but Reece hadn't sniffed hostility when they first met. This repulsion he harbored for her. Nurtured. In calmer times, she thought he'd settled on a lingering, almost clinical fascination with her. Push-pull. He hated what he could not comprehend. Now she knew it was himself he despised. Something he had no control over.

Reece coughs, massaging her throat.

"Ach, you're a faker, you," Uncle says. He sits cross-legged on the floor. He's got two grocery bags. He dropped them by the door when he came in. But he has them now. One's paper—rolled down and wrinkly and looking serious. The other is beige plastic. There's no hiding the bottle inside.

"Business or pleasure?"

"Don't make me bloody beg." It hurts to speak.

Uncle tucks the paper bag behind him. "I know you all too well," he says. He draws the frosty bottle of lemon Stoli from its sleeve. And two shot glasses with price tags glued to their bottoms. He picks at them like scabs.

"What was your impression of the lockup?" He pours.

"Moldy and lacking cheer."

"Ha! But you're out now. You're home again. And there's no putting off what we must do tomorrow."

"What?"

"We've talked about it enough, you and I. Our heart-to-hearts."

"Down with me knickers?"

"Ye degenerate cunt."

"No? I'm lost then, I . . ."

Uncle brings the brown bag to the hollow of his folded legs. He unrolls it, puts his scaly pink hand inside.

"A gun?"

"That it is."

"What do you expect me to do with it?"

"Kill Adrian."

Reece is laughing but she's alone. "You're serious."

"We'll go over together. Remember, I'm going to be at your side the whole time. We're a team."

"Noticed my legal predicament, have you?"

"Fish in a barrel."

"Hullo? Lethal injection?"

"Don't be dramatic."

"Straight now, no more games. We're talking about icing Adrian?"

"Exactly."

"You've gone mad."

"We need the money."

"Just the money?"

Uncle oozes across the apple-beaten, worn boards. He drapes his arm over her shoulders. Reece gets the feeling this is supposed to be an expression of warmth, of kinship. Family.

She shudders.

"It's a lot of fucking money, Zan," says Uncle.

"Call me Reece."

"Ah, how could I forget?"

They sit together. Snug as ticks. Fat on the mere idea of Adrian's blood.

Unquestionably . . . lemon-lime, Reece thinks. "What about Dina?"

"My concern."

"You can't kill Mother."

"Of course not. She'll come 'round."

"Good luck you getting her to do your bidding." Reece takes the gun. *It's heeeeeeavy.* "I should walk up and, like, what? Shoot him?" She aims at her reflection in the oblong mirror. Can't suppress her laughter.

"Hardly more complicated than . . ."

Uncle makes a gun of his finger and drops the hammer. Puts his first soft shot in Reece's head. He's so fucking happy, so proud. Reece doesn't want to disappoint him. She doesn't want pain. His slippery gray eyes snapped tight to her body like rubber.

"How exactly do we do this?"

"There's a good girl." He draws a foil square from his pocket. "For you. For later."

Uncle explains.

Reece listens.

"One, two, three." He's firing bullets again, showing her precisely where—in his invisible world of tomorrow—they will go. They play with ammunition. Uncle teaches her to reload. "In the unlikely event, okay?" he says, then, "Got it?"

She nods.

He pokes the foil with his middle finger. "Do you . . . should I stay awhile?"

"I'll manage," she says.

He leaves the junk. A hypodermic syringe too, and it's superclean. Crackling the wrapper in her palm is bliss.

You need me to tie you off? Reece can't recall if he really asked her that. Did he cook it up? Was he even still there? He unfastened his belt and cinched her bony arm, the uncapped spike T-boned between his teeth. He did that, didn't he? She shoved him off to stop it? No. Think now. Think. About the sequence, the plan, the order. His orders. The solemn promises he'd been making for weeks and weeks. Since everyone started dying.

He goes away. She knows he does. Or is he there?

Reece doesn't shoot. She smokes some of it. Fuuuuck. She's not about to kill anyone. Not in the morning. Not ever. Because she loves, loves, loves junk and she loves the planet and every creature inhabiting its filthy face.

Knows she's not alone . . . can smell Josine's orange and Prometh breath . . . the musk emanating from Patrick's sleeping bag—he lugged that smelly green roll . . .

Booth Family Estate

B.C. was a small city like every small city, Ike thought. It had an inferiority complex lurking like a virus in its bloodstream. You'd see it in the pages of the newspaper and local news broadcasts. Every few weeks, an outbreak. B.C. IS OK! The headline would go something like that, always trying too hard, like the boy with halitosis, the girl who laughed a donkey's bray. Metro area of a half million wasn't big enough for pro sports. They had minor league baseball, a semipro hockey team. Losers, one and all, before they played the first minute of the first game. Perception was king. Ballard was a good *small* school. The city had a branch campus of the state university; the tagline of *at Booth City* followed up the big name like a disclaimer. They weren't NYC or LA, not Chi-town or even beery, bead-throwing NOLA. Plain B.C., like the headache powder Ike saw on the pharmacy shelves as a kid. Outdated. Fortune's wheel had gone around and was not coming around again.

B.C. = Beer (not) Champagne.

He'd seen that on the bumper of a black primer Mercury. The rear end jacked up mercilessly high—so the driver could marvel at the cracked axle—and then the whole bondo-plugged beast was left to die. Lifting its leg in a toll road ditch. An undershirt hung slack from the antenna. Garbage bag for a side window. Nobody around, and nobody coming back. Three pink county tow notices slapped to the windshield. The car stayed there for two weeks.

Made Ike curious about the driver's state of mind. Day comes when the jack is missing, so are the tires. The chassis's sunk in summer weeds. He almost called the Staties. Then the Merc was gone. From the ditch, and his life.

But he still thought about it. Wondered if the entirety of Booth City would go the same route. Broken, abandoned, scavenged upon—then gone. Junked. But where do you throw away a city?

"Gate's open," Eliza said.

"Probably expecting visitors."

She slowed the unmarked and still had trouble turning the full ninety degrees from the road. She saw why. The gate was opened—but only partly. They'd fit. Not much wiggle room, though. She reversed for a running start. Got them centered, and hit the gas. Black leaves slipped under the tires. After the wheels dug through the gravel and mud and found something hard to push against, the car jerked, lurched ahead. And then—just as the windshield of the car emerged from the wall of creeping vines—she stood on the brakes. They rocked forward. Ike punched the dashboard. Runoff bubbled in twin creeks on either side of the lane. At the foot of the lane, where they sat idling, the creeks merged. Pooled. The water looked deep. Cast a dusky shade of purple. A blue-knuckled tree branch poked above the surface. It was easy to imagine the entire tree sunk below.

"Can you go around?" he asked.

Eliza twisted in her seat. "Our butt's between the spikes. I'm going to scrape if I give us any angle."

"Just go through."

"We get stuck, you're pushing."

The car's front end dipped and rose, like the prow of a rowboat.

Dark water spilled over the hood, a bucket of decayed mulch came with it. The rear tires banged hard. The branch thrashed at the undercarriage, then snapped. They were on the other side.

Eliza checked the rearview and noticed the camera perched on the iron fence. "Think the video's still out?" she asked.

"Bet on it."

"They should talk to their security company."

"Maybe they did."

"Think Duval has the brass to show himself?" She didn't know why, but she wasn't afraid to mention him. It was a relief.

"No."

Eliza saw the Camel pack between his fingers. Was the road this bumpy, or did he tremble? The pack disappeared. Ike unwrapped a stick of gum. "Duval's been and gone. That's my guess," he said.

"With the tape?"

"With anything we can use."

Booth Staff Residence

Eliza waited for the maid to finish crying. Talking alone, in the privacy of her room, had been Eliza's idea. They agreed that Ike would sit in for the second go-around if they had something. At the moment, Eliza was thinking the one-to-one was a mistake. Tears started flowing as soon as the door shut. She gave her a minute. Another mistake? They'd find out soon enough. She did what she could to avoid staring at her, hoping the woman would pull herself together. There was a box of Kleenex on the nightstand. Eliza pulled a tissue. Gave it to her.

The maid's room was painted white, but not recently. Start with the simple. *You like living here? It's okay.* The outlets were two-holes. Light switch operated by turning a small black knob. Old. *How they treat you? I don't know. Okay.* A cloth shade canceled any light from the window. There was a garden entrance, but no garden. Tiny concrete patio, rings from a flowerpot that had been moved several times. Arm's length from the twin bed was a second door. Glass doorknob, the room's only ornamentation. *What's through there? Hallway. A bathroom. I share it with the other house staff. Danny, the cook, he lives upstairs. The other two girls are down the hall.* Eliza tried to recall the exact layout of outbuildings. An eight-car garage stood between the staff residence and the main house, shielding it from the circular drive. Danny Montgomery was the only staff member who owned a vehicle. Subaru station wagon. He parked in the garage and drove mostly on weekdays, running errands. *You get into town much? Not really.* The pressing house was a two-minute walk behind the main house, along a path of orange paving stones. Eliza had timed it walking over.

The woman blew her nose. She'd already admitted to placing the emergency call. Eliza needed to know more. Everything. The maid, Sandra Camacho, hadn't anticipated the police questioning her. She thought once she confessed to the call, they'd leave her alone. Her naïveté rankled Eliza, made her more suspicious.

"I didn't know what to do. So I . . . I unscrewed the bolts and I put him in there. He's not so heavy. I lifted him and put him inside. He's okay?"

"He's not okay, Sandra. He might die."

"Oh, my God. I didn't know. Mr. Zan is always drinking and taking drugs. Every night. But he's okay, always. I only wanted . . .

so he would be safe if anyone was looking for him. To hurt him."

"We were looking for him."

"The police?" She was confused.

"Yes, the police."

Sandra showed a flicker of impatience. "I know about the police coming in the afternoon. But I called 911 later because . . . I tell them he's in the . . . *como se dice, la máquina de las manzanas*?"

"The apple press?"

"The apple place, I tell them that. Go and see, he's there."

Eliza didn't stop to correct her. "Sandra, we were searching for him here all afternoon. You had to know about the police. Why didn't you say something to one of the officers?"

"I can't. I'm working for the Booths. I live here."

"But you decided to call this evening?"

"On my dinner break. I borrowed Danny's phone and called. I'm asking why are you not looking for Mr. Zan in the apple place?"

"I don't understand. You say you wanted us to help him?"

Sandra nodded. "Mr. Zan is not bad. He's . . . a very alone person. Nobody cares about him." She expelled a ragged breath. "Oh, God, I didn't think he would be dying. I didn't know. I wanted him to be safe."

"Safe?"

Sandra was rocking slightly, clasping her hands between her knees. She noticed Eliza watching and stopped.

"Safe from who?"

The maid's eyes searched the spotless room for a place to hide.

"From Mr. Duval?"

She looked right at Eliza, her mouth tight. No color in her lips.

"Terry Duval was searching for Zan? Trying to hurt him?"

"No." Her answer was firm, but unconvincing.

"Was he here?"

"Last night. He brings Mr. Zan liquor, I think, and dope. But after that, he leaves."

"How do you know?"

"Because I see them together. Then I see him go."

"But you live on the opposite side of the main house."

Her chin quivered. "I was visiting Gelato. Bringing him some carrots. You don't tell Mrs. Booth, please. She can't know this."

"Gelato? The horse?"

"Mrs. Booth never rides him," she said, becoming indignant. "She doesn't. He's a good animal. Smart. He needs brushing, exercise. My father had horses. But I can't do these things, not here. She wouldn't let me."

"The reason you were outside isn't important. But telling me the truth is. Are you telling me the truth?"

"I bring carrots to Gelato, that's all I was doing last night."

"Well, that's not a crime."

"And you don't report me?"

Eliza shrugged, noncommittal. The Booths would find out. But she needed to keep Sandra talking. A nosy housemaid with a fondness for horses was the least of the Booths' troubles. Adrian had been murdered. Zan was likely going to prison if he ever awoke from his drug stupor. Eliza wanted to fault the woman for her pettiness. But she couldn't. For all she knew, this job was Sandra's last chance at bettering her life. Room and board and a steady paycheck rolled into one. If Eliza's job hung in the balance, would she cover up? She didn't let her introspection delve too deeply.

"Mr. Zan has no shame," Sandra said. "He's a show-off, you know? With his money, his parties, his lovers. He wants everyone to see him. To want him."

"We know he likes to dress up. He has a history of promiscuity with both men and women. Or so we've been told."

"Yes," Sandra said. "He has many affairs."

Words, Eliza thought, not untouched with envy. Was there something more?

She tried to put herself in the other woman's place. It should have been easy. Superficially, they had a lot in common. Mexican women. Not yet forty. Sandra, according to her working papers, was thirty-four. They were both unmarried, childless. They sweated for their bread. Lived alone. Slept alone. Dreamed alone.

The maid's eyes were red from crying. Misty. Soft-focus. But there was coolness lurking underneath. Resolve. These weren't the eyes Eliza saw when she looked in the mirror. But they were too familiar. An older woman's eyes transplanted into a younger woman's face. Same as Mamá's. Seeing the world as it had been, might have been, never would be. Eliza reminded herself not to underestimate people's dreams. Or the power released when dreams were crushed.

"Do you love him?" Eliza asked.

"Oh, no, I never feel . . ." She paused. Another ragged breath. A hiccup. She pressed the Kleenex to her mouth. "But I am only sad for him."

"I need to ask you, was Evan Spivek here? Sailor? He has tattoos, a starfish on his hand. You know this man?" She showed her Spivek's mug shot.

"I know him. I don't see him for many days."

"Sandra?"

"Yes?"

"You were protecting Zan?"

"I tell you this. Yes."

"From who?"

"I can't say anything."

Then it came to her. Marty told her a story before he walked back to his cell. It was a love story. About Terry and the Booths. He told her everything she needed to know. Pointed her to the Tompkins red file. When Leland Tompkins died, who benefited? Duval thought the suicide story didn't wash. What jerk blows his head off in the shower and leaves the water running? Bullshit. He talked to Marty about it. Then he discussed it privately with the dead man's wife. There was a payout. Marty had no details to give. But Terry suddenly finds his way into the Booths' good graces. Life goes on. Baby Zan is born. Dina marries Adrian. Order restored, and a happily ever after too.

Until Zan's friends start dying. And Terry's right there pulling the strings. Pretty soon Dina gets to go shopping for another casket.

Marty put himself in harm's way by talking to her. Eliza didn't realize it at the time. But Terry Duval did. He made the call that killed her father. He had to. Now she knew what was really scaring Sandra.

And who.

The Pressing House

The pressing house started out as nothing more than a barn, a warehouse for farming implements. And to Ike, it still retained the essence of storage. Lacking even a residue of human occupation. Sure there was a hearth, but this was no home. The wooden lid that had covered the apple press was overturned on the floor. Firemen flipped it. Before they hauled up Zan, trying to save his life.

Ike stared down into the old machine.

Booth Orchards had run a commercial cider mill for a century. They had a fruit stand on the riverfront. Sold apples by the bushel, cider by the jug, and during the twenties, bootleg applejack. Ancient Sanford Booth used the profits to buy up land. Land was influence. Influence was always political. Politics went to the church dance with handshakes and smiles. Returned with jangling pockets. Bigger boats floated down the river every year. The valley offered pleasant views. Railroad came through at the right time and some people got rich. Interstate highway, decades later, went the same route. They erected a bronze statue of Sanford Booth on Main Street. He's holding an apple in one hand, the other leveled at the sky.

The hopper was gone, as were the wheels used for rotating the grinder and lowering the press. The inner works had been pulled, probably sold at an antique fair. Left behind: an iron drainpipe and a bucket hook. Ike rubbed his thumb across the hook's rough point. Cold clawing against his skin.

What they chose to save resembled a large, empty hot tub. Vertical slats of oak banded together with iron. The wood seasoned with a hundred years of skins and juice, a mottled jigsaw of yellows and browns. Zan's rescue conjured the odor of bruised fruit. At the bottom of the press, Ike saw mice droppings. Glue traps. Lazy S swirled in the dust where Zan had begun his dying.

He heard the door open behind him.

Damp smells of turf and manure from the corral swirled the room.

Eliza asked him if he talked to Dina Booth yet.

"Super Mario's with her now," Ike said. The dull flash of rain colors—silver, gray, nickel—reminded him of his morning in the canal. An involuntary shiver crept his spine.

"Why's he here?"

"Why you think? He got a call."

"I don't like it."

Ike didn't either. The lieutenant on scene was a clear signal. This case had new weight, a different set of rules. Expectations would change. Not for the better. "Anything noteworthy from Ms. Camacho?"

The door was sticking. Eliza put her shoulder into it. Corner of her eye—a smear of movement passed on the periphery, and then stillness. Nothing. Nobody. Eliza's eyes locked to the vanishing point. The rain acted like a rolling screen.

There. Start-and-stop again, up on the driveway. A person headed away from the main house? Mario? Coming their way. Stopping at the edge of the gravel. Standing there. Man-sized. Not Mario. Wide through the chest, short bowed legs that didn't quite match his top half. Neck muscles bunched to his ears. He pivoted at the waist to look around. Didn't move off in any direction. Stayed put, chewing—a bull in the rain. Turned full circle. Jettisoned a wad of . . . was it gum? Tobacco? Something went flying from his mouth to the grass.

He was wearing a Nestor County Morgue jacket. His hair wet. Long and black and down on his shoulders. Rain drooling over the flat bones of his face, and he didn't bother to wipe it away.

Until the moment his smoke-green motorcycle goggles came off, Eliza hadn't recognized him. He was folding the elastic, putting the goggles in his pocket, and glancing around. Then she knew who he was.

Elvis Fat Bear.

Seeing her. Walking toward her.

Twenty yards. Closing now, a purpose to his step. Eliza took a second to register that there'd been no call to the morgue, no cause for him to be there. They hadn't turned up a body. She saw a Yamaha motorcycle parked next to their unmarked car. Guessed it had to be his.

He waved.

She recalled that day at the park when they were getting ready to load Josine into the van. Other side of the river, the guy in the watch cap glassing them, and Fat Bear waved. She'd questioned him about it.

The precipitation vacillated from mist to drizzle, drizzle to mist.

Her father's voice murmuring softly as he always did, to her, but to himself mostly, his beery breath filling the front seat of the car, thrown back by the dashboard. Quiet times. Water sounds. The comfort of being out of the bad weather—rain drumming on the roof of their Impala, washing down the sides. He'd driven to a playground. Only a block from their house, a good neighborhood in those days; cops and firemen lived in every other house. She was five or six. You've got no sense, girl. 'S raining out. Didja notice? Chasing her from the muddy swing set to the car. It was coming down like this. Even a child had to know it wouldn't stop for hours. Marty called it small rain. He told her angels were crying, but not because they were unhappy, because we were. He had a six-pack between the seats. Four cans left. He opened one and drank. Three.

Wouldja care for a tour, Miss Gahan?

They cruised around. Never going outside the city. He'd slow the car. Take his hand off the steering wheel to point to certain houses. Eliza stood on the seat in her damp sneakers. Listening to him talk and talk.

So she had a few old memories that weren't awful.

Her drunken father showed her where all the bad guys lived.

Was Elvis Fat Bear a bad guy?

Eliza unsnapped her shoulder rig. "Ike?"

"What?" His voice echoed inside the press's empty chamber.

"We got a visitor."

"Kind of visitor?"

He saw her slide right. Getting hard structure between her and whoever was approaching the door. She was throwing a charge Ike swore he could feel.

"Who buzzed County?" Eliza asked the rain. Her words betrayed her. Too loud, too chummy. "There's no pickup today."

Ike pulled his gun, took a position behind the press. He felt like he was hugging a milk pail against his ribs, making it hard to breathe. Slowing him down, spilling cold down his thighs.

"They said you'd be here." *The visitor.*

Close by. His voice was squeaky, like there was emotion boiling behind it. A man dealing with something he didn't want to put into words. Ike couldn't see him.

"Stop right there," Eliza said.

Her gun hand still inside her coat, but she was leaning back like a boxer, guarded, chin tucked, giving herself room to see what was up next. She didn't take her eyes off him. She kicked the door clear with her heel. Pointed her automatic, chest-high.

"Hold it."

He stopped at the threshold.

Big son of a bitch.

Hanging his head. "I need to talk to you," Fat Bear said. He didn't seem to appreciate the gravity of the situation. They were ready to aerate his jacket. He looked at Eliza sheepishly, then over at Ike. "Both you guys."

"Go on," Eliza said.

"Evan Spivek goes to you for this transaction?" Ike said.

"I didn't sell him a shotgun. Or a handgun."

"But you sold him something?" Eliza asked.

Fat Bear throttled his black hair. Rainwater leaked on the boards. He dried his hands on his jeans.

"Totally legal," he said.

"Elvis . . ."

"It was a knife, okay? I sold him a knife." He had a pouch of chewing tobacco. Fished up two fingers' worth, packed it inside his cheek. Talking out of the corner of his mouth. "My brother does these custom designs on the handles. Wood inlays. Rainbow bands, animal icons, initials. They're cool. Pretty knives. If that's what gets you off."

"And Sailor gets off ?"

"Hell yeah." Fat Bear chuckled. "Big time."

"He comes to you to buy a knife?" Ike asked.

"Yep."

Eliza said, "We know about the handles. What type of knife?"

"Combat."

"Is that his usual preference?"

"First time. The other stuff was mostly . . . what you would call collectibles. He used them, though. Sex games. I don't know, seems kind of sick to me, but whatever. He showed me pictures, how he was using them. The blood excited him. He called it his primal urge. What am I supposed to say? I tell him, man that's wild. So he brings somebody by my place for a live demonstration. Josine."

"You went along with it?"

Fat Bear shrugged, then nodded. "That day we're at the Boy Scout Island. I recognized her. Threw me for a loop. I mean she got knifed. Now we're there and I'm seriously wondering. Then I see him. Watching us across the water. I got spooked."

"But you didn't say anything to me?"

"Oh, yeah. Hey, see that guy over there? I sold him knives. And guess what? I watched him cut up this tranny for an hour one Saturday night. C'mon, Detective. I wanted it to blow away. I thought he loved her. That's what he told me. I hoped it was true."

"Any contact after that day at the river?"

"I had a hang-up on my machine from yesterday. Might've been him. I was working. Quiet before that."

"Then he shows up?"

"Like a bad dream."

"When was this?"

"Eight o'clock this morning. I rotated to nights. I'm pretty zoned when the shift ends. That's usually around seven. I grabbed a sandwich at a drive-thru over on Taylor. Came straight home. He's waiting for me in the bushes. No kidding. He's in the fucking bushes outside my duplex. I'm fantasizing about my pillow. This arm reaches out. Tats up to here. Probably some time before eight, that's when he catches me. Fucking Sailor man. I almost pissed my pants."

"Is that everything?"

Fat Bear shook his head. The sheepish look again, as if he were talking about swiping candy bars. "I got two bikes. Yamahas. I loaned him my other bike."

"For what?"

"Said he wanted to go for a ride."

"Brother, you just part with your bike like that?" Ike asked.

"I wanted him gone."

"And so?" Eliza asked.

"I got what I wished for."

Eliza's Apartment

Phone records corroborated Fat Bear's story. The hang-up originated from Spivek's phone at the trailer. They issued an APB on the bike. Eliza told Ike she was going home to shower and eat. They'd meet at the precinct. Stop in and check on Zan together. He was breathing on his own, but he hadn't opened his eyes. The doctors were cautiously optimistic.

Mario made it clear that Dina Booth was off-limits until tomorrow. The topic wasn't open for discussion. She'd been sedated. She didn't know anything. Adrian had spent the night at the office. He did that three, four nights a week. No video. Chariot Security wasn't returning calls.

Eliza was furious. But she kept her mouth shut. For the first time she wondered if Terry had hooks into Mario. Anything was possible. He was connected to the Booths, so why not the lieutenant? She filled Ike in on the Camacho interview. He agreed Dina was top priority. Duval was nowhere to be found. Count him among the missing.

The lab matched the gun in the canal to the Redmon murder and to Regan, the driver; the sniper left cartridges on the mound. They were working on fingerprints. Definitely not the same gun that killed Wayne Poins or Josine Watts. Site search didn't produce the shotgun. They drained the canal. Nothing.

Eliza climbed her stairs. Terry was conspiring with Dina. But why? It was money. But not simply money. On the surface, it didn't seem to be money at all. With Adrian dead, the new riverboat might never open. Terry would be losing business. Word of Adrian's execution under the protection of, and along with, Terry's top bodyguards would send a broadside into Chariot Security's reputation. If Terry had a prearranged deal with Dina, a partnership, then perhaps he stood to gain. But the thing Eliza knew for sure about Terry was that he didn't believe in true partners. He believed in followers. So why would Dina follow Terry? Or, even more bizarrely, why would Terry make an exception and do Dina's bidding? Eliza had no answers. But she planned to get some from Dina once Mario dropped his ridiculous "hands-off" order. What sheer bullshit. If she thought about it any more, she'd drive herself crazy with paranoia.

A hot shower would go a long way toward making her feel human again. And a decent meal might help reset her brain. She needed sleep too. The nightlong presence of a man in her bed hadn't proved especially restful.

While Eliza rushed around her apartment that morning—a toothbrush hanging from the corner of her mouth and a shoe under her arm while she searched in vain for its match—Crispin lay there snoring. She shook him awake. He was hungover. Baggy-eyed. She told him where the coffee was. Spare key. She tossed it to him on her way out.

"Lock up. Slide the key under the door."

"Um, okay."

"I don't know you well enough to say keep it."

"No problem."

"You're not going to get weepy on me?"

"Would you stay if I did?"

She smiled. "You don't know me either."

"I'm learning."

She put her key in the lock. He hadn't done what she asked. The door wasn't locked. She pushed it open. No key on the floor. The lights were off.

Bacon? She smelled the grease in the skillet. He helped himself to breakfast, kept the key, left the door so any neighborhood dirtbag could waltz in and shop around.

Her hand drifted to the light switch. The bedroom door was closed, but she saw a bar of golden light at the end of the hallway.

Steel against her throat. Lump of fear balling up, ready to scream.

"Not expecting me, were you, sweetie?"

Duval. He nudged the gun forward until it hurt.

"You've got a lovely neck."

"Don't be stupid."

"Excellent advice," he said. "Where's your duty piece?" He

disarmed her. Patted her down. She was overwhelmed with a burning wave of shame. How could she have walked into this? The shame mixed with anger at Crispin. How could he have been so careless?

Duval's barrel shifted from her neck to her spine. "No backup? What kind of a cop are you?"

He pocketed her Glock. His gloved hand on her shoulder, a gentle squeeze, and she fought the urge to let an elbow fly. The suppressor—she knew that's what she was feeling under her shoulder blade—prodding.

What was he going to do? What did she see? Drapes cracked to the balcony, a view of the street. He'd been waiting for her. Watching. A kitchen chair was missing.

"Into the bedroom," he said. "Don't get ideas, I'm spoken for."

She turned the doorknob. Duval pushed her. She had to take a step or fall over.

Losing traction as if she'd walked onto an ice rink.

She didn't look down. She steadied herself.

Crispin was sitting in the kitchen chair. The blinds were closed. Near the top, she saw the frayed cords dangling. Duval had bound him across his chest with the long pieces.

Eyes snapping open. Alert. A gag—the straps of Eliza's red under-wire bra drew his face into a grotesque smile. The matching bottoms were stuffed inside his mouth. His jaw was enormous, broken. Eliza stepped on something hard. Teeth.

Her eyes flicked from him to her unmade bed.

Garbage bags. A cut-down .410 shotgun—the butt chopped to a wedge. It looked old, banged-up, used. Good for robbing liquor stores. Killing bodyguards.

Duval shoved her closer.

"You weren't at the shooting party this morning and that surprised me. Got me curious. I hate to ask for help. But I'm jammed up here. I was eager to try some persuading. Rang your bell and got more than I bargained for. But this works."

He wanted to brag.

"Tell me," he said. "Did you think Sailor and Zan went to Adrian for a loan?"

"We were watching Sailor," she said.

"And doing a fine job at that."

"Where is he?"

Duval faced her, cocked his head to the side. His eyes were the color of oyster meat. There was an enflamed blood vessel webbing the left.

"Find the money in the Navigator?" he asked.

They hadn't. He didn't wait for her answer.

"Better off leaving it in plain sight. I worried someone would walk off with a hundred grand. Very tempting. But they were greedy. Zan and Sailor. Maybe Adrian argued. I was willing to let you and Ike put it together. Lovely Zan fucked me by not quite dying. It's a shame. I tried to bring him along, but the boy's addled. Any luck, he stays a vegetable." He nodded, agreeing with his thoughts. The suppressor lifted to his lips, like a contemplative finger. "I dropped the gun in the drink. Bloody fucking gorilla was chasing after me. However, Zan's prints are on the cartridges. I would've had him blast the orchard if I didn't think he'd suddenly smarten up and cap his old . . . guardian angel. Sailor made his break. So, fuck it—new plans. We know the doc had a real interest in Sailor. Young Patrick died from bad smack in his company. He did. But cry me a river. Taking it in the ass would've killed him sooner or later. Our sly dog Sailor blames Adrian who was, as the public will soon find out, dabbling in more than casinos. If it looks like smack and tastes like smack, well . . . I've made preparations, evidence at Adrian's offices to muddy the water. Once we're finished here we'll take care of all that."

He patted her arm.

Eliza saw dried blood on his gloves. His knuckles bulged. Lead kisses buried underneath were effective destroyers of flesh and bone.

"Reason I'm telling you this, Eliza, is because I like you. Always have. Your father was solid as they come. Up until recently. But that was preventable. Wasn't it, girl? Putting your thumb in the pie. Having to make your mark. Spirited. I love it. All is forgiven. Best to keep business in the family. Turn it over to the next generation."

Duval addressed Crispin as he pointed the revolver at him.

"Sweet smart girls with the hearts of warriors. They'll undo us all. Eh, Crispin?"

Crispin closed his eyes.

"You have to see I'm right," Duval said. Confidence bellied his sails. "No clean way out. You've been on Terrible Terry's team from the get-go. Without me, you'd be grilling tortillas. It's going to look like Sailor's mess. We can do that. It's almost too easy."

Eliza sensed that the meter had clicked.

Wherever he was taking them, they'd just arrived.

He said, "Decision time. I can leave you bleeding on the floor. I'd hate to do it, but just the same. Or you can go with me. Need convincing?"

Duval fired a round into Crispin's knee. Eliza jumped at the loud pop.

Wisp of smoke as if he'd extinguished a match.

Crispin screamed against his gag.

"I'll go," she said.

Duval went to her bed.

"Tape a bag over his head," he said.

Eliza took it from him.

She aired out the . . . death hood.

She covered him quickly.

Duval chucked a roll of duct tape at her. She caught it against her chest.

"Do it fast, girl. Then we best boogie out of here."

She wrapped the tape around Crispin's neck. He started to struggle. Three times around, and she tore the end with a bite. Threw the roll back to Duval. He ducked; let it hit the wall. Gun trained on her the whole time.

"Don't get cute," he said.

"I wasn't about to."

He spun the revolver on his trigger finger, offering her the upturned grip.

"You do it," he said. "Show me I'm right about you."

She reached out.

He pulled away.

"All yours," he said. He passed her the revolver with his left hand. Playing games.

He'd lifted her gun from his pocket. Leveling it at her.

The revolver was not big. She was used to the Glock. The homemade suppressor seemed absurdly long. Tiny holes drilled in the cylinder. Front heavy, like it wanted to nosedive. She pressed the cylinder behind Crispin's ear. He tried to jump away. Bucking.

The chair tipped up on two legs. She brought it down. Planted her foot on the brace. A .22 slug behind his ear, just the way Poins got his ticket punched. The slug would go in and rattle around like a marble in a can of spray paint. The cylinder skidded against the bag, made black stars out of the folds. She smoothed the plastic enough to see the shape of his ear. She had no options. Terry had her gun. He'd kill her. She placed the barrel firmly against Crispin's head. He seemed to calm down. Oxygen deprivation hadn't begun. Wouldn't. Maybe he was simply giving up. Giving in. But she was glad for this little change. *He'd kill them both. He'd kill them both if she didn't do it. If she didn't do it. If. She. Didn't. Do it.* She pulled the trigger. Crispin's head snapped left. She felt his blood sprinkle her hand.

His blood was warm. Like tears.

"There's my girl."

"I'm going to be sick."

"You are not." He ejected the Glock's clip. Traded her gun for his. "Goddamn gloves are making my hands itch."

"I don't like leaving him here. My apartment."

Burnt powder sharpness filled her nostrils, making her want to run.

"You'll admit to sleeping with him. But there's no law against that. Poor judgment. Take the official reprimand. Bullshit. Wrist slap. My file was full of them. Nothing's in stone. Believe me. That's going bye-bye when you clear Adrian's murder. They'll kiss your ass. Sailor did this thing. Am I getting through? We'll wrap it up, everything but a fucking bow. Christ, we may be able to sell this as Sailor's handiwork. I'm serious. He could've, using the shotgun and the pistol. That Navigator was a death trap. Trust me, I know. Sailor's deeds, that's our story. He caps the doc. Like he did Poins. Like he did Josine. You dodged him. Whose fault is it the guy's going nuts, blowing people away left and right? That pussy judge let him go. Adrian paid for his own assassination." He touched her arm again. "Eliza, you're on the inside now. Uncle Terry's taking care of you. Thing you need to know is—there's always a way to make it work."

Together they walked into the living room.

"The plate. Is it yours?" she asked.

"Never took my gloves off." He wriggled his fingers.

"But you're not worried about DNA?" She was stalling. She sensed he knew but didn't really care.

"Vacuuming the place, are we? Look, I'm a friend of the family. Your dad and I were partners for years. My hairs belong. My spit and fibers too."

"Asking for trouble."

"You're right. Put the works in the dishwasher. Turn it on when we go."

He tortured Crispin. Then treated himself to a snack. Eating with his bloody gloves on. He was going to kill her anyway. She knew now. He'd take her somewhere and come back later to tidy up. His plans. Perhaps Sailor was dead. She'd be joining him. Isn't that what Ike had said about the shooter in the canal—he'd made too neat a package?

She rinsed the plate, the pan, the fork, and the steak knife, and closed them up inside the machine with the soap. Crispin's blood washed off. She cranked the dial. Heard the water start to fill.

He stood next to her. The .22 enfolded in his arms. "Ready?"

"What about the shotgun?"

"Leave it."

"Why?"

"Enough questions, Detective Ochoa. We need to hit the road."

"I think we should take it along. If Sailor ever—"

He interrupted her. "Be quick about it."

She jogged into the hallway.

He called out, "Sweetie, you know it's not loaded?"

"Why's that matter?"

"Doesn't."

Inside her bedroom, she had seconds. Crispin hadn't budged an inch. She poked her thumbnail against the hood and ripped. Blood trickled out. She was beyond helping him, but at least she could do this much.

She grabbed the shotgun.

Darting back into the hallway.

Duval opened the apartment door. Killed the interior lights. The dishwasher was chugging. The vestibule lamps glowed greenish behind him. Olive walls peeling and Eliza imagined Hell's Gate swinging open to welcome her. She thought something might be wrong with Duval. But Terrible Terry was simply enjoying the moment, unleashing a wide grin.

"Under your coat or you'll frighten the neighbors," he said, pointing to the shotgun.

He lunged at her.

A colorful arm locked under his chin.

Sailor rode him to the floor.

Turning his knife like a giant screw.

Duval scrambled. Seeking some point of leverage. His face flushed orchid. He made gasping sounds. A great balloon of blood exploded from his lips. He reared up.

Sailor was whispering to him.

This time Duval went down slowly. Cracking his head at the end. Sailor pulled the knife loose. He was on his knees, panting.

Eliza felt frozen.

She pointed the shotgun at him.

"You go ahead," he said.

"Drop the knife."

"What?"

"You're under arrest."

He laughed. The knife rolled from his red fingers. He put up his hands. Then reached out and seized Duval by the hair.

Flipped him over onto his back.

Sailor took up his knife again. "Lady, you do what you need to do. I'm not finished with him. But if I heard right, then you got no choice in the matter."

She swung the shotgun like a bat, the twin barrels hitting him.

The roar.

Sailor's head came apart.

She'd never forget the roar.

It was amazing.

Booth Estate—Main House

The cold was making another play for Booth City. Ike bundled up. The car's heater set on high. He parked in front of the main house.

A maid answered the door. It wasn't Sandra Camacho. This woman was older. She offered to take his hat. He declined. She informed him that Mrs. Booth was in the greenhouse. He followed her to a long hallway. Glass panels. Rough-cut stones underfoot. He walked the rest of the way alone.

The greenhouse temperature was fifty degrees hotter than outdoors. He read a thermometer hanging inside the second pair of glass doors. Moisture beaded inside the glass, ran down in rivulets.

"Over here, Detective."

He followed her voice to a narrow aisle.

She was kneeling in a flower bed, working a trowel into the sandy soil. As he approached, she stood. Her gloves were white and dirty only at the fingers. She removed them. Small hands. Small feet too, Ike noted, like a child's. Her throat was rosy, glossed with sweat.

"Let's sit on the bench, if you don't mind," she said.

"I don't."

Dina Booth looked healthier, less frazzled, than the day they spoke to her in the library. The day they arrested her son.

She unclasped her cigarette case. Offered it to him.

"No thanks. Trying to quit."

She lit her cigarette with a slender gold lighter.

"How is your partner?"

"Doin' fine. Taking some time away from the job."

"If what I read in the papers is true, she's very brave."

"No question."

"She shot that doctor in the head?"

"The bullet creased him." Ike showed her where, using his own head as a model. "Nasty scar. His knee had to be replaced. The cap shattered."

"Horrible."

"Might've been worse, of course. If Duval—"

"Don't mention that man's name in my house."

Ike dropped his hat on the bench. Granite was his best guess. Rosebuds carved into the footwork. Too much like a cemetery for his taste.

"Why, exactly, are we meeting today?" she asked.

"I'm retiring."

"Congratulations."

"Thank you. I've had a good run. Your case was my last."

"My case?"

Ike let her question pass. It would feel good to leave when he was finished.

"You knew Terry Duval for a long time."

"Please, I asked you not to —"

"He investigated your first husband's death."

"That's correct."

"The other detective, I'm not sure if you knew, he was Detective Ochoa's father."

"I didn't."

"Did you know Terry taped your phone calls?"

She gave no response.

"How's your son?" Ike picked up his hat. It looked like a cop's hat. He'd need to get a new one.

"Detective Horner, I've tried to be fair to you."

"Simple question. You inquired about my partner, and all I wanted—"

"We're bringing him home. I've hired a nurse. Arranged a room for him, here, in the main house. Good-bye." She stood, holding her gloves. She snatched the trowel from the bench as if he might do it first.

"He's not talking."

"Not a word." She couldn't resist the urge to smile.

Ike produced a small tape recorder.

"I won't give you permission to tape our conversation."

There was a cassette inside.

He punched the PLAY button.

DUVAL'S VOICE: "I know we're talking about your son."

ANOTHER VOICE: "He's your son too."

Ike got what he came for. Pressed STOP.

"That's you."

"Prove it."

"Terry even wired himself up. Like the day you talked about Poins. He was blackmailing you. That had to give you fits. First some transsexual prostitute your son played nasty with, then this cabdriver comes along. You met with Poins at the Aquarium Bar. The date's written in my book. I left that at the precinct, because this is just a social call. We have a witness. Saw you."

"You're a liar."

"Speaking the truth is why I'm here."

"I won't pay for your silence."

"You shot Josine. You were there when Adrian was murdered. Didn't your first husband kill himself with a shotgun? A .410 doesn't have that much kick. Lady your size could manage it fine. It was *your* gun. That's why it went missing from the evidence room. Sentimental value. Am I right?"

She started walking away.

He got up.

"Your son was born prematurely. According to hospital records in New Orleans, two months early. Not one. Was Terry Duval Zan's father?"

She opened the glass doors.

"Or did you just tell him that to get what you wanted?"

She went through.

The greenhouse had a side entrance. Ike walked out. He followed along the orange paving stones. The apple trees were still in winter's grip. They looked like they were trying to burrow themselves back into the ground. Growing downward. The pressing house was dark. The stable had a bright red padlock on the door. She wasn't the type to commit suicide. Maybe her first husband wasn't the type either. The wind gusted, and the glass plates of the greenhouse rumbled.

Big production brewing this morning at the precinct. Everybody wearing what looked like churchgoing clothes. Somebody called the newspeople. Ike had to duck out on the sly. Filing the retirement papers made him yearn for reckless days. Seeing Jamila in Corpus Christi might take the edge off. He was certainly feeling it now. He felt sharp as a brand-new tack.

Lights were flashing in the trees at the bottom of the lane.

He counted the cars.

Stopping at seven.

What did they think she'd do? Climb the roof with a rifle?

Maybe she would.

He noticed they were coming with their sirens switched off, as a courtesy.